CAPTAIN
from
CORFU

Also by Muriel Maddox

CAPTAIN
from
CORFU

A Novel by
Muriel Maddox

SUNSTONE
PRESS

SANTA FE

Sunstone books may be purchased for educational, business, or sales promotional use. For information please write: Special Markets Department, Sunstone Press, P.O. Box 2321, Santa Fe, New Mexico 87504-2321.

Library of Congress Cataloging-in-Publication Data:

Maddox, Muriel,
   Captain from Corfu: a novel / by Muriel Maddox
   p. cm.
  ISBN: 0-86534-287-3 Hardcover
  ISBN: 0-86534-528-7 Softcover (alk. paper)
  I. Title.
PS3563. A339455C36 1999
813' .54--dc21   98-52306
                                         CIP

Published in

WWW.SUNSTONEPRESS.COM
SUNSTONE PRESS / POST OFFICE BOX 2321 / SANTA FE, NM 87504-2321 /USA
(505) 988-4418 / ORDERS ONLY (800) 243-5644 / FAX (505) 988-1025

*T*o the memory of my father
Captain Charles Hamilton Maddox
United States Navy

I must go down to the seas again, to the lonely sea and the sky,
And all I ask is a tall ship and a star to steer her by,
And the wheel's kick and the wind's song and the white sail's
      shaking,
And a grey mist on the sea's face and a grey dawn breaking.

                                  —John Masefield

BOOK ONE

One

The Greeks have a saying: "You cannot escape your fate," and for Captain Nikos Meletis the coming cruise was one that would change his life.

He stood on the bridge of the *Pericles* and looked at the outline of Venice through his binoculars. He was taller than most Greek men and handsome, with black hair tinged with gray on the sides and dark brown eyes, a dashing and romantic figure. For twenty-five years he had been a seaman, a captain for twelve. He seldom saw his wife and two sons in Athens. As soon as the ship docked in Venice he must call home. He would ask his three-year-old, "Fanis, have you broken anything?" Nikos smiled. He was a rascal, that Fanis, always breaking something. His fourteen-year-old son, Evangelos, would still be in school. Evangelos was serious, a good student, he wanted to become a doctor when he grew up. Fanis—who knew what he would be? He loved ships too.

They are good boys, Nikos thought, good boys. He missed them. That was the trouble with the life of a sailor. If you have children you never see them.

This had been a long cruise, twenty days, and the sea was rough crossing the Atlantic. They had picked up the passengers in Venezuela, Germans, he had this same charter group every year and he did not like the atmosphere of the ship when they had Germans on board. It was somber, heavy. They marched into meals, after dinner every night there were lectures in the lounge, sometimes they sang German songs and drank beer, and then early to bed.

When he heard German it reminded him again of the war. As if he could ever forget . . .

Nikos Meletis looked again at the approaching harbor. He was tired. It had been ten years since he had a vacation, not counting November when they were in dry-dock in Piraeus. But then he could not rest because he had to be in charge of repairs to the ship.

They would disembark the Germans in Venice this morning and go right out again this evening with another group, Americans this time, for a ten-day cruise in the Mediterranean and Greek Isles. That would bring them back to Athens the middle of April, just in time for the Greek Easter. He paced the bridge smoking a cigarette. He wondered how things were in Greece, if any of his friends had been thrown in jail by the Junta. Mail was censored, it was not safe for his wife to put anything in letters, but he had heard on the BBC broadcast that only two days ago they had arrested another newspaper editor in Athens. More and more they were suppressing human rights, no Greek was free to speak out in safety against the colonels. For three years now, since April 21, 1967, they had been in power. Where would it all end?

He did not discuss politics with the passengers, though they often asked him about the political situation in Greece. Americans would not understand, they had never known what it was like to be enslaved by a dictatorship. They had never had their cities bombed, their villages burned, their men shot for reprisal.

How could they know of the eternal struggle for freedom that rested on the shoulder of every Greek?

No, he would not talk of these things with the Americans. They would ask him where they could buy the best gold jewelry in Athens, what nightclubs to go to, what restaurants, and he would tell them. He would dance with the ladies and they would ask the ship's orchestra to play the music from *Never on Sunday* and *Zorba the Greek*. There would be the usual women wanting to have a flirtation with

had some difficulty with English, but when he did not understand he
would just smile and nod, pretending to listen.

For the voices he would be hearing would not be those of the
ship's passengers but the voices burning beneath the soil of Greece,
the immortal cry in every Greek heart. The Greek people despised
the Junta with their signs 21 APRILIOU everywhere, they mocked
the colonels, they were playing for time.

And as it had in centuries past, Greek courage and pride would
rise again against the oppression. Greece would be saved.

He looked over his shoulder nervously. He must keep these
thoughts to himself. It was not like when he was nineteen and in the
Greek Resistance. Twice he had been captured by the Nazis, twice he
had escaped. Now he was forty-seven, he had a family to think of.
He must be more cautious. Youth was reckless, willing to take chances.

But still, he was Greek. To be a Greek was something to be proud of.

They were nearing the harbor now. He blew the ship's horn.
The stewards had piled the luggage on the decks. The passengers
were standing around, many with cameras. Some were climbing up
to the bridge deck. He ordered the second officer to put up the rope
blocking off the bridge. He did not want the passengers obstructing
his vision when he was trying to dock the ship. Especially Germans.

He looked through his binoculars. The pink palaces of Venice
rising from the sea, a city unlike any other. How many times had he
seen it now? He had forgotten. The voyages followed one after the
other, with only a few hours rest between.

Tonight at the captain's cocktail party he would give the same
speech of welcome to the new passengers. It would begin all over
again . . .

*   *   *

The chief steward opened the doors of the Dionysus Lounge and the passengers started to file past.

"Good evening, Captain."

"How do you do."

After so many cruises they all looked much the same, mostly middle-aged couples, businessmen who had been persuaded by their wives to take the trip and who would rather play golf or fish than look at Greek ruins. And then always the elderly widows, traveling in pairs or alone. He nodded politely as the ship's photographer snapped a picture of him shaking hands with a passenger. They always wanted to buy a picture of themselves with the captain to show to their friends at home. He forced a smile. This was the part of his job that he disliked the most, yet it was a very important part. He saw an older woman with a cane approaching followed by a young girl in a mini-skirt and long straight blonde hair.

"How do you do, Captain. I'm Mrs. Winthrop Pearson and this is my granddaughter, Daphne. I'm so looking forward to showing Daphne the Parthenon and Delphi. I was in Greece years ago with my late husband. We sailed around the Aegean on a friend's yacht—"

"Yes?" He must keep the line moving. "That is very nice. I hope you enjoy the cruise."

He held out his hand to the next passenger and without warning something long forgotten stirred in his memory. The woman was blonde with a fragile loveliness and large blue-gray eyes framed in long dark lashes. Even though she was smiling there was a strange sadness in her face and she seemed to be traveling alone.

"How do you do?"

"How do you do, Captain."

He was surprised at the firmness of her grip, unlike the limp handshakes of many of the lady passengers. The faint scent of her perfume lingered after she had disappeared in the crowd. The line continued, and finally he had greeted them all. Now for the speech welcoming them to the ship and introducing the other officers. He walked up in front of the orchestra and the cruise director called for attention.

"Ladies and gentlemen, I would like to present the Master of the *Pericles*, Captain Nikos Meletis, who will say a few words to you."

Nikos took the microphone and adjusted it to his height.

"On behalf of the company and the crew and myself, I want to wish you a very pleasant cruise. If at any time there is anything we can do to make your voyage more enjoyable you have only to let us know. And now I would like to introduce my officers. Mr. Georgios Christopoulou, the chief purser, Mr. Vasilios Papadakis, the chief radio operator . . ."

He continued with the introductions and then he saw where she was sitting. In a corner with the elderly woman with the cane and the young girl.

"And now I would like to give a toast in Greek." The steward handed him a glass of champagne and Nikos raised it. "*Kalo taxidi.* A good voyage."

There was polite applause and he handed the mike back. Now he must circulate around the room, sit with one group for a few minutes, then join another group. If he showed too much attention to any one person there could be letters of complaint to the line, so he was always careful. He picked out a group of several middle-aged couples sitting together and walked over to them and pulled up a chair.

"This seems to be a very well-run ship," Mrs. Pearson remarked. "And the captain is most charming. I wonder if he plays bridge."

"Here he comes now," Daphne said. "Why don't you ask him?"

"May I join you?" Nikos asked.

"Please do." Mrs. Pearson smiled coyly. "Captain, do you play bridge?"

"Bridge?" He looked puzzled. "Yes, I must go to the bridge soon," he said. He pulled out a pack of cigarettes and passed them around. "Nobody here smokes?" He smiled. "You are more smart than I am. I try to stop." He shrugged and lit a cigarette. "It is very difficult. So many hours on the bridge."

Mrs. Pearson tried again. "No, Captain, I meant do you play bridge, the card game?"

"Oh, no. I have never learned. No time."

"My grandmother's a real bridge fiend," Daphne said.

"Oh?" The word "fiend" seemed to bother him. He looked around and noticed that the glasses at the next table were empty. He snapped his fingers and a steward came over quickly. He said something in Greek and motioned. He looked angry. *"Tora,"* he said. "You are not drinking your champagne?" he asked.

"Oh yes, it's delicious," Mrs. Pearson said.

His eyes, dark and intense, focused on the blonde woman, and she quickly took a sip of her champagne.

"Would you like something else?"

"Oh, no thank you, Captain. This is fine."

He continued to stare at her. "This is your first trip to Greece?"

"Yes. My husband and I always wanted to come, but he could never get away."

He looked at her wedding ring. "Your husband is not with you?"

"No," she said quickly. "I'm a widow. My husband . . . died last year."

"I am very sorry."

"Captain, are you going to teach us how to do the Greek dances?" Daphne asked.

"You would like to learn?"

"Yes. I think they're groovy."

He smiled. "I will arrange with the cruise director to have a class. Then you can show to your friends when you return home."

Daphne laughed. "They'll be a gas in Philadelphia!"

"Gas?"

"My granddaughter means that they'll cause a sensation," Mrs. Pearson explained.

"Oh, I see." He turned to the blonde woman. "Are you also from Philadelphia?"

"No, my home is in Greenwich, Connecticut."

"Greenwich. I have heard of it. The village where many painters live."

"That is a different place," she said, smiling. "It is part of New York City. This is a town in Connecticut."

"Ah, I understand. It is confusing."

The steward poured more champagne for everyone. Nikos raised his glass. "Enjoy yourselves," he said. He stood up. "I must go now. Many things to do."

He made his way through the crowded lounge, past the reception desk, and started up the stairs.

He stopped in the radio room for messages and a weather report. Rain along the Dalmation Coast, the sea was choppy off Dubrovnik. That meant they could not anchor near the old town, it would be too rough for tenders to go ashore. Instead he would have to take the ship to the dock on the other side and have the passengers take taxis to the walled city. It was some distance but it could not be helped. Weather he could not control. The ship, yes.

The blonde woman bothered him. Who was it she reminded him of? Long ago, it was during the war. He had tried not to stare at her, but there was something . . . what was it?

He had been married to Katina for fifteen years now. Evangelos was fourteen and Fanis three. Katina was a good Greek wife, she sat at home and raised the children and waited for him. He saw her once a week during the summer when they cruised the Mediterranean and not for five or six months when the ship was in the Caribbean. She did not complain that they were apart so much, she knew he loved the sea, that this was his work.

American women he had met were different. They were spoiled. It was the men's fault that they were like that, in a Greek family the man was the boss. He was like a king. The children obeyed him, the wife also. It was the way things should be.

Like the ship. One person in control. The captain.

Two

*A*t dinner Alexa Hollister sat with a middle-aged couple from Cleveland named Overstreet, Beverly Sullivan, a red-haired girl from Buffalo, and two elderly spinsters from Boston. The stewards wore white gloves when they served. Alexa looked over at the captain's table. It was empty. Presumably he didn't come down to dinner with the passengers the first night out.

An announcement came over the intercom from the tour director. "There will be slides and a lecture on Dubrovnik in the main lounge after dinner."

"I wonder if we'll need visas for Dubrovnik?" asked Mrs. Overstreet. "After all, it's a Communist country."

"I'm sure the ship's purser will take care of everything," one of the spinsters from Boston said. "I don't think we need to worry."

Alexa wondered if they were sisters. She hadn't caught their names. One was frail-looking and spoke in a timid voice, the other was heavy-set, with bobbed gray hair, and wore a wristwatch with a wide leather band.

"When Winifred and I were in Africa last year we had the most glorious time," continued the plump spinster. "Have any of you been there?"

No one had.

"I'm just dying to go on a safari," said Beverly. "With one of those handsome white hunters."

"Some friends of mine went to Kenya several years ago," Mr. Overstreet said. "One of them shot a lion. Only trouble was the lion's mate was hiding in the brush and almost got him."

"Every time Ellwood tells that story it gets better," his wife said.

"Well it's true, Martha. It's all true."

The steward passed around the menu for dessert. "We have chocolate ice cream, apple pie, and baklava."

"Isn't baklava a Greek pastry?" Alexa asked.

"Yes, Kyria," the boy said. "You like?"

"Yes, I think I'll try that."

"Is very good. Made with honey and nuts." He beamed.

Everyone decided to have baklava except Mr. Overstreet, who wanted chocolate ice cream.

"Honestly, Ellwood, you'd go into a Polynesian restaurant and order lamb chops!" said Mrs. Overstreet.

"Well why not, if that's what I wanted?"

The steward brought the dessert and poured coffee.

Dinner was finally over and the spinster ladies said they would see everyone in the lounge for the slides on Dubrovnik. Mrs. Overstreet wanted to go back to her cabin first, so her husband said he would meet her in the bar.

Beverly looked at Alexa. "Do you want to have some more coffee? I think I'll have some."

"Fine. The lecture doesn't start for another half hour."

"And I'm not anxious to sit with them again. God, what a grim group!"

Alexa smiled and said nothing.

"I haven't seen any single men yet, have you? Unless they're hiding someplace."

"I really didn't expect to find any."

"The sexiest man I've seen on this ship is the captain." Beverly looked around. "I wonder where he is?"

"Probably on the bridge directing the ship."

"Let's see what we can find. I know one thing, I'm not going to get stuck at a table with this dull group again. How about you?"

"Maybe the chief steward can move us to another table. I think there's an empty one over by the window."

"Now you're thinking. I've saved for this trip for months and I'm going to make the most of it. By the way, what's your first name?"

"Alexa."

"Mine's Bev. Do you work, Alexa?"

"No. Do you?"

"Sure do. I'm a secretary, but I'm kind of in between jobs right now. I want to get something in New York when I get back. I've gone about as far as I can in Buffalo."

"I've never been there."

"You haven't missed a thing, honey. Look, I want to go to my cabin for a sec. I think one of my false eyelashes is coming loose. What deck are you on?"

"Hermes. Where are you?"

"Juno. Why don't I meet you right outside the lounge in say ten minutes?"

"Fine."

"And if you latch on to anything interesting, see if he has a friend!" Bev winked and stood up.

"I'll try." Alexa laughed.

He sat at the desk in his cabin going over the stack of papers beside him, the endless details that had to be attended to at the beginning of every new cruise. And since the Junta there were new forms to fill out, more complicated. He had to account for everything. When they were in port they had to know where he was every minute so they could reach him if something went wrong with the ship. It was the law. He was never free to do what he wanted. He could never sleep without someone knocking on his door and saying, "Captain, you are wanted on the bridge."

For a crazy moment Nikos Meletis had a wild desire to be a

simple sailor again, to sail the seas he loved without the heavy responsibilities that had been his so long.

He had been a captain for twelve years, the youngest captain of
the Delphinaki Lines. At first, no one would believe he was a captain.
If he appeared stern and shouted at the men it was necessary. The
captain had to have authority, his word must be unquestioned. Otherwise the sailors and the other officers did not have respect for him.
The staff captain had gray hair, was older than he, the chief engineer
also. Often he had the feeling they resented him. That he could not
help. He, Nikos Meletis, was the captain and they had to take his
orders.

His dinner lay on a tray beside him, hardly touched. He was
not hungry.

He lit a cigarette. On the wall above his desk were framed pictures of his family, one of Evangelos and Fanis alone, another of them
together, and a separate one of Katina. Katina had the photographs
taken before he left for the Caribbean in December. "To remind the
lady passengers that you have a wife and sons," she said.

He opened the ship's log and wrote the date: April 4, 1970. In
two weeks would be the Greek Easter. The officers' families always
came on the ship that week and it was a big celebration with red eggs
and the special Easter soup. Even the colonels had not been able to
do away with that.

Nikos glanced at his watch. It was almost time for the BBC
broadcast. He finished writing his report and turned on the radio,
wondering what the news from Athens would be tonight.

There was a knock on the door.

"*Embros,*" he said. "Come in."

It was Panayiotis, the chief steward. He was holding a plan of
the cabins and had a worried expression.

Nikos sighed and turned off the radio. Like always, more problems. "Yes?" he said. "What is it?"

"Some of the passengers are unhappy with their cabins,"

Panayiotis said. "They want to change. It is not possible. The ship is full."

Every trip this happened. The cabins were smaller than they looked on the brochures. If they wanted large cabins let them take the *Sagafjord* or the *Statendam*, Nikos thought. Those were larger ships with more luxurious cabins.

"They want to see the captain," Panayiotis said. "They say they are friends of the owners."

The ship's owners were always offering free trips to their friends and were given the cabins that were left over. Naturally they were not the best cabins on the ship. Those were booked months in advance by tour groups.

"I can do nothing about the cabins," Nikos said, "but put them at my table for dinner tomorrow night."

"Yes, Captain." Panayiotis did not move.

Nikos looked up. "There is something else?"

"Two ladies are missing their luggage."

"Perhaps it was put in the wrong cabin. You have checked the ship?"

"The bags are not on the ship. The ladies have not seen them since they boarded the plane in San Francisco. They changed planes in London and the airline said they would check the luggage straight through to Venice, not to worry. So now the bags, they are not here—"

"Ah, then it is fault of the airlines. Ask the purser to send a cable to them and have the bags forwarded to Malta."

"That is three days from now. The ladies—"

"You have a better solution?" Nikos shouted.

"No, Captain." Panayiotis looked at the captain's tray. "The fish was not good?"

"I am not hungry."

"Can I get you something else?"

"Nothing. Yes, maybe a Campari and soda."

"Yes, Captain."

Panayiotis picked up the tray and left.

As soon as he had gone, Nikos turned on the radio. The news from Athens was just coming on.

Bev had taken off the jacket of her white cocktail suit, revealing a tight, low-cut sheath. "I just peeked in the bar," she said, "and saw the most gorgeous hunk of man sitting there. He has a deep tan and he's wearing a dark suit. "Let's go in and order a drink."

Alexa hesitated.

"Come on. You don't want to spend your time with a lot of dried-up old school teachers, do you? I intend to have fun on this trip."

"Well, all right. But I think we're going to have the slides in a few minutes."

"Oh, by the way, speaking of fun, have you seen the honeymoon couple?"

"No. But I suppose there's one on every ship."

"Not like this one. They're seventy if they're a day. She's carrying a faded bunch of flowers and they walk around holding hands like a pair of teenagers. I suppose that's all they can do at this stage. They're really quite sweet. They have the cabin next to mine. The door was open and they were toasting each other in champagne when I passed."

"Maybe they were lovers who were separated in their youth and who finally found each other again."

Bev laughed. "Alexa, what a romantic you are! The truth is they're probably a widow and widower who married each other for companionship in their old age."

"Maybe." Alexa smiled. "But I like my version better."

The tanned man at the bar turned around. "May I buy you ladies a drink?"

"Thank you, we'd love one, wouldn't we, Alexa?" Bev slid onto the barstool beside him.

"What will you have?" he asked, glancing at Bev's low neckline.

"Two stingers. That is if they can make one. It's not a Greek drink, is it?"

"I'll just have Dubonnet," Alexa said.

The man said something in Greek to the bartender. He looked puzzled and shrugged his shoulders.

"Look, if it's too complicated I'll have something else," Bev said.

"It's all right, I've just explained to him how to make it."

"You're the first blond Greek I've seen on this ship," Bev said.

"Perhaps it's because I'm not Greek."

"Oh?"

"I carry a British passport."

"Where are you from?" Alexa asked.

"I was born in Cape Town. British father, Dutch mother."

"How did you learn Greek so well?"

"I've lived in Athens for several years. And I really don't speak it that well, but thanks for the compliment. I can understand them and make myself understood. By the way, my name is Geoffrey Reid. Geoff to my friends."

"I'm Bev and this is Alexa."

"Are you traveling together?"

"No, we just met at dinner this evening," Bev said. "We were stuck at a table with the Geritol set."

Geoff laughed. "I know what you mean. We don't usually get many young and beautiful ladies like yourselves on these cruises."

"Are you connected with the ship?" Alexa asked.

"I work for the shipping line. I'm not always on the *Pericles*, they change me around to different ships. I do a little bit of everything. I'm what is known as a trouble shooter."

"I like trouble," Bev said, leaning toward him.

"I'll remember that." He smiled. "I wish I didn't have to get off at Crete."

"Where do you go then?"

"Fly back to Athens and pick up the *Achilles*. It's their newest ship, maiden voyage and all that." He raised his glass. "But we don't get to Crete for five days. Perhaps I can arrange a storm to slow us down. Are you girls good sailors?"

"I don't know," Bev said. "This is my first cruise."

He turned to Alexa. "What about you?"

"My father was a captain in the Navy and I grew up around ships. I wouldn't dare get seasick." She laughed.

"That's the spirit. We shall expect to see you on deck in the roughest seas."

Bev looked worried. "I thought the Mediterranean was calm in April."

"It is. Usually. Don't worry. I'm just pulling your leg. Besides, we have a good captain. He'll see us through."

"Where is the captain?" Bev asked.

"I guess he's where he should be, on the bridge. He's pretty tired. We had a long trip. But he's quite a ladies' man. You'll see him."

A woman in her sixties, with thin penciled eyebrows and scarlet lipstick painted in a cupid's bow, was weaving her way toward them. She had on a long orange and yellow chiffon dress with a scarf trailing from around her neck to the floor and she held a drink in one hand.

"Here comes trouble," Geoff whispered. "Isadora approaches."

"Is that really her name?" Bev giggled.

"It's my name for her," Geoff said. "Did you see the film about Isadora Duncan?"

"I did," Alexa said. "It was playing in Greenwich just before I left."

"Then you see what I mean, don't you?"

Alexa nodded.

"Oh, there you are, you naughty boy!" The woman tossed her chiffon scarf over one shoulder. "I was wondering where you'd escaped to." She gave Alexa and Bev a withering look. "I was once young and beautiful myself. When I worked for Mr. de Mille he said to me—"

A voice over the ship's intercom interrupted. "We are now ready to show the slides on Dubrovnik in the main lounge. Will all passengers wishing to learn what to see in Dubrovnik tomorrow please assemble in the main lounge now. We will also give you landing tags. This is very important. Thank you."

"I think we'd better go in now and get seats," Geoff said. He turned to the woman. "Is your husband coming?"

"Who knows that that S.O.B is doing? He didn't want to come on this trip anyway. Just wanted to stay home and count his money. I told him, 'Maury, you can't take it with you.'"

"If you'll excuse us we'll go in," Geoff said. 'We'll see you later."

"Go right ahead." The woman made a sweeping gesture with her arm. "I'm going to sit here and have a drink with this cute bartender."

Geoff took Alexa and Bev into the lounge.

"Here are some good seats where you can see the slides well. I wish I could join you, but I'd better keep an eye on Isadora. If she falls off that barstool and sues the Delphinaki Lines the captain will have my neck."

"Maybe she'll rape the bartender instead," Bev laughed.

"Anyway, enjoy the lecture and I'll look for you girls later." Geoff waved and was gone.

"I wonder what cabin he's in?" Bev said. "Too bad he's getting off the ship at Crete. Well anyway, that gives me five days. And then there's the captain . . ."

The cruise director stood up at the microphone and introduced himself. He told a few jokes and then the slides and lecture started.

Alexa leaned back. She was suddenly feeling tired from the long plane flight. She stifled a yawn. As soon as the lecture on Dubrovnik was over she planned to take a stroll around the deck for some air and then turn in. Let Bev stay up and party if she wanted to.

The slides continued. The cruise director explained about changing their money into dinars, but that they were always happy to take American dollars.

"That's good," Bev whispered. "We won't be there long enough and I don't want to get stuck with Yugoslavian money."

It turned out that individual visas would not be needed as had been expected, the ship's purser would take care of everything. But the Yugoslavian authorities would board the ship when they docked and issue landing cards to all the passengers, which must be returned.

"And each passenger has a landing tag hanging on the bulletin board in the reception opposite his name. Don't worry, ladies, we haven't printed your age beside it," the cruise director said. There were a few giggles. "Now, you keep this same tag for the whole cruise. Each time you leave the ship you take it with you and when you return you put the tag back on the bulletin board. That way I can check who is back on board. The *Pericles* sails promptly and the captain will not hold the ship for any latecomers. You will feel very foolish standing on the dock seeing us sailing away without you." More laughter. "Oh yes, one last thing, there will be a lifeboat drill at eleven in the morning and all passengers must attend. You will find a lifejacket in your cabin and instructions as to the location of your lifeboat station. Now, I'm sure you're all tired, so we'll see you in the morning."

"Well he may be tired but I'm not," Bev said. "Let's go in the bar and have a drink."

"I think I'm going to turn in, Bev."

"Oh, come on. Don't tell me you're going to be a party pooper."

"I'm afraid so," Alexa said. "Tonight, anyway. I'll see you at breakfast."

"Breakfast! Are you kidding? I'll get up in time for the lifeboat drill."

The lounge was full of smoke and Alexa was beginning to get a headache. I need some sea air, she thought. I'll take a few turns around the desk and then go to my cabin.

"Good night, Bev," she said. "I'll see you in the morning."

He stood looking out at the sea, smoking a cigarette. He hoped the Yugoslav authorities would not give them any trouble tomorrow. Tito was not as bad as some of them, he was anxious to make a good impression, but he was after all a dictator and it was a Communist country.

The news from Athens had depressed him. More arrests. Unspeakable tortures for those who spoke up against the regime. The Americans would not see this. The colonels were anxious for the tourists to bring money to Greece.

He lit another cigarette. The doctor had warned him to stop. If he was not careful the ulcers could start again. He had tried to cut down but it was difficult.

The Junta had ordered Greek school children to sweep the streets of Athens. "Keep Athens Clean Week," they called it. Any parents who objected would be severely punished. He was glad Fanis was too young. Evangelos would do it, but never Fanis. He was a rebel, Fanis. Already at three. Nikos smiled. He is like I am, he thought.

Katina was a good mother. He had known her family all his life. Her brother, Costas, was his best friend. It was understood from the time they were children together on Corfu that one day he and Katina would marry.

The names were handed down. Evangelos, named for one grandfather, Fanis for the other. In Greece if your name goes on you will never die. Greek men were attracted to foreign women, often they fell in love with them, but they married Greek women. The family. That was what marriage was. Love was something else.

There had been a woman once, blonde, it was during the war, they thought they were in love. It was like a delirium. She was a student at the University of Athens. Her parents were English. He had been crazy enough to think of marrying her, he had told his mother and father.

"She is not Greek?" his mother asked.

"It is impossible," his father said.

He enlisted in the Royal Greek Navy, he became an officer, and then he transferred to cruise ships. The pay was better. He married Katina when he was thirty-two and she twenty-five. She had waited for him, and finally, she had won. They were married in the Church of Saint Spiridon on Corfu. He turned the narrow gold band on his right hand. It felt tight.

A passenger was walking around the pool at the stern of the ship. The breeze caught her short blue chiffon dress and he could see that she had good legs. He liked to look at pretty legs. Most Greek women had heavy legs and they put on weight after the first child.

The woman walked toward him. She was blonde and he realized it was the woman he had talked to earlier, the one who reminded him of . . . yes, that was who she was like. She had the same delicate bone structure, the high cheekbones as Patricia. Patricia. It was a name that was hard for a Greek to pronounce. She used to tease him about it. They were both very young. It was a long time ago.

The sea was starting to get rough and the blonde woman grabbed the railing. Her hair blew across her face. She walked along toward the bridge, slowly, and he could see her face now, and she was not afraid. She seemed at home on a ship. Some passengers got frightened the moment the ship pitched, they asked him nervous questions, as if he could do something about the sea, make it calm. Who could know the sea, understand its moods, like a woman . . .

"Hello, Captain." She stood before him, smiling.

"Hello. You are good sailor."

"I'd better be. My father was a Navy captain. I wouldn't dare get seasick!"

He laughed. "What is your name?"

"Alexa Hollister."

"Alexa. Is very pretty. I like. The little daughter of our king, she is named Alexia. She was born at the Royal Summer Palace on Corfu."

"Corfu." She looked up at him. "I hear it's a beautiful island. Is it?"

"Yes, very beautiful." He paused. "It is my island. I was born there."

"I've wanted to go to Corfu ever since I read a book about Elisabeth of Austria. I want to see the villa she built there. What is it called?"

"Achilleion Palace."

"Yes, that's it. They say she used to wander in its gardens and write poetry. Sad poetry. They called her 'The Lonely Empress.'"

"She had very sad life, Sisi. Much tragedy. But on Corfu she was happy."

"I hear that the island is lovely in spring, that it is covered with wild flowers."

"It is."

"Tell me about it."

He looked down at her. How to describe it to her, Kerkyra, his birthplace, his beloved island? It was difficult for him in English.

"In Greek we call it Kerkyra," he said, "not Corfu."

"Oh, that's much prettier! It has a musical sound. Say it again."

"Kerkyra." He smiled. "You like the name?"

"Yes."

"It is very green, Kerkyra. Not like the other Greek islands. Now the almond trees will be in blossom and everywhere wild flowers." He paused, searching for the words. He thought of the white beaches of Palaiokastritsa, of lambs grazing by a stream, of Easter with lighted candles and the gay scarves of peasants dancing in the town square. Kerkyra. No matter to what foreign port he sailed, his heart always returned. When his days on the sea were finally over, it was there that he would be buried. "Yes," he said, "it is very beautiful."

"Do you have brothers or sisters on Corfu?"

"No more. I am the only one left." He paused. "We were three brothers. My oldest brother was killed by the Germans, the youngest in the Greek Civil War fighting the Communists."

"I'm sorry."

He shrugged. "It is life."

"And your parents?"

"My mother, she died ten years ago, my father not long afterwards. Of my family, I am the only one left."

There was a silence and then she asked, "We get to Corfu the day after tomorrow?"

"Yes. Monday."

"I can hardly wait."

"My wife and my youngest son, they fly over from Athens to meet me there for the day. I have not seem them for five months."

"You will be happy to see them."

"Yes." He could smell the perfume of her hair, a scent like roses and jasmine. It was silky, like spun gold in the moonlight. Katina's hair was coarse and black and always smelled of olive oil. "Yes," he repeated. "Very happy."

"I think I'll go down to my cabin now," she said.

"Goodnight. Sleep well."

"Goodnight, Captain."

She turned and went down the stairway to the deck below, holding carefully to the rail. He watched her until she disappeared from sight. Then he went back to his cabin.

Slowly, not bothering to turn on the light, he took off his uniform. He lay down on the narrow bed in his shorts and undershirt. He lit a cigarette and lay on his back, staring up at the dark.

Memories rose, a key turned in him. Yes, she was like Patricia, the same delicate blondness, the large blue-gray eyes, the sensual mouth. He had wanted to reach out and kiss her, to bury his mouth in her hair. It was as if a craziness had come over him. He must be careful. He was married to Katina, he had a family, a reputation, the pattern of his life was set. Not that he had been faithful to Katina during the fifteen years of their marriage. That was not expected of a Greek man. There had been airline hostesses, tour directors, casual one-night things, no one took it seriously, no one was hurt.

He knew there was something missing in his life, but there was nothing he could do about it.

He watched the smoke curl upward in a spiral as he had seen it over bombed cities during the war. It was a long time before he was able to get to sleep.

Three

*I*n the dream her father was alive and she was a child again waiting for him to return from the sea.

She heard the front door slam and his deep voice in the hall.

"Anybody home?"

Then the whistle, the special whistle he had for her mother, a melody of four notes, exclusively his, she had never heard it since.

"Daddy!"

The hugs, the presents, the stories of adventure. The sailor home from the sea.

No. Home was the sea. The house was where he hung his jacket with the four gold stripes. Where her mother and her brother and she waited.

His home was the ship. That big gray ship that took him away from them. At Christmas, on her birthday . . .

"Daddy, why can't you stay at home like other daddies?"

The sad look. To love the sea is always to be torn in half. It was in his blood. Forever.

"Daddy, don't go!"

She woke up. Her father had made his final voyage, she was no longer a child but a woman with children of her own, and she was on a ship, a Greek ship in the Adriatic Sea.

The cabin was warm and she could feel the ship rolling beneath her and hear the sound of the engines. Her alarm had not gone off and she turned and looked at the small travel clock on the bureau between the beds. Eight-thirty. Next to the clock were photographs of Brooke and Cicily. Brooke had her thirteenth birthday just before she left and she was getting so grown up. Cicily, at ten, had her hair in a ponytail and her mouth tightly shut so her braces wouldn't show. Alexa felt a sudden pang of homesickness at being so far away from them. It was the first time she had left them since . . .

She must not think about that awful night, she must block it from her mind. What had happened could not be changed.

It was over. Keith was dead.

And she was alive. Somehow she must pull herself together and go on living. Time heals, everyone told her. The only thing they did not say was how much time.

It's really stuffy in here, she thought, I must have some air. Some of the passengers had complained of feeling chilly the night before, so they had probably turned on the heat. She got out of bed and tried to open the porthole. Then she noticed the sign that passengers were not to try to open the portholes themselves but to call the cabin boy. It was printed in Greek, English and French.

She decided to get dressed and have breakfast. Afterward she'd take a stroll around the deck. The ship gave a sudden lurch and she fell against the other bed. Through the porthole she could see white-caps and the sky was a misty gray. They should be going along the Dalmation Coast now, but she couldn't make out the shoreline.

The bathroom door had flown open and was banging the wall. She closed it and opened the closet. Several dresses had fallen off their hangers and she hung them up again. She took out a yellow Italian knit suit and a matching scarf, then rummaged around in the bottom of her suitcase for a pair of comfortable low-heeled shoes. The cruise brochure had suggested rubber-soled shoes for the ship, but she didn't have any, other than tennis sneakers, and she didn't want to bring those.

She went in the bathroom and splashed water on her face. The bathroom door, which she had left ajar, kept swinging back and hitting the closet doors every time the ship rolled. She pulled it tight and then turned on the shower. Only a trickle of water came through the nozzle and she turned it around trying to get a heavier spray. Finally she gave up and sponged herself with a washcloth. She would have to get them to fix it after breakfast.

The shelf above the basin where she had put her bottles of make-up and cologne had a narrow chrome bar around it to keep things from falling off. The water carafe and two glasses were securely anchored in a corner.

The ship lurched again and she heard the slapping of a huge wave against the bow. She wondered if the captain had put the stabilizers down.

The captain.

There was something tragic and lonely about him. She suddenly wondered what his wife was like.

I will never, ever, fall in love with a Naval officer, she had once told herself as she watched the Navy wives at Coronado waiting for their husbands' ships to return after long months at sea.

And so she had grown up and married Keith, Keith, who was the opposite of her father . . .

Alexa ran a comb through her hair. I have a feeling there won't be too many at breakfast this morning, she thought.

She opened her cabin door and saw an elderly woman wandering down the corridor. Her hair was wild and her dress was buttoned crookedly.

"I can't find my cabin," the woman said plaintively. "It's somewhere around here. Isn't this Juno deck?"

"No, it's Hermes."

The glass door of the fire extinguisher on the wall had swung open and was banging back and forth each time the ship rolled. Alexa tried to close it but it wouldn't stay.

"My land, I must be on the wrong deck," the woman said. "I thought this was Juno." She looked around and her eyes had a vacant look. She grabbed Alexa's arm. "Can I just tag along with you?"

Just then the cabin boy appeared.

"Young man," she said, "I can't find my cabin."

"Here, let me help you. What is your cabin number?"

"J-27."

"That is one deck below. Here, lady, take my arm."

"Thank you. Isn't he nice?" she said to Alexa. "They're all so nice on this ship." She turned to the cabin boy. "If you could just ask the captain for me, young man, to please keep this ship a bit steadier—"

"Captain Meletis very good captain. I sail with him many times. Sea rough, that is all. Will be better soon."

"My land, I hope so."

A man wearing green, pink, and white striped trousers and a bright green shirt came down the corridor. "Good morning," he said. "Is there some way I can get tea for my wife?" he asked the cabin boy. "She's not feeling very well."

"I will see about it as soon as I take this lady to her cabin. What number are you?"

"H-31." He pointed.

"I will see to it right away, sir."

Alexa started toward the dining salon. There weren't many passengers about and the dining room was deserted. She chose a table by the window. Outside she could see the ocean rising and then disappearing. A steward came quickly over and handed her a menu. She noticed the white gloves again.

"Would you like some melon? Very nice." He smiled.

"Yes, thank you."

"And ham and eggs?"

"No, I'm not that hungry. Just rolls and coffee, please." She handed him back the menu.

"Bacon? Very good."

"No, that's all."

He looked disappointed. Other stewards were standing around at empty tables.

"Am I early or late?" Alexa asked.

He looked puzzled.

"I don't see many people. Have they all eaten?"

"Oh, no. Not many come for breakfast."

The sea rose and disappeared from view again. Alexa decided not to look out.

The steward poured coffee. "My name George," he said. "You take cream?"

"No, thank you. Just black." Another wave slapped the side of the ship. "I guess if this keeps up we won't have the lifeboat drill at eleven."

George smiled. "Oh, the captain, he hold it anyway." There was pride in his voice.

"Oh?" Alexa took a sip of coffee, trying to keep it from spilling. "Do you know if he has the stabilizers down?"

"No stabilizers. Slow speed too much. Then we be late at Dubrovnik."

"I see."

"If it gets bad, captain use stabilizers. We cross Atlantic on *Pericles* in December. Big seas then. This nothing.

He came back with hot rolls. "You take jam?" He passed it and then stood next to her chair with a napkin over his arm. He seemed eager to talk to someone.

"You must be happy to be getting back to Greece after five months, George. Do you have a wife waiting for you?"

He grinned. "No wife. Girlfriend. Maybe I get married—sometime."

She spread jam on a roll.

"This is your first trip to Greece?" he asked.

"Yes."

"You will like. Everybody like."

The man in the striped pants came in the dining salon, looked around the room, and walked over. "May I join you for breakfast?"

"Please do."

He sat down. "I'm Frank Griffin."

"Alexa Hollister."

"These seas don't seem to bother you."

"No, but then I grew up in the Navy."

"I was in the Navy myself during the war. Saw duty in the Pacific."

"How is your wife feeling?"

"Not too well. The cabin boy just brought her some tea. I see your husband didn't make it either."

"My husband?"

"Is he seasick too?"

"Oh, no, I'm—" She would have to get used to questions like that. "I'm traveling alone," she said.

"A pretty woman like you?"

Just then Mrs. Pearson came in leaning on her cane and assisted by Daphne. A steward rushed up to them and led them over to the table.

"Good morning," Mrs. Pearson said. "Not many hardy souls like ourselves up for breakfast."

Alexa noted that Daphne looked rather pale and there were blue circles under her eyes.

"No. Mr. Griffin's wife is under the weather."

"Oh, I'm so very sorry." Mrs. Pearson took in the green, pink, and white striped pants. "I do hope she's better shortly."

"Well actually my wife's not much on cruising," he explained. "She wanted to cancel out at the last minute and stay in Milwaukee. We've just had our first grandchild."

"Congratulations," Mrs. Pearson said. Daphne stared out the window listlessly. "You must be very happy."

"We are. But I told her, 'Edna, you'll have lots of chances to baby-sit with him, but how often do you get to go to Greece?'"

"Very sensible," Mrs. Pearson said. She handed Daphne the menu. "I left my glasses in the cabin. Would you read this to me, please?"

Daphne started reading in a monotonous voice.

"My, everything sounds so delicious. This sea air really gives me an appetite. Herring, I think I'll have that. I hope it isn't frozen. And scrambled eggs and whole-wheat toast."

Daphne turned white and put down the menu. "Excuse me, I'm going back to the cabin and lie down." She made a hasty exit.

"These young people today, they just can't take it," Mrs. Pearson said. "When I used to cross the Atlantic on the *Ile de France* it was much rougher than this. What business are you in, Mr. Griffin?"

"I sell plumbing fixtures."

"Oh. Very interesting."

"Well there's always a need for them. It doesn't fluctuate the way some businesses do."

"No, indeed. Which reminds me, I wonder what the stock market is doing. I don't suppose there's an American newspaper on this ship?" She turned to the steward. "Where could I find a newspaper?"

"Maybe in ship's library." He looked doubtful.

"Where is that?"

"Next to reception office."

"Good, I'll go there after breakfast. And then I must write some postcards."

"Excuse me, I think I'll take a few turns around the deck," Alexa said.

"Hang on to the railing," Frank Griffin said. "You don't want to be swept overboard."

She smiled and got up. "I'll see you later. Probably at the lifeboat drill."

There were several sailors on deck mopping up water that had come over the side. She decided to go to the top deck and walk around by the pool. A stiff breeze was blowing and she tied the yellow scarf securely around her head.

Hanging tightly to the stair railing, she climbed up. A sailor was busy polishing the brass. She smiled and said the one Greek word she had learned. *"Kalimera."* She wondered if she was pronouncing it correctly.

He beamed. *"Kalimerasas."*

She saw someone watching her. He had on a black turtleneck sweater and at first she did not recognize him.

"Good morning," he said.

"Good morning, Captain."

"You speak Greek?" He seemed amused.

"I've learned one word. Good morning. *Kalimera.* Is that right?"

"Very good. Is very difficult language, Greek."

"Yes. I can't even read the alphabet. What does that say?" She pointed to one of the lifeboats.

"M.T.S. PERICLES. Piraeus."

"I'd never know it."

He smiled.

"By the way, are you still planning to have a lifeboat drill at eleven?"

"Of course. Why not?"

She held out her hand. "It's starting to rain."

"So?"

She saluted. "Yes, sir. I'll be there."

He threw back his head and laughed. "You are very sweet. And you salute very well. Where you learn?"

"My father taught me. He ran a tight ship. I don't know if you have the same expression in Greek. He believed in discipline, every-thing ran according to schedule."

"Is necessary."

"I agree."

"You are good sailor, I see. Are many of the passengers sea-sick?"

"A few."

"If I put down stabilizers and cut speed we do not make Dubrovnik in time. It will be dark. No good."

An officer walked over and said something in Greek. The captain seemed annoyed. He replied in an angry flow of Greek, gesturing. The officer answered.

It's so frustrating not being able to understand a word they are saying, she thought.

"Excuse me," the captain said. "I must go now back to the bridge."

She returned to her cabin and wrote postcards, the ones she had bought yesterday in Venice in Piazza San Marco. She chose one of a gondolier on the Grand Canal for Cicily, a view of Saint Mark's Cathedral with its many pigeons in the square for Brooke, and the Bridge of Sighs for her mother.

She read over the cards and then went to the purser's office to mail them. Eric, the cruise director, was in the main reception talking to one of the ship's officers.

"Good morning," he said. "I haven't seen your friend around today."

"She told me last night she was going to sleep late," Alexa said. But she'd better check on Bev and see how she was.

"Don't forget the lifeboat drill at eleven. In half an hour."

"I won't."

She gave her postcards to the purser.

"I'd like these to go airmail," she said. "Will they be mailed at Dubrovnik?"

"Of course, my dear."

"And can I change a traveler's check into Yugoslavian money?"

"When we get to Dubrovnik the officials will come on board with a bank. You can change your money then." He leaned over and took her hand. "I go off duty soon. Would you like to have a drink with me?"

She withdrew her hand. "Thank you, I can't now."

A twinkle appeared in his eyes. "Later, perhaps?"

"Perhaps. I must go now."

The two Boston spinsters came over to the purser's desk and his manner changed abruptly. "Can I help you?"

Alexa smiled to herself. Out of the corner of her eye she saw him counting one dollar bills with a bored expression. Eric and a fat Greek officer were discussing the landing in Dubrovnik, and the senile lady was wandering down the corridor again in a dazed manner. Alexa decided to take another stairway to her cabin and call Bev.

Bev answered on the fourth ring in a sleepy voice.

"What time is it?"

"Almost eleven," Alexa said.

Bev moaned. "I've been seasick all morning. Geoff and I stayed up drinking until three and then the ship started to pitch . . . oh . . ." She moaned again.

"The lifeboat drill is in ten minutes."

"My God! Do we really have to go to that?"

"The captain said so."

"Tell him I'll go down with the ship. I can't get out of bed."

"I'll make an excuse for you. Stay there."

"Thanks." The phone clicked.

Alexa opened the closet and took out the orange lifejacket stored on the top shelf and read the directions. Suddenly there was a long shrill blast, followed by several more. She put on the jacket and fastened it. Passengers were running out into the hall, giggling and fumbling with their lifejackets.

"Mine won't fasten," a fat lady said.

"Where's lifeboat station six?" one woman asked.

"You'd know if you'd read the directions in your cabin," her husband said.

They assembled on the top deck beside the lifeboats. In Alexa's group there were fourteen women and three men.

"Who is going to do the rowing?" laughed one of the women.

"I'm glad this isn't the real thing," someone said.

"On the *Andrea Doria* the crew panicked and jumped for the lifeboats ahead of the passengers," another volunteered.

"Those were Italians. These are Greeks."

The ship's officers marched around the decks inspecting. Alexa was amazed to see Bev suddenly appear two lifeboats away. The bright orange jacket contrasted strangely with the sickly pallor of her face. Her hair had been neatly combed and she was wearing lipstick. Alexa wondered how she had managed. Bev waved wanly.

There was an announcement over the intercom. "Two of the lifeboats will now be lowered."

The sailors stood in place beside them and there was a loud, grinding sound as the boats came down.

"I've been on a lot of cruise ships," a man said, "and I've never seen the lifeboats lowered before. This captain is really thorough."

Alexa looked down at the choppy sea with its white caps and was glad they weren't being asked to abandon ship at that moment.

The lifeboats were raised back into position and there was another announcement that the drill was over. Bouillon would be served on the covered deck below.

Bev came over.

"I thought you were going to stay in bed," Alexa said.

"I was. I think the least the captain could have done was to take part in the inspection after I got all dressed and appeared on deck."

So that was the reason for the lipstick, Alexa thought. "He's probably on the bridge," she said.

"Have you seen him?"

"Earlier."

"Oh?" Bev unfastened her lifejacket. "Let's go and have some bouillon. I guess I'd better try to get something in my stomach."

They started down the stairs. Suddenly Bev pointed. "Oh, my God, look who's coming. That batty woman. Geoff told me that she's senile and her son sent her on this trip. At home she has a companion who lives with her. He should have sent her along too. As it is someone on the ship has to keep an eye on her every minute. She's always getting in the wrong cabin."

"Who is she, do you know?"

"A Mrs. Fitzgerald from Chicago."

"Yoo-hoo!" Mrs. Fitzgerald waved. "Where do we go, girls?"

"The lifeboat drill is over," Alexa said.

"My land! You mean I've missed it?"

"I'm afraid so," Bev said.

Geoff appeared suddenly and took Mrs. Fitzgerald by the arm. "Why don't you sit down in this deck chair and have some bouillon?"

"Why how nice of you. That would be lovely."

Geoff beckoned to a steward.

"You look a little pale," he told Bev.

"I've been seasick all morning. Doesn't this boat ever stop pitching?"

"You'd better not call it a boat in front of the captain. You just haven't gotten your sea legs yet. Why don't you girls sit here with Mrs. Fitzgerald and have some bouillon and crackers? That will make you feel better. Did you take some Dramamine?"

"Yes, but it didn't do any good."

"My husband and I used to take so many sea voyages together when he was alive," Mrs. Fitzgerald said. "We went to the Orient by ship, and another year we went around South America. Mr. Fitzgerald loved to travel."

"You must have seen a lot of interesting places," Alexa said.

"Oh, my yes!" Her voice became wistful. "But it's not the same without him."

Bev was nibbling gingerly on a cracker, trying not to look at the swelling waves.

"I've never been on a Greek ship before," Mrs. Fitzgerald said. "It seems to be very well run, and everyone is so nice."

"The Greeks were pioneers on the seas," Geoff said.

A large wave slapped against the side of the ship. Bev stood up suddenly. "I think I'll go back to my cabin. I feel sick again."

"Do you want me to go with you?" Alexa asked.

"No, I'll be all right." Bev turned and ran.

"I'm so sorry your friend isn't well," Mrs. Fitzgerald said.

"Luckily the sea never bothers me. We went through a typhoon once and Mr. Fitzgerald and I were the only ones who were able to get up for breakfast. Half the crew was seasick too."

"I'd better go and see if there's anything I can do," Alexa said. "Excuse me."

"Let me know how she is," Geoff said. "She had quite a bit to drink last night, so it may be the combination."

Alexa nodded. "See you later."

"How did it go?" Nikos asked.

"Most of the passengers came to the drill," the second officer replied. "We had ten missing."

"Like always. They do not think it necessary. Too much trouble." He looked at the list. "They think it big joke. Then if anything happens—" He made a gesture of cutting his wrist. "The captain's fault. You have latest weather report from Dubrovnik?"

"Rain. Heavy at times."

"Then we cannot anchor near the old town. It is too dangerous for the small boats. We dock at pier instead." He paced back and forth, then picked up his binoculars and looked at the coastline. "Fog. And we are late now."

He studied the chart and then lit a cigarette. It could not be helped. The weather. He tried to bring the ship in on schedule. If they were late the passengers would complain. But it was too risky to open speed.

"I will go speak to the chief engineer," he said.

Four

*D*ubrovnik. She could see the outline of the ramparts rising from the sea and the grove of dark cypresses in the hills beyond. The fog had cleared but the rain continued. Heavy waves pounded against the cliffs and the massive white walls of the ancient town with its red-tiled roofs.

As the ship approached, passengers crowded on deck, some with cameras.

Mr. Overstreet was adjusting his light meter. Finally he gave up. "It's too dark," he said.

"What a shame the sun isn't shining," his wife said.

"Guess you'll just have to buy postcards, old boy," a heavy-set man with a red face remarked. "I never bother with a camera on trips. Too much trouble."

Bev appeared in a raincoat with a scarf tied round her hair, still looking somewhat pale.

"How are you feeling?" Alexa asked.

"A little better, I guess."

Alexa saw Mrs. Pearson, leaning on her cane, and Daphne, still with her bored expression.

"I wonder if that poor girl's going to have any fun on this trip," Bev whispered.

"She seemed under the weather this morning."

"I don't blame her with that watchdog with her all the time."

The ship gave a blast as it swung around past the old town and headed toward the dock, its blue and white flag blowing in the wind.

"Did you see the pilot come on?" Bev asked.

"No, did you?"

"Yes, I was looking out my porthole. A small boat pulled alongside and they let a ladder down and he climbed up. He's with the captain now on the bridge."

Eric came on deck. "Do you have all your landing tags?"

"I'm going to get mine now," Alexa said. "And my umbrella."

"I'm all set," Bev said. "I'll wait here for you."

Alexa took her landing tag off the bulletin board and went back to her cabin. There was a white envelope under her door containing an engraved card with her name written in ink.

"Captain Nikos Meletis, Master of the *M.T.S. Pericles*, cordially invites you for dinner tonight at eight," it read.

He tried to conceal his growing irritation with the chunky Yugoslavian pilot standing beside him in the wheelhouse giving orders as if he were the master of the ship.

The pilot might know the waters of this harbor better, Nikos Meletis thought, but he does not know how the ship handles. Only I, her captain, know her. I know every inch of her, how many degrees to turn her, how she will handle in any circumstance.

They passed a buoy in the outer harbor.

"Okay, Captain, two hundred and forty-seven degrees true, half speed," the pilot said.

Passengers were climbing up the narrow stairs to the bridge to get a better view. They were crowding on the starboard side so it was difficult for him to see. Nikos shouted an order in Greek to an officer to clear them.

The officer ran and stretched a rope across. "Captain's orders," he said. "Please go below."

There was a Russian freighter in port flying the hammer and sickle and it gave him a chill. If there should be an accident in a Communist port with a Greek ship . . . he did not like to think about it.

Always one foot in a prison. The story of his life.

An officer was standing at the top of the gangway and sailors were getting ready to lower it as soon as the ship pulled alongside the dock.

He saw taxis waiting in the rain to take the passengers to the old town. The drivers were standing around in groups arguing and waving their hands. No matter what price they agreed on before, he always heard tales later from the passengers how they had been over-charged.

Sailors were getting ready with ropes to throw to the men on the dock below. An officer on the Russian freighter was watching them through binoculars.

Always problems, he thought. Soon the immigration officials would be boarding, more questions, papers, everything must be in order. They always tried to find something. All the passports of passengers and crew must be cleared before anyone got off the ship.

He paced the bridge tensely smoking, shouting orders through a megaphone. What are those men doing down there on the pier? he thought. Idiots! Catch the ropes! The ship came alongside the pier. He could see all the Russian sailors standing on the deck of the freighter watching.

The gangway was lowered and the officials started up it. An officer was holding back some passengers eager to disembark. He hoped they would all be back on the ship on time. A sailor placed the sign with the departure time written in Greek, English, French and German at the top of the gangway.

Now would begin the endless procession of people coming to see him about something. For the captain, never a rest. He must give the final decision on everything. The chef wanted to see him about something later. Also the purser. He buttoned his jacket. The officials were here.

He held out his hand. "How do you do? I am Captain Meletis. Welcome aboard."

*   *   *

Alexa, Bev and Geoff walked down the dock to the waiting taxis. The rain was coming down heavier and Geoff was in the middle trying to hold Alexa's small travel umbrella over the three of them.

"Why don't you get a real English-sized umbrella?" Geoff asked. "One of those big black ones that really covers you."

"I know. This folding travel one seemed great when I bought it, but at least it's better than hers." Alexa pointed to Mrs. Griffin, whose umbrella had blown inside out. Mr. Griffin, still in his wildly-striped pants and with a look of annoyance on his face, was trying to straighten it.

They stepped over several mud puddles into a taxi, and after a brief discussion about the price and whether the driver would come back for them afterward, they took off, careening at a wild speed down the narrow, muddy road.

"I wonder how you say 'Go slow' in Yugoslavian?" Bev asked, holding on to the seat.

Geoff said something to the driver, but it had no effect. There weren't enough taxis to go around, so he was rushing to leave them off and go back for more passengers.

Finally Geoff said something in German that the driver understood, but by that time the walls of the old town were in sight.

The driver agreed to pick them up at six at the main entrance.

"I hope he understands," Alexa said. "It's a long walk back to the ship."

"Don't worry, luv, he'll be here."

They crossed the bridge and walked along the cobblestone streets. Groups of young men were standing around watching them. They went in an old church, the town hall, and looked in the windows of shops.

Some of the passengers from their ship passed.

"All the shops are closed," one of the ladies complained.

"That's the best news I've heard today," her husband said. "You can't see anything in all this rain. That looks like a bar and it's open. Let's go."

"There's a beautiful church down this street," Geoff said. "And I think there might be a Mass going on."

"You mean they still allow church services in Yugoslavia?" Alexa asked.

"Oh yes, Tito's not as strict as the other Communist dictators. Are either of you girls Catholic?"

"I am," Bev said. "But not a very good one. My sister makes up for it. She's a nun."

Geoff looked surprised. "Well let's look in, if you'd like."

They pushed open the heavy doors of the cathedral. Rows of women in raincoats and kerchiefs were praying on the wooden benches. They were mostly old with heavily-lined faces. A priest with a rich, low voice was speaking in Serbian and they repeated after him, fingering their rosaries.

What things they must have seen in their lives, Alexa thought. They had survived the war, the German occupation, and now the Communists. At least they were still permitted their religion. There were very few men in the congregation and she wondered if they had all been killed in the war.

"Do you know where they are in the Mass?" Geoff whispered to Bev.

She shook her head. "I can't understand what he's saying. It's High Mass, that's all I know."

A woman came in by a side door, crossed herself with holy water, and knelt in the row ahead of them.

I hope we don't seem like tourists, Alexa thought. She wanted to be part of the service, to mingle with these people, to absorb the atmosphere. In this ancient dark church with its flickering candles, the old priest's voice chanting, there was beauty and peace.

"We'd better go now," Geoff whispered. "The show at the theatre is in five minutes."

The tourist office had arranged a program of folk dances for the ship's passengers. It had already begun when they arrived and they found seats in the back of the darkened theatre. The dancers

were young and attractive and wore costumes from different parts of
Yugoslavia. The music was stirring. An interpreter explained each
dance and said that they had been handed down from generation to
generation. The costumes were gay and colorful and Alexa thought
how she would love to buy a costume for Cicily and Brooke.

Tomorrow the stores would be open, but they would be gone.
That was the trouble with tours like these, there was never enough
time.

A man was singing now and playing a native instrument. He
had a beautiful voice, that of an operatic tenor.

She thought again of all the things these people had endured,
horrors that Americans had never known, and she was sure that it
was the music and dancing that had kept them sane.

There was clapping, the singers and dancers bowed, and the
show was over.

The cruise director stood up.

"Now, all passengers from the *Pericles,* the taxis will be waiting
by the bridge outside the main entrance to take you back to the ship.
Remember that the ship sails promptly at seven. If you cannot find
the main entrance just say to anyone, *'Gdja taxi?'* Now, I want to hear
you all repeat it after me, *'Gdja taxi?'"*

"*Gdja taxi?*" There was giggling.

"Fine. See you back at the ship. Don't forget to turn in your
landing tags."

They were all seated at the table when the captain arrived. The
men stood up and he shook hands with each one. The steward had
placed a list with the passengers' names beside the captain and he
glanced at it briefly. Alexa was seated on his left. At his right was
Mrs. Winthrop Pearson and across the table her granddaughter
Daphne. Also at the table were the Overstreets, an elderly man who
seemed to be by himself, and the two ladies whose luggage was missing, still in their tweed traveling suits.

The steward poured wine and the captain raised his glass.

"To a good journey," he said. His eyes caught Alexa's for a moment, then moved around the table.

The captain's chair faced the rest of the dining room and was placed in the center so that he could hear all the conversation. He listened politely to the questions about Greece, he asked his guests which part of the United States they were from, and Alexa had the feeling, that even though he was polite and attentive, this was the part of his job that he liked the least.

Mrs. Pearson asked him how long it had been since he had seen his family.

"Five months. My wife, she is flying to Corfu tomorrow from Athens with my youngest son."

"What a happy reunion that will be for you, Captain," Mrs. Overstreet said.'

"Ah, yes. It will." He avoided looking at Alexa.

"You must get very lonely away from your family so much," Mr. Overstreet said.

"Yes. But it is my work."

"When we get to Athens will you have several weeks off to be with them?" Mrs. Pearson asked.

"No." He sipped some wine. Alexa noticed he did not eat very much. "You see, we go right out again that evening on another cruise."

"But that isn't fair!" one of the ladies in the tweed suits exclaimed.

The captain shrugged. He glanced around the table. "No one drinks his wine?" He raised his glass. *"Yiassou!"*

They all raised their glasses and drank.

"Very good wine, Captain," Mr. Overstreet remarked.

The captain looked pleased. "You like? It is Greek."

They finished dinner and the captain stood up. "Thank you very much for dining with me."

"Thank you, Captain."

He shook hands again with each one. "Good night." He went up the stairs in back of the table.

Alexa joined Bev and the others in the lounge.

"I noticed you at the captain's table," Bev said. "How was it?"

"Very pleasant."

"Yes, the captain is just charming," Mrs. Pearson said. "Just think, he hasn't seen his wife for five months, poor man."

"I wonder if he's going to come in the lounge tonight?" Bev said.

"He's probably going to bed early to rest up," Mr. Overstreet remarked slyly.

"Ellwood!" admonished his wife."

"I think he's groovy," Daphne said. "Maybe he's not happy at home. He may like being at sea all the time."

Alexa wondered about that. If he wasn't happily married it was the ideal set-up. His wife sitting at home raising his family, all the attractive women on shipboard. He couldn't be faithful all that time to a wife he seldom saw. Geoff had implied that the captain was a ladies' man. And he was Greek. She didn't know much about Greek men but she knew that Italian men all played around.

"Oh, there he is," Daphne said.

Alexa turned around and saw the captain standing in the doorway at the entrance of the lounge. He towered over the stewards and the other officers. He paused for a moment and then walked slowly across the lounge, smiling and greeting passengers.

"May I join you?" he asked.

"Please do, Captain," Mrs. Pearson said.

There was an empty chair next to Alexa. He sat down.

"We were wondering where you were, Captain," Bev said.

"We thought you might be resting up for tomorrow," Mr. Overstreet said.

His wife glared at him.

"Rest? I am not tired." He turned to Alexa. "Would you like to dance?"

"I'd love to."

He stood up. "Excuse us," he said to the group.

He led Alexa to the dance floor. He pulled her to him so that her forehead was against his chin and hummed as they danced. Over his shoulder Alexa saw the purser come over and ask Bev to dance.

"You are a good dancer," he said.

"Thank you. So are you, Captain."

"Ah, on Corfu, everyone they love to dance. We have Greek show one night on ship. You will see."

"But isn't it true that only the men dance in Greece, not the women?"

"No. The women too."

"In the movies I've seen the men are dancing in a row and there are no women. Like in *Zorba the Greek*."

"Ah, that is different. But the women, they also dance."

"Have you been to Malta before, Captain?"

"I was there once. In a submarine." He pulled her closer so that his cheek was against hers. "You are very sweet."

They continued to dance and she noticed Bev watching them. The ship rolled slightly and he held her tighter. The dance floor was at a slight angle.

The orchestra was playing a Greek song.

"What's the name of that song?" she asked.

He listened. *"Oneiro Demeno."*

"I like it. What does it mean in English?"

"Dreams . . . how do you say . . . tied?"

"Tied dreams?"

"Attached. Like the ship when she is tied to the dock."

"Oh." It didn't quite make sense. "It's very pretty. I'd like to get a record of it."

"Is very well-known Greek song. I will write down name for you."

The vocalist with the ship's orchestra was singing the words.

"It sounds sad," Alexa said. "Is it a love song?"

He smiled. 'All Greek love songs are sad."

The music stopped and he led her back to the table.

"Thank you very much," he said. He called a steward and said something rapidly in Greek. The steward came back with a pad and pencil. The captain started to write, then hesitated. "You do not know Greek alphabet?"

She shook her head.

"I write it both ways. You take it into record shop in Athens and show them this."

Bev leaned forward, her breasts almost falling out of her dress. "Captain, when are we going to learn how to do the Greek dances?"

"You like? I arrange a dancing class. We have two days at sea between Tunis and Crete."

"That would be fun," Alexa said.

"And you teach the class, Captain," Bev said. "You'd have every woman on the ship signing up for them."

He looked uncomfortable and ran his hand through his hair. Alexa noticed again the gold wedding ring that he wore on his right hand and she wondered if that was a Greek custom.

"I've read that the Greeks believe very much in fate," Mrs. Pearson remarked. "Is that true, Captain?"

"Ah, yes, we have a saying in ancient Greek, 'To moraion phigin adinato.'"

"What does it mean?" Bev asked.

"It means the fate—" He paused, searching for the right word. "It is impossible to escape fate." He looked at Alexa.

"Then they believe in astrology in Greece?" Daphne asked. "You know, reading your fortune by the stars."

"The stars?" He smiled. "No. But the women, they sit in the *kafenion* and drink the Turkish coffee, then they turn over the cup and read what it says."

"Like tea leaves?" Mrs. Overstreet asked.

"Yes, but they do it with coffee instead."

"And only the women believe in this in Greece, not the men?"

"Yes, only the women." He shrugged. "The men, they have other things to do."

"Right on," said Mr. Overstreet.

"The men dance and the women sit around reading their fortunes in coffee cups. Did you ever have your fortune read, Captain?" Bev asked.

"Once. I had an aunt who could read the coffee cups."

"Was she good?"

"Yes, very good."

"What did she tell you?"

"Ah," he smiled, "I do not remember." He looked at Alexa and again she could feel his eyes burning through her. "It was a long time ago." He stood up. "I must go now to the bridge. I read the stars to find out where we are."

Five

*I*t always gave him a strange feeling to return to Corfu.

So many happy times he remembered from before the war. Diving through the seaweed for colored shells, catching crabs, playing in the olive groves where he and his brothers chased lizards hiding in the moss-covered walls. Listening to the cicadas and goldfinches and the buzzing of insects in the thickets of myrtle. There was nothing better to be a boy growing up on an island and to be a Greek.

Nikos paced back and forth on the bridge of the ship smoking a cigarette.

So long ago now, those good times with the family. His father, tall, severe, his mother singing in the kitchen while she baked bread, his two brothers . . .

They were all gone now.

He still had the ikon of Saint Nicholas, his patron saint, that his mother had given him the first time he went to sea. It had protected him during the war and on many voyages since.

They were passing through the narrow channel between Albania and Corfu. There was bright sunshine, the air was warm, a beautiful day. The sailors were happy. A Greek ship returning to Greek soil after five months in the Caribbean.

He looked through his binoculars. He could see figures waiting on the dock, waving at the ship. He gave a blast of the whistle.

He wondered if Fanis had changed much. At this age there were always changes. They would telephone Evangelos in Athens. He was in school and he would see him in a week. At Easter the shipping line let the officers' families travel on the ship. The purser was not married but all the other officers were. For a Greek man, the family came above everything. The sons. When you get old, they are your tomorrow. If you have no sons, there is nothing.

A girl on the dock was waving a long white scarf. She was young, the girlfriend of one of the crew. The sailors were leaning out of the portholes cheering.

He even liked the pilot who had come on. But then he was Greek. Nikos smiled. It was good to be back in a Greek port. Seagulls were following the ship. Greek seagulls.

They pulled alongside the dock. He saw Katina and Fanis. She was wearing a red sweater and a brown skirt. She had put on weight. Fanis was jumping up and down. He waved to them.

Fanis started to run toward the ship. Katina caught him just as he neared the edge of the dock.

Nikos smiled. You always had to run after Fanis. He was crazy about ships, about water. Not Evangelos. Evangelos, plump, studious, his head always in a book. He took after Katina's family.

He waved again. It was good for a man to have sons.

Alexa looked up and saw the captain waving from the bridge to some people on the dock. She followed his eyes and saw a woman holding a small boy by the hand. The woman was dark, very Greek-looking, her heavy black hair escaping from a coil at the back of her neck, and Alexa judged her to be in her early forties. Alexa wondered if she had been pretty when the captain married her. The woman walked down the pier holding tightly to the little boy who was trying to pull away. The boy was dressed neatly in gray shorts and a blue sweater with high white socks and polished black shoes, and Alexa wondered again at the European custom of dressing up their children in their Sunday best, while the women were indifferent about the way they looked.

Somehow she had pictured the captain's wife differently.

She moved away from the rail. The sailors were shouting and laughing and calling greetings in Greek to the people on the dock.

Then she saw the sign: *21 APRILIOU.*

April, she thought, I can read that much in Greek, but today isn't the twenty-first, it's the sixth of April.

The purser had come on deck and was standing at the top of the gangway. She went up to him.

"What does that sign say?" she asked, pointing.

His face darkened. "The Junta," he whispered. "It is when they took over. Three years ago. They put the signs everywhere so we do not forget. As if we could forget." He stopped suddenly.

"I see," she said. She had heard that it was not safe for any Greek to speak against the colonels. They never knew who might report them, turn in their names as traitors to the regime. "I understand," she repeated. She would not mention it again.

21 APRILIOU. Like the swastika over Nazi Germany, she thought. It was like a gray cloud suddenly descending.

She took her landing tag from the bulletin board. The other passengers were forming in groups, waiting to board the sightseeing buses that had been chartered.

Eric clapped his hands for attention. The chattering continued. He picked up the microphone by the reception desk.

"Ladies and gentlemen, we are about to disembark at Corfu. Be sure to pick up your landing tags before you leave the ship. The buses are waiting. You will be served a box luncheon at Kanoni after we have seen Achilleion Palace. The temperature is warm. It is a beautiful day. Welcome to Greece."

Alexa looked out the window of the bus. Groves of olive trees and fields of wild flowers, yellow, purple, and white. A peasant woman walking along the road in a gray dress with a black kerchief, carrying a blue basket on her head. Stucco houses, white with blue shutters, pink with green shutters, tile roofs, wisteria, calla lilies, laundry hanging out to dry in the bright sunshine.

"Oh, look," Bev said. "How adorable!"

A baby goat was drinking from a stream. Two old women in black dresses and kerchiefs looked up at the bus and smiled. One waved, and Alexa could see that she had two teeth missing in front.

They passed a young boy pulling a donkey. There were clumps of poplars and in the distance they could see Mount Pantokrato.

"Did you read Lawrence Durrell's book about Corfu?" asked the man sitting across the aisle from them who was an English teacher at a boys' prep school in Connecticut.

"No, but I'm going to when I get back," Alexa said.

They started up the hill toward Achilleion and were met by another tourist bus coming down. The road was too narrow for them to pass so both buses stopped while the drivers yelled at each other in Greek, waving their hands.

"This is interesting," Bev said. "We may be here all day."

Finally their driver made a gesture with five fingers extended, turning his open palm to the man. The other driver did the same thing and spat.

"I think that's the gesture they warn tourists not to use if they're counting on their fingers," Alexa said. "It's supposed to be one of the worst Greek insults."

Shouting more obscenities in Greek, the driver of their bus backed down the road and pulled over so the other bus could pass.

"I'm glad they settled that," the English teacher said. He took out his guide book and started reading a description of Achilleion to his wife.

They pulled up outside the gates of the villa and let everyone off the buses. Achilleion was a smaller version of Schönbrunn Palace in Vienna and painted the same Hapsburg yellow. In front of the entrance was an oval bed of bright red tulips. There were statues everywhere, on the balconies, the stairways, in the gardens, dominated by the favorite of Empress Elisabeth, the dying Achilles. It was all garish and overdone, Alexa thought, but the setting was superb. Looking out over the sea toward the coast of Albania, there were winding paths with wildflowers and purple iris, old pines and cypress trees, and birds and butterflies. She could picture the empress wandering through these gardens, lonely and tortured, mourning the death of her son, the Crown Prince Rudolph at Mayerling, and somehow finding peace here.

"Now let's go inside," said Anastasia, the Greek guide.

The interior of the villa was decorated in monstrous taste with much gilt and marble. The upstairs was roped off, and Alexa was disappointed, as she wanted to see the bedroom of Elisabeth.

"This is the chapel where the empress spent much time praying for her son," the guide said.

There was a beautiful painting of the Virgin and Child above the altar and on the ceiling a large painting of Christ and his disciples. The chapel was tiny but it had an air of peace and beauty. Alexa was sorry they had to rush on so quickly.

They went through the other rooms, each more hideous than the last.

"This is Kaiser Wilhelm's desk," said Anastasia. "You must remember that the Kaiser had the palace after Elisabeth, and much of the heavy furniture that you see belonged to him."

There were photographs of the Kaiser and his family and pictures of the royal yacht. In glass cases were letters and jewelry belonging to Elisabeth and the Hapsburgs.

The group stood in front of a large oil painting of the empress.

"As you can see," Anastasia said, "she was one of the most beautiful women in Europe."

The eyes of the tragic Elisabeth looked down on them.

"But unfortunately," continued the guide, with some satisfaction, "beauty is no guarantee of happiness. Now, back to the buses." Anastasia wore heavy horn-rimmed glasses and on her upper lip there was the hint of a mustache. "Please, ladies and gentlemen, do not stop to buy postcards or souvenirs now. We are due at Kanoni and we are late. Come." She beckoned to the group and said something in Greek to the guard, shrugging her shoulders hopelessly.

*   *   *

Nikos walked slowly along the beach holding his son's hand. There were herring-gull tracks in the sand and the cove was deserted except for an old fisherman.

"We must get back to the house now, Fanis," he said. "It is time for luncheon. Mother will be waiting."

It was precious, this time with his son. They climbed the steep path, rocky and winding among the myrtle groves. At the top of the cliffs he looked back and the sea had become a deep emerald.

"Can we go fishing afterward?" Fanis asked.

"Perhaps for a little while. I have to get back to the ship."

Fanis looked disappointed.

He rumpled his son's dark curly hair. "I think there will be time."

Fanis smiled.

To the boy, Nikos thought, the touch of the father is different from the touch of the mother. The mother is gentle, she protects him, but he needs the father. The father must teach him to be strong, brave, to be a man. A Greek man.

"Look!" Fanis pointed. A brown and yellow shell lay in the path, and then a wrinkled, scaly head appeared cautiously and bleary eyes blinked at them. "A tortoise!" He ran toward it.

The tortoise blinked again, then he spread his legs, rose slowly, and ambled down the path toward a clover patch under a cypress tree. They watched him. The tortoise's mouth opened, he tore off the clover leaves and sat there munching happily.

"Come," Nikos said. "We must eat too."

They walked on. A swallow-tail butterfly pirouetted in the sunshine. The tinkling of lambs' bells came from the olive groves.

Ah, my son, he thought, may you never lose the wonder and joy in being alive that you have now.

"Nikos! Fanis!" It was Katina's voice calling them.

"We are coming."

He saw her standing in front of the white stucco house with its blue tile roof and shutters. The house of her parents.

"Stelios and Manolis are here," she called.

"Ah, good." His cousins. He had not seen them for a long time. They would sit around the table and talk, tell stories, find out what had happened to everyone. And then suddenly, as always, he would become restless, he would want to get back to the ship. "Hurry, Fanis," he said. "We are late."

Six

*T*he passengers trouped up the gangway. Many of the women were carrying woven Greek bags and large blue *komboli* or worry beads.

"These will cause a sensation in Buffalo," Bev said.

" I bought some smaller ones." Alexa showed Mrs. Pearson and Daphne some pale green beads on a loose chain ending in a tassel. "They're supposed to be made of olive wood."

Daphne had a bright blue bag woven with designs in yellow, green, and white. It was knotted and casually slung over one shoulder. "I can use this to carry my books at college," she said.

Mrs. Pearson had bought several books about Corfu. "They say this is where Ulysses was washed ashore," she said.

Alexa saw the senile lady, Mrs. Fitzgerald, carrying a reproduction of an ancient Greek vase.

Bev nudged Alexa. "I bet those people can't wait to see the tourist buses unload to sell them all this junk! How is she ever going to get that in her suitcase?"

"Maybe she intends to carry it with her."

Mr. Griffin was still wearing his striped pants and had several dozen worry beads. "The girls at the office will get a big kick out of these," he said. "And I can give the rest to clients."

Another person was taking some worry beads back for "my friends who are going to psychiatrists."

The captain passed them and Alexa noticed that he was not in uniform but had on gray slacks and a blue shirt.

"Did you have a good day?" he asked her.

"Yes. Corfu is beautiful."

"I am glad you like." He seemed preoccupied. He glanced down at the dock. Alexa saw his wife and little boy standing next to an elderly couple in black. They were waving.

Alexa wondered if he had been alone with her, if they had made love after the long separation. It was hard to picture anything romantic between them. "Let's watch us pull out," she said to Bev.

He was up on the bridge now with the megaphone giving instructions to the sailors on the dock. They started to take up the gangway.

"I bet the captain's sorry to be leaving," Bev said. "His little boy's cute, isn't he. He looks like him."

"Yes," Alexa said.

"I'd hate to be his wife, though. She never sees him. And you know there must be two or three women on every cruise."

Alexa didn't reply.

"Let's go in the lounge and have a drink. But first I want to put all this stuff in my cabin."

"Go ahead. I'll be with you in a little while. I'd like to take a shower and change."

The ship gave a whistle and the distance separating the shore grew larger. Alexa stood leaning against the railing. The people waving on the dock were now small specks. Finally Corfu disappeared from sight and she went inside.

"Today the military court in Athens sentenced newspaper publisher, Ionnis Kapsis, to five years in prison for printing an interview in *Ethnos* calling for the restoration of democracy in Greece," said the clipped voice of the BBC announcer.

Nikos turned up the broadcast.

Today Katina had told him about a close friend of theirs, Petros

Gleridis, who was arrested in December. He was picked up on his way to work and taken to the *Asphalia*, headquarters of the security police on Bouboulinas Street. There he was questioned and subjected to *falanga* and other tortures. A motorcycle machine was run next to the interrogation room to drown out the screams of the victims. He was sent to Averoff Prison and kept in a cell not fit for an animal. After three months, they released him, a total wreck. He still was not told why he had been arrested in the first place.

But then the Junta did not need a reason.

It was worse than the war when you could at least fight back. This way your enemy waited in the shadows and you did not know who he was. They said that the harbor master of Piraeus was one of them.

He switched off the radio. He must put on his uniform and go down to the cocktail lounge. The passengers would be expecting him.

"Did you have a nice visit with your family, Captain?"

"Yes, very nice. Thank you."

"You must have seen changes in your little boy."

"Ah, yes. Fanis, he has grown very much."

"What is his name?"

"Theofanis. We call him Fanis for short. It is—how you say in English—?"

"Nickname."

"Yes, nickname."

"Tell me, Captain, is it true that in Greece you celebrate your saint's day instead of your actual birthday?"

"It is true. Fanis, he celebrates January sixth. It is the twelfth day after Christmas when the cross is thrown in the water and they dive for it. The feast of Saint Theofanis."

"Then your saint must be Saint Nicholas, Captain."

"That is right."

"When is his day?"

"The sixth of December."

"But that is not your real birthday, is it Captain?"

"No. No, I am born in February." Out of the corner of his eye he saw Alexa coming in the lounge. She was alone. He stood up. "Excuse me."

She saw him walking toward her.

"Good evening, Captain."

"Did you enjoy your day?"

"Yes, very much." She wondered if he had enjoyed his. "I like Corfu. Kerkyra. Am I pronouncing it right?"

"The accent is on first part. Kerkyra." He smiled. "I am glad you like." His eyes went over her, dark and intense. "How beautiful you look."

"Thank you."

"Would you join me for a drink?"

Without waiting for a reply he took her arm and led her over to a sofa in the corner.

"Let us sit here," he said. "What would you like to drink?"

"A glass of Perrier, please."

"That is all?"

"Yes."

He smiled. "I see you are big drinker. Like I am."

He snapped his fingers and a steward came over. He said something to him in Greek. More passengers were coming in the lounge. Across the room she saw Bev with the purser. Mrs. Griffin, obviously drunk, walked by and almost fell as the ship rolled. She clutched a post and a steward took her arm and guided her to her seat. Alexa noticed a look of disgust on the captain's face.

"I see her come on board this afternoon with big bottle of vodka," he said. He looked around. "I wonder where is the husband?"

"He won't be too hard to find in those striped pants," Alexa said. "Oh, there he is."

Frank Griffin was standing near the dance floor talking to

Daphne. At the same time the captain noticed him and said something in Greek to a steward.

"If she have a fall I am responsible. She could sue the line."

"Yes, I know." His eyes seemed to burn through her and she started to feel uncomfortable. "How long have you been a captain?" she asked.

"Twelve years. I was the youngest captain of the line. Nobody would believe I was a captain." He shrugged and took a sip of Campari and soda.

Again she noticed the gold band on his right hand.

"Tell me, Captain, is that a custom in Greece?"

"What?"

"To wear your wedding ring on your right hand instead of the left?"

"Yes. We wear it on the left hand when we are engaged."

"I see. Does your wife ever come on the cruises?"

"Sometimes in the Greek Islands. But she gets seasick."

"Do you bring your sons on the ship?"

"Yes, the little one, Fanis." He smiled and a special light came into his eyes. "He is crazy about ships."

"Does he want to have his own ship some day?"

"Ah, I do not know. I do not know if I want that life for him. Then he will be like I am, never free, always tied to the ship."

"But you would not want any other life."

"Maybe not. It is all I have done. I do not know anything else. We sailors, we are so stupid. We know only the sea. On the land they take us in business."

"I don't know what it would be like to have sons. I have only daughters."

He seemed surprised. "You have children?"

"Yes."

"How old are they?"

"Brooke is thirteen and Cicily is ten."

"You must have been married very young."

"I was nineteen."

"Nineteen." He paused. "When I was nineteen I was in the Resistance."

"That must have been dangerous."

"Life is dangerous." He shrugged. "Everyone in Greece was in the Resistance during the war. Twice I was captured and sentenced to be shot. Twice I escaped."

"Were you captured by the Italians or the Germans?"

"The Germans. On Corfu."

"How did you escape?"

"I made friends with a young German guard and he let me go out one day to work. I was not supposed to go out. I was in a cell with the ones who were to be shot. So I escape. I swim across the channel from Corfu to Albania, then I walk through the mountains to Northern Greece. There I am captured again, but I got away."

"You were not meant to die then."

"No." He touched her cheek with his fingers. "Alexa. It is like a Greek name. How did you get it?"

"I was named after my father. His name was Alexander."

Some passengers were coming over.

"Would you like to dance?" he asked quickly.

"Yes, I'd love to."

He pulled her close to him on the dance floor, his chin touching her forehead, and again he smelled the perfume of her hair and felt the softness of her body. He was hardly aware of the other passengers dancing near them, only of the music and holding her.

"You are very sweet," he said.

He held her tighter and he knew that he wanted her and that he should not. She was not like many of the women who came on the ship who wanted only a casual fling. With her love was serious. He thought of a friend of his, the captain of the *Amphitryon*, who had fallen in love with an American woman, divorced his Greek wife, disgraced his family. There was a terrible scandal and the company had fired him. He had been with the line twenty years. And after all that the woman had left him, first humiliating him with other men.

"You are very serious, Captain. Are you thinking of problems with the ship?"

"Ah," he laughed. "Always."

Captain Leptakis of the *Amphitryon* had killed himself. His first wife was willing to take him back, but his sons would no longer speak to him. He had disgraced the family.

The ship pitched and a couple bumped into them.

"Sorry, Captain," said the man. "Can't you keep this boat from rolling?"

"Yes, it's really getting rough," his wife said.

The same stupid questions. Nikos forced a smile. "I will see what can be done."

"What time do we arrive in Malta, Captain?"

"The afternoon."

The couple left the dance floor, complaining that it was too difficult to dance with the ship rolling.

He must go up now and check on things. There was really nothing to do but the passengers would expect it. They would write letters to the company that the captain was dancing with a pretty girl and not concerned about their safety.

The music stopped and he led Alexa off the dance floor. "Thank you very much," he said. "I must go now to the bridge to fix position of the ship."

The sky was powdered with golden stars, the wind full of the whispers of distant rain, and billows of emerald foam came almost as high as the bridge. She felt like a figure out of ancient Greek mythology standing on the prow of the ship, she wanted to sail the seas forever. So this is the hold it has on men, she thought. Now I understand.

She did not know how long she was there before she sensed someone watching her. She turned in the dark and saw a figure standing in a dimly lighted doorway. He walked toward her and she saw that it was the captain. He had taken off his jacket and tie.

"The sea is rough tonight. You are not afraid?" he asked.

"No." She smiled.

He looked up and down the deck. All the passengers had gone to bed and the officer on watch was in the wheelhouse with the helmsman.

"Come," he said, holding out his hand. "It is starting to rain. You will get wet." He pulled her into his cabin and closed the door.

The cabin was small with a desk, a chair, and a sofa against the wall. There were some books in Greek on a shelf and several American paperbacks of popular novels. The door to the next room was open and she could see a narrow bed with the covers turned back.

He pointed to some framed pictures on the wall.

"That is my family," he said. "My sons." There was pride in his voice.

She walked over to take a closer look at the pictures. There were photographs in separate frames of the boys and one of them together with their arms around each other. The older boy was very dark and looked nothing like him, the little one had brown curly hair and a roguish smile. She tried not to stare at the other photograph, a woman with black hair in a heavy coil and large dark eyes that had a melancholy expression. His wife.

"They are handsome boys," she said.

"Ah, yes. They are good boys. Fine sons." He pointed to the sofa. "Sit down."

She saw his eyes on her again.

"Would you like something to drink?"

"No, thank you."

He reached over and took her hand. "You are very beautiful," he said. "Why you come on this trip alone?"

"Because I wanted to get away."

"From what?"

"I don't know." From the past, she thought, from all that happened that I am still not able to face. "A change, I guess. To see new places. I've always wanted to go to Greece."

He had not taken his eyes from hers but he did not seem to be listening to what she was saying.

"You know I am very attracted to you," he said. "From the first moment I saw you."

His right hand was stroking hers and she saw the gold wedding ring.

"I must go down to my cabin now," she said quickly. "It is late."

He held her hand tighter. "Do not go. I do not want you to go yet, Alexa. A little while longer. I cannot sleep."

I cannot sleep either, she thought, but I am afraid. I am afraid of what will happen between us. It can have no happy ending and I do not want to be hurt again.

"I want you," he said.

And he took her in his arms and she felt herself trembling as he kissed her mouth and her neck. His hands went over her, caressing her gently, he murmured things in Greek that she did not understand, and yet she knew the meaning. I want him, she thought, I want to surrender to him completely, now and forever. His fingertips stroked her face, she did not know anyone could be so gentle yet at the same time so intense.

"I will never hurt you, *Alexa mou*," he whispered. "Come."

They lay side by side on the narrow bed in his cabin feeling the ship rolling beneath them. She saw his jacket with the four gold stripes on the back of a chair, her dress tossed over it like a cloud of lilac chiffon, her silver slippers on the floor. Now, she thought, now is all that matters. She felt his lips all over her, the ship was rolling from side to side and she could hear the waves slapping the bow.

"Hold me," he said. "Like this. Ah, that is good. Yes, yes . . ." he moaned. "You like?"

"Yes," she whispered.

"You make me crazy."

"You make me crazy too."

"Darling . . . now, now. Yes, yes, like that, come now, darling, now."

It was as if they were one, nothing mattered but this moment. She felt the ship rising and falling and him holding her, closer and closer, and then there was only him . . .

The storm continued, but neither of them was aware of it.

Finally she said, "What time do you have to get up?"

"Five o'clock."

"That's not very long from now. I'd better go."

"Do not go yet." He stroked her face. "Alexa. *Alexa mou.* Do you know what that means in Greek?"

"No."

"My Alexa." He kissed her. "*Alexa mou.*"

"I must go."

He held her close. "Come up tomorrow night."

"Do you want me to?"

"Yes. Every night."

Every night, she thought, and a sudden chill came over her. You mean every night until the end of the cruise. After that we will never see each other again.

In the dark she could barely see the gold band on his right hand. But it was there. Yes, it was there.

She wondered if it made him feel safe. This way any woman knew exactly what she was getting into. He was not like some American men who pretended they were single when they were really married.

He pressed her hand and she could feel the ring.

"I must go," she repeated, and reached for her clothes.

Seven

This is not real, she kept telling herself when she awoke. It has no bearing on your real life. Your real life is Brooke and Cicily. The house in Greenwich, Connecticut. Your friends.

You make me crazy. Ah, Alexa mou.

Last night. The storm. His arms around her.

I love him, she thought. I love his voice, the way he speaks Greek, everything about him. I love him, and I must not. How did everything happen so fast?

For a year she had felt dead inside, going through the routine of living as if under anesthesia. And now . . .

There had been a wildness, a complete abandon, they were alone together in the storm sailing endlessly, touching no port, suspended in time.

She threw back the covers and got out of bed. The storm had passed and it was a beautiful sunny day. She watched the foam the ship made as it sped toward Malta. She wondered if he was on the bridge now and what he was thinking.

I have taken leave of my senses, she thought. Completely.

She got dressed and went down to the dining room. Bev was sitting alone at their table drinking coffee.

"What happened to you last night?" Bev asked. "You just suddenly disappeared."

"I decided to go to bed." Alexa picked up the menu and studied it.

"I didn't see the captain around either."

"Oh? What did you have for breakfast?"

"Juice and coffee. I called your cabin but there was no answer."

George came over beaming. "Good morning. You sleep well?"

"Yes, thank you, very well."

"We have today fresh tiny strawberries from Corfu. Very good."

"I think I'll have them. And scrambled eggs, toast and coffee."

Eric's voice came over the intercom. "Good morning, everyone. For those of you interested in learning Greek dancing, we will have a class in the main lounge at eleven. We will dock at Malta right after lunch. Correction, the captain says around three o'clock. Thank you."

"I wonder if the captain's going to teach us the Greek dances?" Bev said.

"What?"

"Where are you today, Alexa? You seem in a trance."

"Sorry. I was thinking of something else."

"Obviously. Well, I'll see you later." Bev got up.

Alexa finished breakfast and walked around the deck. And then she saw him. He was coming down the stairs from the bridge with another officer, the chubby gray-haired one who was second in command of the ship. He looked worried.

"Good morning," he said, his voice impersonal.

"Good morning." She started to add "Captain" but it seemed strange to call him that after last night.

The other officer looked at her and nodded. She had never heard him speak English and she wondered if he did. He was much older than the captain, or appeared so, and she wondered if he resented taking orders from him. He also wore a good wedding band on his right hand, but she didn't care about his wife or whether he was happy with her. The only one who mattered was the captain. The captain. She wondered how many other women on cruises had been attracted to him. She should have held him off longer, played harder to get . . .

"It is a beautiful day," he said. His eyes revealed nothing, he might have been making conversation about the weather to any of the passengers, not a woman to whom he had made love the night before. She suddenly felt angry.

"Yes, Captain. The storm is over."

They walked on speaking Greek, their voices rose, he was shouting something. She wondered if there was some problem with the ship.

Already I am feeling possessive and I have no right, she told herself. How did I expect him to act?

Through his binoculars Nikos could see the fortifications of Malta in the distance.

He had not been to Malta since right after the Greek Civil War when he was a sailor on a submarine in the Royal Navy. He was not married to Katina then. He had gone ashore with the others, they had walked through the cobblestone streets of the old town and seen the cathedral and the churches and the Maltese Cross of the Knights. They had looked for women . . .

The pilot boat was approaching. The sailors put the ladder over the side. There were many ships in the harbor. Nikos looked again. A German freighter was tied up at the pier where the *Pericles* was supposed to dock.

The pilot waved to him. He was a short man with a bald head and dressed in a brown suit. Two other men were with him. They were wearing uniforms and had some suitcases. Suddenly he heard shrieks of joy and then clapping against the rail.

"Mabel, it's our luggage! I can't believe it!"

"It's all there, Gladys!"

One of the officials held up a suitcase from which a B.O.A.C. Airways tag fluttered in the breeze. He beamed. There was more clapping and laughter. The two ladies from San Francisco were crying now with happiness and hugging all the passengers.

At least that problem is solved, Nikos thought. The ladies now have their missing luggage.

But what about our dock? What is the German ship doing there?

The pilot came up to him with his hand out.

"Captain," he said, "there has been a little problem with the dock."

"So I see."

"Unfortunate, but it cannot be helped. We will go round to the other side."

"But the rocks? I have studied the chart and it is not possible with this ship. The tides—"

"Captain, I will direct you."

Idiot! Nikos thought. You do not know this ship. He looked down to where the pilot boat was bobbing alongside them. It was about to scrape the side of the *Pericles.*

The pilot had a disagreeable expression now. Like all small men, he craved power.

"It is not up to you, Captain, it is up to me to decide."

"It is up to me! Do not touch the ship!" Nikos shouted to the men in the pilot boat.

They moved off just in time.

"We will anchor in the harbor and disembark the passengers by tenders," Nikos said. "I do not take chances with my ship running aground."

The pilot walked away angrily. His face was red and a vein throbbed in his forehead. "Damned Greeks!" he muttered. "They think only they know the sea."

Alexa looked up. She had heard the shouting on the bridge, but most of it was in Greek, so she did not know what was going on.

Then there was the sound of the anchor going down.

"I wonder what's happening?" Bev said. "I thought we were supposed to dock."

"I did too. I guess plans have changed."

Bev glanced up at the bridge. "The captain was madder than hell about something. He sure has a temper."

Eric's voice came over the ship's intercom. "We will be going ashore by tender. The first launch will be leaving in fifteen minutes. The buses will be waiting for us on the pier. All passengers taking the first launch please be ready at the gangway and don't forget your landing tags."

"Save a place for me," Bev said. "I'll be right back. I want to get my camera."

Malta looked like one vast fortress, Alexa thought, with no grass or trees in sight. She remembered a postcard her father had sent her from Malta when he was in command of a cruiser on their way to Gibraltar. She had kept all the postcards he had sent her and all the dolls from foreign countries. Her brother had his medals.

She saw Nikos coming down the stairs from the bridge. He walked over to her and smiled.

"Did you sleep well?" he asked.

"Yes, very well."

He started to say something else but Bev suddenly reappeared with her camera.

"Captain," she said, smiling coyly, "you didn't come back to the lounge last night after dinner. We missed you."

"I had many things to do. Reports to write."

The chubby radio officer came up and spoke to him in Greek.

"Excuse me," he said. "Enjoy your afternoon."

Beg glanced over her shoulder as the captain walked away. "You know," she whispered to Alexa, "I think he's shy."

Their guide was a woman of about fifty, short with dark hair, and a mole on her cheek. Her eyes were bright with enthusiasm as she explained the story of her island, the Maltese language, the history of the Knights. She obviously loved her job, Alexa thought, unlike the guide they had on Corfu.

As the bus drove through the narrow streets they saw shabbily-dressed children huddled in doorways looking at the tourists with large dark eyes.

The guide told of being cut off from supplies during the Second World War and how the people came close to starvation.

"Now we are coming to the cathedral," she said. "We will stop here. Please stay with me when we get out of the bus and do not wander off."

They went in the cathedral and the guide showed them part of a German bomb that had fallen through the dome while a Mass was going on.

"It was a miracle that no one was hurt," she said.

The guide led them to a small chapel. She went up to the altar, knelt and crossed herself. She remained with closed eyes for a few minutes while everyone looked at the decorations and paintings, then she crossed herself again and rejoined the group.

"I always say a prayer," she said, "wishing all of you a safe journey home."

They left the cathedral and the guide pointed down a street. "That is the main shopping section. You will find some shops selling Maltese lace and also jewelry. The buses will wait for you here." She glanced at her watch. "We will leave in half an hour, so please be on time. We still have to see the old town and the cross of the Knights."

They passed a shop selling brass ornaments. In the window was a door knocker shaped like a dolphin.

"Let's stop in here, Bev," Alexa said. "I want to price that."

"It's awfully heavy, don't you think? Unless you're planning to send it."

The shop owner said they would be delighted to ship it.

"I really think it would look marvelous on my front door," Alexa said, writing out a traveler's check.

"And you can say to everyone in Greenwich, 'Just a little something I found in Malta.'"

"Where would you like to go now?"

"I'd like to find some lace tablemats for gifts." Bev said. "I think our guide mentioned a good shop down the street."

They started down the hill.

"Look over there." Bev pointed.

Mrs. Griffin was coming out of a liquor store carrying a brown paper bag.

"I wonder where he is?" Alexa said.

Just then Mr. Griffin appeared waving a newspaper.

"I finally found an American newspaper," he said. "Hi, folks," he waved. "You can get the *New York Times* there. A week old, but what the heck!"

"Let's hurry," Bev said. "We don't have too much time."

In the lace shop they ran into Mrs. Pearson and Daphne and Mrs. Fitzgerald. Mrs. Fitzgerald's blouse was buttoned crookedly and her purse was hanging open.

"Isn't this lace lovely?" she said. "I'm getting some for my daughter-in-law."

"Here," Alexa said. "You'd better close your purse. You might lose your passport or your money."

"My land, wouldn't that be something?" She looked around vacantly. "What time does the ship leave Corfu, girls?"

"We're on Malta, Mrs. Fitzgerald," Bev said.

"Malta?" With palsied hands she made an attempt to close her purse, after taking out some Greek drachmas.

"I'm afraid we don't take those here," the salesgirl said.

Mrs. Fitzgerald looked blank.

"Do you have Maltese money? Or American Express checks?"

"But isn't Malta a Greek island?"

"No, Madam."

"I thought this was a Greek Island cruise." She turned in bewilderment to Alexa and Bev. "Where is Malta?"

"It's an independent island," Alexa said. "In the Mediterranean." The salesgirl had wandered off to wait on some other customers. "They'll take a traveler's check. You have some with you, haven't you?"

"Oh my, yes. My son made me get some before I left." She opened her purse again with trembling hands. "See?"

"That's fine. You just sign one of those and give the salesgirl the address. I'll get her."

"Oh, I don't trust the mails. Too many things are lost. And there was a postal strike in Chicago just before I left. I'm going to take everything with me."

Alexa threw Bev a quick look.

"Have you decided now, Madam?" the salesgirl asked.

"Yes," Mrs. Fitzgerald said. "And thank you, girls. I don't know what I would have done without you."

"That's all right. We'll see you back on the bus."

When they got out in the street Alexa said, "Maybe we should stay with her. Do you think she can find her way back to the bus?"

"We're not her keepers. If we start that we'll be stuck with her the rest of the trip."

"I guess so. Can you imagine any son sending his eighty-year-old mother off all alone on a trip like this?"

"Especially when she doesn't know where she is half the time. He sounds like a beaut." Bev glanced back at the shop. "Mrs. Pearson and Daphne are still there."

"The blind leading the blind."

They saw their guide standing at the end of the street, waving frantically.

"I think our bus is about to leave." Bev said. "I'll go back to the shop and get the others. You go ahead."

"Ladies, ladies," called the guide. "Please come now."

"And tell her we'll be right there," Bev said.

Nikos stood near the gangway talking to the second officer, watching the passengers get out of the tender. He always worried that some older person would have a fall. Like the woman with the cane down there. He shouted to the sailors to help her.

They came up the gangway holding on to their souvenirs, beaming happily.

"Hello, Captain."

"Did you have a nice day?"

"Oh, yes."

"I am glad."

"Didn't you go ashore, Captain?"

"To do . . . what?" He shrugged and smiled.

The man in the striped pants was coming up the gangway carrying some newspapers and his wife was following him. He noticed she had a brown paper bag with the top of a vodka bottle showing.

"We're all ready for the cocktail hour now, Captain," the man said. He waved a newspaper. "Anyone want one? I bought several."

"I'd rather not know the news," said a passenger who had remained on the ship. "I take these cruises to get away from all those unpleasant headlines."

"I can't wait to get to my cabin and take off my shoes," a plump lady announced. "I've never walked through so many churches, and all those cobblestone streets! My ankles are starting to swell."

He looked down. Alexa was not in the first tender. He saw a second tender loaded with passengers approaching the dock. Now he could see her blonde hair blowing in the breeze as the launch came closer. She reached up a hand to push it out of her eyes. He smiled.

The other one was with her, the redhead. She made him uncomfortable with her obvious approaches. He tried to be polite to all the passengers, he did not want to offend, but he wished she would not be so forward. It was a quality about American women that he did not like.

It was up to the man to make the first moves, the woman to follow.

When a woman chased him he wanted to run. The cruises were

not long, they always ended, and with them the affairs. If they wrote him letters afterward, he did not answer.

Once a woman had called his home and spoken to Katina. It had upset her. "It is part of my job to be nice to the passengers," he had explained. "Can I help it if she misunderstands? The woman is crazy."

The woman asked her husband for a divorce and came back to Greece. He had a terrible time getting rid of her. Nikos shuddered. He did not want any more problems like that.

They were usually escaping something, the women who went on cruises. Unhappiness in a dull marriage, looking for a quick fling . . .

Then they went back home, they resumed their lives, they drove their children to school, they went to their clubs, they listened to their husbands discuss business. He had been told that American men discussed business even in bed.

He wondered about Alexa, about her life. Most Americans told you everything about themselves right away. She did not. There was something closed off, a reserve, and yet she was not cold. What about the husband? How had he died? In Vietnam? He could not ask, it was not polite. Only the father had she spoken of, and her daughters. She was beautiful, charming, surely there were many admirers in—where was it?—Greenwich, Connecticut, for a beautiful young widow.

He was strongly attracted to her, much more than he wanted. It was crazy. He had not felt this way for a long time, many years . . . since Patricia. That had ended in tragedy, this also was hopeless.

He must be careful.

He did not want to hurt Katina. She was a good woman, the mother of his sons, but he had never pretended, even to himself, that he was in love with her or ever had been. There were many marriages like that in Greece based on mutual respect and family ties. Men were expected to have their little side steps, but the family remained together.

Alexa was climbing up the gangway, her blonde hair blowing back from her face, her blue eyes bright and happy.

"Hello, Captain," she said.

"Hello." Deliberately he made his voice impersonal. "Did you like Malta?"

Her eyes suddenly had an expression he could not fathom. He noticed they were the color of the sea, a blue-gray tinged with green.

"Yes," she said. "It was very interesting."

"Good. I must go now to the bridge. I will see you later." He reached out and touched her hand. *Alexa mou*, he wanted to say, but there were people listening. "Later," he said.

He went quickly up the stairs, not looking back. It was time to sail.

Eight

*A*pril 8ᵗʰ, *she wrote.* Tunis. We docked early in the morning. Saw the museum, the ruins of Carthage, the village of Bousaid with its white stucco houses, blue doors and grilled windows. Men wearing red fez caps, women in white robes and veils covering their faces so that only their eyes showed.

Alexa closed her travel diary, the one Brooke and Cicily had given her for her trip.

"So you won't forget anything," they told her. "Since you aren't taking a camera."

How far away that world seemed now, her home in Greenwich, her children. It was almost as if they didn't exist, she felt detached, floating, the ship was her real world as she drifted from port to port—with him. How many more days were left now? She did not want to think about it, she did not want the cruise ever to end.

Nikos. She said his name softly to herself. Only when they were alone, in those stolen moments together in his cabin, was she able to call him Nikos. She thought of how he was when he made love to her, the things he said to her in Greek that she did not understand, and the look in his eyes that needed no translation.

Two weeks ago I did not know he existed, she thought. Now I will never be able to look at the sea without thinking of him.

The sea was rough leaving Tunis, with no wind, and Nikos gave the order to cut speed. Even with the stabilizers down the ship rolled from side to side. The weather report was for more bad weather. We will be late arriving in Heraklion, he thought. Even with smooth seas the distance from Tunisia to Crete was two days. It was bad planning by the company who had chartered the ship, but he had to try to do what they wanted.

He went back to his cabin and lay down. They knew where to get him and he wanted to take a nap. He closed his eyes, but he could not sleep.

He sat on the edge of his bed and smoked a cigarette and thought of her. Alexa. He wanted her and he should not. It was a craziness, what he felt for her. On the wall through the open doorway he could see the pictures of Katina and his sons. He crushed out the cigarette.

For years he had prided himself on his discipline, his ability to hide his inner feelings. It was necessary to survive. What could she know of his life, or his narrow escapes during the war, and afterwards the Greek Civil War? He had come through it all, he had achieved a position of authority and respect, he had produced sons to carry on the family name. He could not throw it all away.

What was he to do?

He got up and paced back and forth.

Six more days remained of this cruise and then it would end. They would say goodbye and he would not see her again. And that same day another cruise would start with new passengers and another and another . . .

The pattern of his life. It went on and on. He was a prisoner, he walked a chalk line and he had no choice. He pounded his fist on the desk. He wanted to explode, to yell at the top of his lungs. It is my nerves, he thought, so many years at sea, the constant responsibility, worrying about the weather, the passengers.

I worry about everyone, but who worries about me?

He walked to the porthole and looked out.

She was leaning on the rail with her back to him away from the others and the wind was blowing her hair. She had on a bathing suit.

He opened the outside door to his cabin and stood there in his trousers and undershirt and then she turned round. He looked first to see that no officers or passengers were near, then he beckoned to her silently.

She walked over and he pulled her inside and locked the door.

"What were you doing there?" he asked.

"I like to watch the sea. And it is quiet back of the lifeboats."

He smiled. "That is the only reason you were there?"

"No. It is not the only reason."

He stroked her face with his fingertips. *"Chryso mou."*

"What does that mean?"

"My golden one."

"Am I?"

"Yes."

Suddenly he pulled away. "Ah, what is the use? What can we do about it?"

"We have now."

"Now. Six more days. And then it ends."

"Are you sorry we met?"

"No."

"Or that this happened?"

"I did not say that." He held her close. "I need you. *S'agapo.* You understand what s'*agapo* means in Greek?"

"I think so."

"I love you." He put his hand under her chin so that her eyes looked directly into his. "Do you love me?"

She hesitated. "Do you want me to?"

"It is not a matter of wanting. Do you love me?"

"Yes, Nikos."

"Then say it. *S'agapo.*"

"*S'agapo.*"

"Do you want me to make love to you always?"

"Yes."

He saw her glance quickly at the pictures of his sons on the wall. "I would give you nice sons," he said. "You would like?"

"Yes, but . . ."

"If you like me you would like the sons. If you do not like me . . ." He shrugged.

She smiled. "I like you."

"Come," he said, leading her to the bed in the next cabin. He closed the door and took off his undershirt.

"You are very tan," she said.

"I swim in Caribbean when I can get away from the ship. Will you come to Caribbean in the winter?"

"Maybe."

"Do not say maybe. Tell me you will come."

She did not reply.

"There is a reason you cannot come? You have a job?"

"No. Not yet. I was thinking of taking a real estate course."

He frowned. "Real estate?"

"To sell houses."

"Ah. Then you could not come to Caribbean." He pulled down the straps of her bathing suit.

"You know I will come," she whispered. "I will meet you wherever you want. I know it's crazy, but I don't care."

Later, he asked, "Has anyone ever made love to you like this?"

"No, never."

"Ah, darling. *Glika mou.* My sweet one. I do not want you to leave me ever."

Nine

*A*head she saw the jagged blue-brown mountains of Crete and below the white town of Heraklion. Nikos came out of the wheelhouse and she noticed that he was wearing a whistle around his neck. He nodded briefly at her and walked back in again. A sailor was running up the flags and she could hear shouting in Greek from the engine room intercom. The ship's horn gave a blast. They were still quite far from the harbor. Nikos came out on the bridge and looked at the flags. The first officer brought out the walkie-talkie.

Nikos put his hands on his hips. *"Ola aristera!"* he shouted. The ship turned slowly to the left.

He was born to command, Alexa thought, watching him. For him nothing existed now but the ship.

More passengers were coming up the stairs to the bridge to watch the docking. A large military plane flew overhead. Taxis and tour buses were waiting on the pier and she saw the same signs that she had noticed on Corfu: *21 APRILIOU*. The Junta made its presence known everywhere.

Bev and Geoff came up the stairs.

"I get off here," he said. "But maybe we'll meet again on another cruise. I'll give you girls my address in Athens. I keep an apartment there and someone always knows where to reach me."

"I wish you didn't have to leave," Bev said.

"That's the way it goes, luv."

A car pulled up alongside the taxis and a fat Greek woman got out. A man with her took a red suitcase out of the back. They both looked up at the bridge and waved to Nikos. He waved back.

"Who are they?" Bev asked.

"He's the ship's agent in Heraklion and the woman with him also works for the line. She's getting on here."

"What does she do?" asked Alexa.

"I'm not sure," Geoff replied. "I just know that she comes on the ship quite often. She's a good friend of the captain's wife."

The captain's wife. Alexa felt a chill go through her. The woman was staring at her. Will she be watching us the rest of the cruise? she wondered. We have so little time left together.

Geoff held out his hand. "Goodbye," he said. "Have a nice cruise."

Nikos saw Soula Vassilakis get out of the car belonging to the ship's agent and wondered why she was coming on the ship. Did Katina suspect something? Now he would have to spend time with her, have her at his table. He had never liked her. He cursed under his breath.

"Is something wrong, Captain?" the first officer asked.

Always people watching him, everywhere.

He blew the whistle. "The dock," he said. "Why do the men not catch the ropes? Stupid!" He blew the whistle again and muttered a Greek oath.

Alexa wrote in her diary:

Crete. The palace of Knossos. The museum. We only catch the highlights as it closes at six. A quick shopping tour. In the town we pass a bust of Nikos Kazantzakis, the great Greek writer. He was born on Crete. Somehow Crete seems rather dreary, but we have only seen the port of Heraklion, not the countryside, which they say is lovely in the spring.

Back to the ship—and him.

*   *   *

That evening was the fancy dress parade and those who wished to participate were asked to gather after dinner in the ship's library to get a number and register.

"Where's your costume?" Bev asked Alexa. "Or are you going to change after dinner?"

"I wasn't planning to wear one. But I like yours."

Bev was dressed as a belly dancer in veils and beads and the stewards were looking at her and making remarks in Greek.

"Just a little something I whipped up in my cabin," Bev said, pulling a veil across her face and wiggling her stomach. One steward nudged another. "Hope it doesn't shock this stuffy group. The stewards seem to approve anyway."

Alexa looked over at the captain's table. The guests were all seated waiting for him and she noticed the Greek woman who had boarded at Crete seated on his right.

"Here comes the captain," Bev said. "This outfit should catch his eye, don't you think?"

"I'm sure it will." Do women throw themselves at him on every cruise? Alexa wondered. She saw him looking at her and then he looked quickly away. Five more days. That is all we have left. She took a sip of her wine and tried not to think about it.

"I still think you should wear a costume," Bev said.

"No thanks. I'd rather just watch everyone else. And besides, you need an audience." There were enough people in costume so that she didn't feel guilty not joining in. The two sisters from Boston were each wearing African safari outfits which they had obviously brought with them and several men had used the ship's sheets to make Roman togas.

Next week when I am back home he will be here at another costume party, and another . . .

"I would give you nice sons," he had said. *If* he were free, which he was not. They both knew it was impossible. She could come on the ship from time to time, but where would that lead? He had no other life, it was all that he knew.

"You're looking very pensive," Bev said.

"Was I? Sorry, I didn't mean to."

"Maybe there's some secret thing you've got going that I don't know about?"

Alexa laughed. "Of course not! With whom?"

"With whom is right. The men who aren't senile on this cruise are gay. Except for the ship's officers and crew—" She paused, her fork in mid-air. "Wait a minute. The captain?"

"Don't be silly." She felt her face flushing.

"I know he's married, but so what? He'd be exciting to have a fling with."

"Bev, you're imagining things."

"I'm not so sure. He keeps looking over here, by the way."

"Does he? I hadn't noticed."

"He seems bored. I bet he gets tired of the same old questions all the time. But then, if he's not happy in his marriage, the ship is a good escape."

"Where did you hear that?"

"What?"

"About his marriage?"

"Oh, it's general knowledge. See, you are interested."

"I wonder how people think up all these clever ideas for costumes," Alexa said, quickly changing the subject and looking round the dining room.

They finished dinner and Bev went to the library to register and Alexa went in the lounge. The chief steward came up to her as she walked in.

"Captain would like you to be one of the judges. Please come this way."

He led her to a table directly on the dance floor that had a reserved sign on it. Mrs. Pearson was also there and another couple she had seen around the ship but had not met. They introduced themselves and then Alexa saw Nikos walking in the lounge with the fat Greek woman who had been on his right at dinner.

"Good evening," he said. "This is Mrs. Vassilakis."

The Greek woman nodded and smiled.

Nikos sat in the center seat next to Alexa and Mrs. Vassilakis in the empty one on the other side of him. A steward came over quickly.

"What would everyone like to drink?" Nikos asked.

The steward took the orders and Alexa noticed that Nikos avoided looking into her eyes. He said something to Mrs. Vassilakis in Greek and she laughed, showing a gold tooth.

"Excuse us for speaking Greek but Mrs. Vassilakis does not speak English."

The chaperone, thought Alexa, as she noticed the Greek woman looking her over. Mrs. Vassilakis was wearing a long black dress with an antique gold necklace and her gray-black hair was in a coil. Her laugh was like a cackle and Nikos called her Soula.

"Soula is a good friend of my wife's," he explained. "We have known each other for many years."

Was that explanation for the group or for me? Alexa wondered. He was like two different people, last night the ardent lover, now the disciplined captain of the ship. Will we always have to hide what we feel for each other, carry on a masquerade? She suddenly wanted to scream, but instead she picked up the piece of paper in front of her and studied the categories. It is his job, she reminded herself, and he must not jeopardize it.

"Have you ever seen so many marvelous costumes, Captain?" Mrs. Pearson asked. "It will be hard to choose."

Nikos smiled. "Yes. They are very good. On the last cruise we had a lady who dressed up as me. A German lady. She was the captain." He turned to Mrs. Vassilakis and translated for her. She laughed and said something in a quick flow of Greek.

The cruise director walked up and took the microphone and the costume parade began. They were to judge for the most original, the funniest, and the most beautiful costume. The contestants walked around with numbers on their backs.

"And now the captain will present the prizes," Eric said as Nikos walked up. The ship's photographer was busy snapping pictures.

"I'm not sure that it makes one very popular with the other passengers to be a judge," Mrs. Pearson remarked. She stood up. "I think I'll turn in now. We have a long day tomorrow at Ephesus. Goodnight, everyone."

The other couple said that they were going to their cabin also and left, leaving Alexa alone with Mrs. Vassilakis. Nikos came back and sat down.

"What would you like to drink?" he asked. He called the steward and ordered. "Now," he said in English, "we cannot speak Greek. Do you speak French?"

"Yes," Alexa said.

"Ah, good."

The three of them started to talk in French when one of the officers came over and said something to Nikos in Greek. He shouted back in Greek, gesturing. He appeared angry.

"Excuse me," he said. "Always something. I must go now to the bridge. I will be back in a little while." He got up quickly and left.

"I have known the captain for many years," Mrs. Vassilakis said. "He misses his family very much."

"I'm sure he must," Alexa replied carefully. "He is at sea so much."

"Captain Nikos has two fine sons and a beautiful wife." She threw Alexa a slanting glance. "A very beautiful wife."

These Greek women stick together, she thought, and wondered what she was supposed to reply. She had not spoken French for a long time and it was difficult for her to express herself. "Captain Meletis is a very good captain," she said. "All the passengers like him."

"The captain is thinking of retiring in two years. So that he can spend more time with his family."

"Oh?" She took a quick sip of her drink. Was that the wife's idea or his? She could not picture Nikos sitting around doing nothing. Or working in an office. He was part of the sea, he was born to command ships. He would be restless, lost.

Like her father, who paced the house like a caged lion after he retired. To his dying day he missed the sea . . .

"You have a family?" Mrs. Vassilakis asked.

"Yes, I have two daughters."

"How nice." Mrs. Vassilakis smiled. An anchor. Something to keep her at home and not chasing a ship. "I am sure that you will be very glad to see your daughters again. How old are they?"

"Thirteen and ten."

"But you look so young."

"I am thirty-five."

"You do not appear it."

If only Nikos would come back and I could escape from this woman, Alexa thought. This friend of the wife's who is so intent on pointing up the captain's happy marriage. Does she suspect anything between us or is she just warning me in case?

"American women are very different from Greek women," Mrs. Vassilakis said.

"I guess so." How can I end this discussion? She looked round the room and then she saw Nikos standing in the doorway. My love, she thought.

"There is the captain now," said Mrs. Vassilakis.

He walked through the lounge, stopping here and there to greet passengers, and then sat down at the table.

"I think I will go to my cabin now, Nikos," Mrs. Vassilakis said. "I am tired."

Nikos helped her up. "I will walk with you to your cabin, Soula." He turned to Alexa. "Are you leaving now?"

"Yes."

He looked at her but she was not sure of the message in his eyes.

"Then goodnight," he said. "Sleep well."

"Goodnight, Captain."

Ten

*D*awn over the Turkish hills. A flock of birds against the pink sky. A lighthouse. The Turkish pilot boat flying the red flag and in the distance the port of Kusadasi with its red-roofed houses and minarets.

She took the excursion to Ephesus with the rest of the passengers and they were suddenly back in another century, as if time had not changed. From the bus window as they drove along country roads she saw women working in tobacco fields, dark swarthy men, fig trees. They walked with a Turkish guide through the ruins of Ephesus, of what had once been a thriving city, and she wondered about the people who had lived there. A civilization, a people long dead, forgotten, unearthed now for others to wonder: Could this, too, happen to us? Will we vanish as they did, suddenly?

The Turkish guide was talking but Alexa found her mind going back to the ship and him. What was he doing now? She had not seen him last night after they parted in the lounge. At least Mrs. Vassilakis was not on the tour, so she would not have to try to make conversation with her. There was something about the heavy Greek woman that she did not trust.

"Now we will have twenty minutes to buy souvenirs and then back in the bus," the guide announced.

Outside the gate there were stands where merchants were selling Turkish slippers, brass ashtrays shaped like camels, small prayer rugs, blue beads to ward off the evil eye, and other tourist souvenirs.

Alexa bought some postcards for Brooke and Cicily and then went back in the bus to wait for the others.

He stood on the dock next to the ship as the passengers filed back on board carrying their various purchases, tourist junk.

"Hello, Captain."

He nodded. Where was she? She had not come up last night. He had waited and finally he realized that she was not coming. He had too much pride to call her cabin. What had that devil Soula said to her? There was a Greek word for her, *karakatsa*. Magpie. Always she liked to cause trouble. He wished that Katina would not see so much of her.

The next bus pulled up and he saw Alexa get out. He turned and went quickly up to the bridge. If she wanted to speak with him she would see where he was.

In a few minutes he saw her coming up the steps.

"Hello," he said, his voice deliberately cool. "Did you enjoy Ephesus?"

"Yes. It was fascinating."

He walked closer, looked over his shoulder, then said in a low voice, "You did not come up last night."

"You didn't ask me to."

"Yes, I said, 'Are you leaving now?'"

"But I thought you had to go on duty. On the bridge."

"On duty?"

"To work, I mean."

"That is what I meant when I asked you if you were leaving. With Mrs. Vassilakis beside me, how else could I say it?"

"I'm sorry, I misunderstood."

He shrugged. "Is all right."

"I wasn't trying to avoid you. Really."

Just then the second officer came out and handed him the walkie-talkie.

It was time to sail.

*   *   *

"What time do we go through the Dardanelles, Captain?"

"Two o'clock in the morning. It will be dark. Nothing to see."

"Captain, isn't Rupert Brooke buried on some island around here?"

"Who?"

"Rupert Brooke, the English poet."

"Ah, yes. On the island of Skyros is his grave."

"This bed is too small, Captain," she teased.

"You do not like? We can be closer this way."

The sea was rising and falling beneath them. He felt the warmth of her body against him, their legs entwined on the narrow cot, their hearts beating as one.

"Like this," he said. "It is good?"

"Yes," she whispered.

"*Alexa mou.*"

The waves were pounding the ship. Her arms tightened around him.

"You are not afraid?"

"No."

"I want you always. Always."

He stood on the bridge with his binoculars watching the ferries blowing black smoke passing back and forth in front of the ship. The currents were treacherous and he could feel his heart pounding. If he were to have an accident here, he a Greek, they would throw him in a Turkish jail forever.

The sky was gray over Istanbul, as it usually was. He could see the Blue Mosque and the minarets of Saint Sophia. A small fishing boat crossed in front of him and he blasted the ship's horn.

Now the Turkish pilot boat was approaching.

Out of the corner of his eye he could see Alexa. What could he offer her? Nothing. Nothing but unhappiness.

It came back to him what his aunt had told him long ago, the one who read the coffee cups.

He was in a gray mood today. Istanbul always depressed him. Black smoke from the ferries filled the sky. A dirty city. He wondered why the passengers all wanted to come here. Usually afterward they were disappointed and told him so. The ship would remain here overnight, then sail at noon the next day for Delos and Mykonos.

He glanced at Alexa again. Only three more days.

This evening he would be expected to have dinner in Istanbul with the ship's agent and Mrs. Vassilakis. There would be people coming on board he would have to entertain. The captain must always be available.

Alexa was looking at him. He pretended not to see her.

Three more days . . . and they would not be able to be alone tonight. It was too risky.

He grabbed the microphone. *"Ola aristera!"* he shouted down to the engine room.

The ship turned slowly to the left to meet the pilot boat.

Istanbul was not the exotic, mysterious city she had always pictured. Everywhere there was dirt and litter, black smoke from the ferries and factories, honking of horns. Even though it was warm the women wore coats, head scarves tied in Turkish fashion, coarse stockings with runs in them. From the bus window, as they slowly made their way through the heavy traffic up the hill to Topkaki, she saw vendors selling rolls with seeds like bagels, a boy carrying a basket of tomatoes, an old man shining shoes. Noisy Turkish music blared forth from an open tavern, men with dark evil faces, tobacco-stained teeth, black mustaches. She could understand how the Greeks feared the Turks when they descended on a village, there was something cruel-looking about them.

The bus pulled up in the courtyard of Topkaki and everyone got out.

"Now follow me," the Turkish guide said. "We are going first to see the porcelain collection, then we will look at the jewels and costumes of the sultans."

"Are we going to see the harem?" one of the men asked, pointing to a sign.

"I am very sorry, but the harem is closed at this time for repairs," said the guide. "This way, please."

When they had finished the tour of the museum they got back in the bus and drove to the Blue Mosque.

"You will all please leave your shoes outside," the guide said.

"But suppose someone steals them?" a man asked.

The guide looked shocked. "It is a most serious offense to steal shoes from outside a mosque. And ladies—" she noticed a woman in a sleeveless dress among the group—"you must have your arms covered. Please take a jacket with you."

When they came out of the mosque Mr. Overstreet said, "Someone has gone off with my shoes."

"But, sir," the guide said, "you have your shoes."

"No. They look like mine, but they're too small. They pinch. Someone must have taken mine by mistake." He looked around the group.

"Ellwood, are you sure?" his wife asked.

"Of course I'm sure. I know what my shoes feel like. Someone is walking around in shoes that are too big and I just hope he's in our group and not on some other ship."

"Well if you don't find him you can always buy some Turkish slippers at the bazaar," someone suggested.

Alexa looked across the nightclub and saw Nikos sitting at a table with Mrs. Vassilakis and another Greek couple. He looked bored as the fat belly dancer performed.

Then he saw her and their eyes locked for an instant before he looked quickly away.

He reveals everything with his eyes, she thought. We do not need words. If only we could run out of here, go someplace romantic and be alone, instead of me sitting here with the rest of the passengers and he still doing his official duties with Mrs. Vassilakis and what she supposed was the Greek ship's agent in Istanbul and his wife.

The performance ended and there was applause.

The lights went on.

Alexa glanced over at the table where Nikos had been sitting with the other Greeks.

It was empty.

He could not sleep. He tossed and turned in the narrow bed. Somehow it was easier for him to sleep when the ship was moving, it had become a habit since most of his life had been spent at sea. Now with the ship anchored in port . . .

He heard voices of passengers coming back on the ship after the night tour of Istanbul. He wondered if she was back yet. He thought of calling her cabin. But no, there was no way she could come here or that he could go to her, too many people were walking around the ship. And if he should be needed for anything while in a Turkish port and they found him with a woman in his cabin . . .

It was too dangerous.

He had built his career slowly, years of working with no days off, giving up his vacations and taking the money instead for his family.

The family.

For every Greek man the family meant his sons.

While you are young you build for yourself, he thought, but when you are older you build for your sons. They are your tomorrow. If you have no sons, one day your dreaming ceases.

Responsibility.

It was a word that he had accepted very young. He remembered when he had been the first officer on another ship. It was the maiden voyage and there were two captains on the bridge, one the regular captain and another older captain who was on the cruise to supervise. They were docking the ship and the two captains could not agree on where to put the ropes. In the meantime the ship was drifting and about to collide with the dock. Suddenly he grabbed the walkie-talkie and took charge as the two captains continued to argue. A few months later he was promoted to captain, the youngest one of the line.

That was twelve years ago.

Alexa. He desired her and he loved her. He wanted her in bed with him now, to feel her responding to his lovemaking, together to reach the heights of ecstasy . . .

He picked up the phone and dialed her cabin.

There was no answer.

In the dream he was on Corfu with Alexa. They were making love on a small beach in one of the island's hidden coves. Their bodies were golden in the sunlight and there was the faint scent of pine and orange blossoms and the sound of waves gently lapping the shore.

Then suddenly, on a cliff above them, there stood Katina.

Her eyes were wild, her clothes smeared with blood. In one hand she held a knife and in the other . . .

He gasped.

In the other was the severed head of Fanis, dripping blood.

Eleven

They sailed from Istanbul at noon, again across the Sea of Marmara and through the Dardanelles. That evening was Greek Night and the Captain's Dinner. The dining room was decorated with grape vines and Greek and American flags and the stewards were in Greek costumes.

Alexa looked over at the captain's table. They were all Greeks. Tonight and tomorrow night, she thought, and then Athens. The end of the cruise.

The menu was all Greek specialties. Then the lights went out and the stewards entered bearing flaming desserts. Everyone applauded.

Eric brought the microphone over to the captain's table and adjusted it for his height as Nikos stood up and took a glass of champagne.

"We have only one more day left of the cruise," Nikos said, "and I hope that you have had an enjoyable time and will return home with pleasant memories of Greece." He raised his glass and for a moment his voice faltered. "And now for myself and the officers and the crew I would like to propose a toast. *Yiassou!*"

"*Yiassou!*" everyone repeated, raising their glasses.

*   *   *

Alexa saw him coming across the dance floor to where she was sitting.

"Would you like to dance?" he asked.

"I'd love to."

The orchestra was playing a Greek song. He hummed to it.

"You did the Greek dances very well," she said.

He shrugged. "All Greek boys, they learn them."

"Do you perform on every cruise?"

"Not always. Sometimes."

"This one is special?"

"Very special." He lowered his voice. "I am leaving in a few minutes. Wait half an hour and then come up" He raised his voice. "Did you buy many things at the bazaar in Istanbul?"

"Only a pair of earrings. These that I'm wearing." She pointed to the delicate gold and turquoise drop earrings.

"Very pretty. I like."

The music stopped and he led her back to her group.

"Thank you very much."

"I enjoyed it, Captain." She tried to keep her voice as impersonal as his.

"Goodnight," he said.

He stroked her body, he entered her slowly, and there was no space between them anymore, only warmth and closeness and the sound of the sea through the half-open porthole, they rose and fell with the waves as the ship sped toward Mykonos.

"I want you to come first," he said. "I will hold back. Yes, move like that . . . yes, ah yes . . . do you like?"

"I love it."

"Now, let us come together. I cannot wait any longer. Yes, now, darling. Ah . . ."

Nothing mattered anymore, horizons swept away, they were intertwined and borne on clouds, the crescendo mounted higher and higher and exploded like fireworks of many colors, and then they lay exhausted, limp, in each other's arms.

Finally he said, "This will have to last us."

"There's tomorrow night."

"Ah, the last night I have always much to do. Reports to write, people coming to see me all the time. It is impossible."

"And then?"

He sighed. "Who knows."

"You do not think we will ever see each other again . . . after this cruise?"

He felt her trembling and he put his hand under her chin and looked into her eyes. "Do you love me?"

"You know I do."

"Say it."

"I love you."

"I do not want you to leave, *chryso mou*. But what can we do?" His voice was without hope.

"I will come to the Caribbean this winter. We will be together again."

"That is eight months from now."

"I know. But it is better than nothing."

Better than nothing . . . a small consolation. Suddenly he wanted to strike out at something. "Why is there no happy life?" he said. "Only moments of happiness."

Twelve

"We are very sorry," came Eric's voice over the intercom, "but the captain says that it is not possible to disembark at Delos. The waves are too rough."

There were sighs of disappointment throughout the dining room.

"I guess that's what 'weather permitting' means in our brochures," one passenger said.

"Instead we will have more time at Mykonos," Eric said. "We will arrive there earlier and there will be more time for shopping."

The ladies applauded.

"Sorry about that, husbands," Eric said.

As they approached the island of Mykonos, Alexa could see small, white-washed houses and windmills on a hill, then gaily-painted fishing boats, the only touches of color against the stark white. Two other cruise ships were anchored in the harbor.

A small boat was pulling up alongside the *Pericles* and a short man with a deep tan got out carrying a briefcase and ran quickly up the stairs to the bridge. Nikos came out of the wheelhouse and they embraced and Alexa heard them speaking rapid Greek. She wondered who he was.

Nikos picked up the megaphone. The anchor was going down and the sailors were getting the lifeboats ready for the passengers to disembark. The waves looked choppy and there was a strong breeze.

Eric got on the intercom and gave his usual announcement about the departure of the boats for Mykonos and what time the last boat would return to the ship.

Nikos walked up to her with the man who had come on at Mykonos.

"This is Lukas Yiannoulis, the ship's agent at Mykonos," Nikos said. "Alexa Hollister."

Lukas smiled, showing very white teeth. He appeared to be about thirty. "I hope you will join the captain and me for dinner. There is a very good fish restaurant that we like to go to. The owner is a friend of mine."

Alexa hesitated and looked at Nikos. She wondered where Mrs. Vassilakis was and if she was also joining them.

"Yes, please come with us," Nikos said.

"Fine, I'd love to."

"We will be going ashore in about an hour. We will meet you in the lounge."

The restaurant was on a back street not frequented by tourists and was very small. The owner greeted them and showed them to a table.

"You pick out the fish you want," Lukas said, pointing to a case of freshly-caught fish, "and they fry it for you. That and a *horiatiki salata*—a village salad—and a bottle of Greek wine . . ." Lukas kissed his fingertips in the air. "Food for the gods."

The owner brought a basket of coarse brown bread and a bottle of retsina.

"We call this peasant bread," Nikos said, breaking off a piece. He was dressed in blue denim trousers and a black turtleneck sweater. "Here, try some. You will like it."

A group of young Greek men were sitting at the next table. One of them was twirling red glass worry beads. They called the waiter over and ordered ouzo.

"Excuse me for a few minutes, but I must telephone to Athens," Nikos said, getting up from the table. He walked over to the telephone on a wall in the corner.

"The captain wants to call his family," Lukas explained. "Have you met the captain's wife?"

Alexa felt a knife go through her. "No. What is she like?"

"Very beautiful. Not just because she is dark, but she has large eyes and very white teeth. And because she comes from Corfu her voice has a lilt."

Alexa said nothing. She could hear Nikos' voice speaking Greek. He sounded very animated. "Do you live on Mykonos all year round?" she asked Lukas.

"No. In the winter there are no tourists. I go to the Caribbean on one of the ships."

Nikos returned to the table. "My son, he tells me that he had chocolate ice cream for lunch." He smiled.

Chocolate ice cream, Alexa thought. Children are alike the world over.

Lukas said something to Nikos in Greek and he answered, smiling and shrugging.

"Please excuse us that we speak Greek," Lukas said. "I said to the captain that you are very beautiful and I hope that you will come to the Caribbean. This winter I will be on the *Pericles*. I will see that you have a good time."

Before she could reply the waiter arrived with the fish. Alexa noticed that they were served with the heads on and the eyes staring up at them.

"Ah, beautiful!" Nikos said. He looked quickly around the restaurant. "There are no passengers from the ship here? Good." He picked up the fish in his fingers. "I like to eat it with my hands."

Lukas laughed. "The captain is not as serious as he has to be for his job," he explained. "On the ship it is different."

I've never been with him away from the ship, Alexa thought, and she wondered again what the future held for them.

"It is the same for me," Lukas said. "With my job I have to be serious. But I like to have a good time."

"You are not married?"

"Me? Married?" Lukas threw back his head and laughed.

"Lukas is a bachelor," Nikos said. "He likes many women."

"Speak for yourself." Lukas turned to Alexa. "Did they warn you about the captain?"

"Do not believe it," Nikos said. "Lukas is a big—" He paused, searching for the word. "He likes to joke." He slapped Lukas on the back and said something in Greek.

Just then two women passengers poked their heads in the doorway of the restaurant.

"I do believe that's the captain of our ship," one said to the other.

"The man in the turtleneck? No, you're wrong, Sally."

The two left.

"You see why I do not wear my uniform ashore," Nikos said. "Well, I guess I should return to the ship. Many things to do always the last night of the cruise."

The last night of the cruise, she thought. The return to reality.

Lukas called for the check and the three of them left. The lights of the cruise ships in the bay were outlined against the dark sky and reflected in the water, cicadas chirped in the oleanders.

If only Nikos and I could stay here and make love in a little whitewashed house covered with bougainvillea, swim together at a deserted beach, hold hands in a taverna and listen to bouzouki music . . .

"It is better if we go back to the ship separately," Nikos said, after they had thanked Lukas for the dinner. "I see some of the passengers."

"All right."

"I will expect to see you on the ship in the Caribbean," Lukas said.

"Maybe."

He kissed her hand and left.

"Lukas likes you," Nikos said.

"He's very nice."

"Yes, he is a nice boy. Human being. Not like me."

"And what are you?"

"Me? I am chained to the ship. Twenty-four hours a day. You call that a normal life?" The purser was approaching with the radio officer. Nikos sighed. "Now it begins. I will try to see you later."

"We did not see the pelican, Captain."

"He is around. Somewhere."

"Did you see him?"

"Earlier. When you look for him he disappears. Once a week I come to Mykonos and always I see this pelican, Petros. Then I come with my son—the little one—I want to show him the pelican. But where is he? He is hiding. We cannot find him."

The passengers laughed.

"Excuse me, I must go now."

He went up the stairs to the bridge. It was good that he had a lot to do. He would not have time to think about anything but his work and the ship. Tomorrow morning she would leave the ship at Piraeus and then . . .

Who knows if they would ever see each other again?

Tomorrow night Katina and his sons would be on the ship. Greek Easter Week. The family. That was what was important to a Greek man.

He must get hold of himself.

In her cabin Alexa waited for the call that did not come. She finished her packing and put her large suitcase outside the door. Then she undressed and got into bed.

It was lovely and it is over, she told herself. He made no promises and now it has ended.

She put the pillow over her head so that no one would hear her sobs.

*　　*　　*

In her dream Keith is alive again, as if nothing has happened. She starts to say to him, "But you're dead," and then she stops.

It is summer. She has taken the girls to Nantucket to spend July and August with their grandmother. Keith is going to join them on weekends and the last two weeks of August. Then—what makes her do it?—she decides to come back to Greenwich in the middle of the week to surprise him.

She opens the door with her key and walks in the house. Keith is in the bedroom and he has on a pair of her lacy panties, the elastic stretched round his waist almost to the breaking point. On the bed is a satin slip and her pink chiffon negligee. She puts her hand to her mouth to suppress a scream. No, no! It's not true!

He looks at her in horror. Please understand, his eyes plead. I tried to tell you, but I couldn't find the words.

There are no words.

My husband—a transvestite. How could I not have known?

She turns and runs out of the room, down the stairs, out into the garden. There is a pain in her chest, it rises to her throat, it is choking her.

The children, their father . . .

Is it possible to suffer like this and go on living?

She runs down to the edge of the garden beside the brook. The air is sweet with honeysuckle, she wants to wind it in her hair and play Ophelia, float in the cool water until it closes over her and she feels no more.

Help, someone help me!

Daddy, where are you? I need you. Tell me what to do.

But her father will not come sailing home on his gray destroyer. There is no one. She must bear it alone and no one must know. Her mother? Never!

She is so ashamed. What could she say?

She presses her face against the cool grass, clenching and unclenching her hands. Her tears soak the ground.

Then, suddenly, a shot. From the direction of the house. She looks up and listens.

Silence.

She stands up. She is trembling. Slowly, she walks back. Through the French doors leading from the dining room, up the stairs, into the bedroom.

She screams!

He is lying on the floor. He has changed back to his Brooks Brothers seersucker suit, a white shirt, a striped tie. But he has no head. There is only a bloody mass and a shotgun lying beside him.

There is no note. None is needed.

The lingerie is gone.

She screams again, louder and louder, she cannot stop screaming . . .

The telephone ringing by her bed awoke her.

It was Nikos.

"I cannot sleep," he said. "I want to see you, but the stewards are putting the suitcases on the deck. Too many people around, running up and down the halls, it is not safe. Alexa? . . . Do you hear me?"

"Yes. Yes, I . . ." She yawned. It was still dark out.

"We will be coming into Piraeus soon. I must be on the bridge in a few minutes. But I want to say—I want to ask you . . ."

"Yes?"

"You will come to Caribbean this winter?"

"If you want me to."

"I want. Very much."

"Can we write to each other?"

There was a pause. "It is difficult . . . while I am in Greece," he said finally. "But when the ship is in Caribbean you can write to me in care of the ship's agent in San Juan. He will give me the letter and no one else will open it first. You understand?"

"I understand." Did he mean that if she wrote to him in Greece the Greek censors might open the letter—or his wife?

"So let me know when you will come. I will be waiting for your letter." He turned away from the phone and shouted, *"Amesos!"*

"What was that?"

"They want me now. I must go." He hung up quickly.

She stood waiting at the foot of the stairway that led down from the bridge. Dawn was just breaking over Piraeus and the port bustled with activity.

Then she saw him.

He had changed from his uniform to a dark suit. His face was haggard and there were deep circles under his eyes, as if he had not slept at all.

He came over to her and his eyes had a tender and sad expression. "I am going into Athens now," he said. "Thank you for . . . good companionship." He took her hand pressed it. "Have a good flight home."

And he turned and walked quickly down the gangway, not looking back at the ship or at her.

She watched him disappear into the customs house and she dug her fingernails into her palms. I must not cry, I must pull myself together. Goodbye, my love, until we meet again.

The other passengers were starting to mill about. She did not want to see anyone, she wanted to get off the ship now as fast as possible.

Then she heard the sound of Mrs. Pearson's cane tapping on the wooden deck as she approached.

"Hello there. Hasn't it been a lovely cruise? It went so quickly I can't believe it's over already."

Alexa smiled and hoped her voice didn't betray her.

"Yes," she said. "It was a lovely cruise."

BOOK TWO

BOOK TWO

Thirteen

*I*t had been snowing when she left Connecticut. Now she stood sweltering in the tropical heat of the San Juan airport, her heavy winter coat over her arm, while she waited for her luggage to be taken off the plane.

In an hour I will be back on the ship, she thought.

With him.

She saw her suitcases and pointed them out to the porter. "And I'd like a taxi, please."

The cab driver had worked in New York for several years, he told her, but he missed Puerto Rico and returned home.

"There's your ship," he said, as the harbor came into view.

Several large cruise ships were tied up at the dock, but the *Pericles* was easy to recognize with its blue smokestack with the yellow dolphin. My ship, she thought, and she leaned forward to catch a better glimpse.

"What nationality is that ship?" the driver asked.

"It's Greek."

He drove on to the pier and stopped. "This is as close as I can get," he said. "There are some porters." He beckoned to one.

Alexa paid the driver and gave him a large tip.

"Have a good cruise," he said.

"Thank you, I will."

He was coming up the stairs from the engine room with the

chief engineer when he saw her. At first he could not believe his eyes. But yes, she was here. She was back on the ship. And she was as beautiful as when they had said goodbye in Piraeus that April morning nine months ago.

Nine long months.

He had tried to forget her, to put her completely out of his mind, but she would not go away. In his dreams she returned to haunt him, when he lay beside Katina and tried to remind himself of his family responsibilities.

And now . . . here she was.

Their eyes met and he knew he must be on his guard. The chief engineer's wife was a friend of Katina's, there were stewards who would gossip around the ship.

She was coming toward him.

"Hello," he said, holding out his hand, making his voice deliberately casual. "Welcome back to the ship. I am glad to see you." He turned and spoke in Greek to the chief engineer, then said to Alexa, "Come and have a drink with me in the lounge."

They sat at a corner table in the lounge.

"Why did you not write me that you were coming?" he asked.

"I thought I'd surprise you. Are you glad I'm here?"

"I am very glad. It has been a long time."

"Nine months."

"And do you still—" The steward was approaching with their drinks and his voice suddenly changed. "How is the family?"

"Fine, thank you."

"Did you have a nice Christmas?"

"Yes." She took a sip of her drink. "Did you?"

He shrugged. "I was here. On the ship. I am always on the ship at Christmas."

"I've noticed some new officers."

"Yes, some of the men, they do not want to come to the Caribbean, to be away from their families for so long."

"When did you leave Greece?"

"The end of November." He looked at her tenderly. "I have missed you. I did not know . . ." He stopped.

"What?"

"If I would ever see you again."

"I said I'd come. And now I'm here."

"Tell me what you have been doing all this time?"

"Well, let's see. I took a real estate course and I have a job with an office in Greenwich. I've already sold two houses."

He seemed to be only half listening, watching passengers coming in. Then a man in greasy brown coveralls appeared in the doorway of the lounge, the man he was with before.

"The chief engineer wants to see me again," Nikos said, getting up. "I will see you later."

He covered her body with kisses.

"*Alexa mou*," he murmured over and over. "*Chryso mou.* How much I have wanted you."

They were lying on the narrow bed in his cabin while the ship moved up and down beneath them, catching their rhythm.

"I've wanted you too. So much."

He moaned. "Take me where you want, do with me what you will, break me in pieces."

It seemed as if they could not get enough of each other. Their caresses made them hunger for more and more . . .

"*M'agapas?*" he asked.

"Yes, I love you. *S'agapo.*"

"You are beautiful," he said.

No one had ever made her feel this way. No one ever would again. They moved as one. They were one.

It erased the dark nights of her childhood, all that she had known since. They were meant for one another.

Her body was alive again after all the empty months. Nothing mattered but him, these moments of delicious intoxication that she wanted never to end.

"There is no one like you," he said. "You make me crazy."

The long separation had made them feverish. Her pleasure mounted with his.

A warmth spread over her, she felt drugged from lovemaking.

Later, as they lay exhausted, watching the full moon through the porthole of his cabin, she told herself: We have a right to be happy.

And she wondered again about the great love stories.

Why were they always tragic?

Fourteen

The first island on the cruise was Saint Maarten, half Dutch, half French. She was waiting for the ship to anchor off Phillipsburg on the Dutch side when a short man with a mahogany tan came running up to her smiling.

"Welcome, welcome! You came after all to the Caribbean."

"Yes, I—"

"I am Lukas. Remember, on Mykonos?"

"Of course. How are you?"

"Busy. I have to see the captain now, but let us have a drink together later. You are going ashore?"

"Yes. Is it a pretty island?"

"There are pretty beaches. I hope to have time to go swimming. I will see you later."

Alexa got her landing tag and waited with the other passengers on the deck.

"The sea looks rough," an older woman said worriedly.

"I heard that the *Mermoz* was here earlier this morning and the French captain wouldn't let his passengers disembark," a man said.

Alexa heard the anchor go down and the sailors were getting the lifeboats ready.

"It looks like this Greek captain's going to let us go ashore."

"Have you seen him?" one woman said to another. "He's so handsome." She pointed up to the bridge where Nikos was leaning over the railing watching the sailors lowering the boats.

"I guess we'll meet him at the cocktail party tonight," her friend said. "I can't wait."

The passengers filed into the lounge and a photographer took pictures as each one shook hands with the captain.

Alexa saw a tall blonde in a tight, low-cut dress near the beginning of the line. She appeared to be in her twenties and was alone. The stewards were giving her interested looks.

"I didn't know they were working ships these days," Alexa overheard an elderly woman ahead of her say.

"I guess there's too much competition in New York," her companion replied. "Only last week the husband of a friend of mine was accosted right in front of the Plaza Hotel. And in the middle of the day, brazen as you please!"

The line moved quickly as a hostess Alexa had not seen before introduced passengers to the captain.

"Mrs. Hollister, Captain Meletis."

"How do you do?" His eyes betrayed nothing.

A flashbulb exploded as the photographer took their picture. "How do you do, Captain," she said.

She looked around the room trying to decide where to sit when Lukas rushed up to her.

"Please join me over here."

"Oh, fine." I hope he doesn't try to monopolize me, she thought. It will be difficult enough as it is for Nikos and me to be alone together.

"Did you like Saint Maarten?" Lukas asked, as the steward passed them drinks.

"Yes. Did you go swimming?"

"Just for a short time."

"I'll go swimming tomorrow at Martinique," she said. "I want to work on my tan."

"You must be careful at first," Lukas warned. "The Caribbean sun is very strong. But if you like, I know a lovely beach."

I would like to go to a beach with Nikos, she thought, as she saw him still shaking hands with passengers. I wonder if he will be able to get away?

"We can invite the captain to join us," Lukas said, noticing her glance.

The statuesque blonde was sitting on a sofa and was apparently trying to reserve the place beside her for someone.

"Is she one of the ship's entertainers?" Alexa asked.

"Sonia? No, she is a passenger. She was on the last cruise as well. She is an airline hostess for Lufthansa. She has been on the ship before. She is a friend of the captain's."

I wonder if that's who she's saving the place for? Alexa wondered. "How was the last cruise?" she asked.

"A disaster. It is lucky you did not come then."

"What happened?"

"Almost everyone on the ship was sick. The flu. One of the passengers brought it and it spread rapidly. Even the captain was sick. And then there was trouble at Grenada. The ship's carpenter, right near the dock, was attacked by a native with a knife. He is in the hospital there now."

The receiving line ended and Alexa saw Nikos looking around the room. The airline stewardess was watching him also.

"Let us rescue him," Lukas said, getting up quickly. He brought Nikos over to their table. "Your friend is waiting for you," he said with a wink.

The stewardess downed her drink angrily and ordered another.

"I will sit down for a few minutes," Nikos said. "Then I must move around." He asked the steward to bring him a Campari and soda. Then he said something to Lukas in Greek and they both laughed. "Excuse me, we must not speak Greek, it is not polite."

"I will teach Alexa some Greek," Lukas said.

"Be careful of him. Let me know first what he has taught you to say." He smiled.

"You do not trust me, Captain?"

"Not with the ladies." Nikos quickly finished his drink. "I must move around now and sit with some of the other passengers. Perhaps we can have a dance after dinner?"

"Why, I'd love to, Captain," Lukas said.

"*Koutos!* I was not speaking to you."

Lukas laughed.

"What does that word mean?" she asked Nikos.

"*Koutos?* It is what he is. Crazy!" He punched Lukas in the ribs. "I will see you both later."

"I like to joke with the captain," Lukas said, as Nikos moved off. "He worries so much about the ship, always so much responsibility. It is good for him to laugh more often." He looked at her. "The captain likes you."

"He's very nice," Alexa said carefully.

"All the ladies like the captain. But then—" he paused significantly, "—he always goes home to his wife. Like any Greek husband."

The bell rang for dinner and Alexa was glad to be rescued from this conversation. She got up.

"I have to go down to dinner now," she said.

The S.O.S. came without warning. Nikos left the lounge and ran up the stairs to the radio room.

"When did you get the message?" he asked.

"A few minutes ago," the chief radio operator said, handing him the report.

The *S.S. Verona*, an Italian cruise ship with five hundred passengers aboard, was on fire off St. Vincent.

Quickly Nikos calculated the distance. Even if they increased speed to the maximum it would be at least six hours before they could reach St. Vincent.

"Are there no other ships closer?" he asked.

"I haven't picked up any."

"Give the *Verona* our position and tell them we are on the way."

*   *   *

Juanita, the cruise hostess, went to the microphone at the reception desk.

"Ladies and gentlemen," she said, "if you have noticed that the ship seems to have increased speed a great deal, you are right. The ship that was docked next to us at San Juan, the *Verona*, is on fire off the island of St. Vincent. As you know, one of the first rules of the sea is to aid any other ship in distress, and we are now going to her rescue. The main lounge is being prepared to take on passengers. The captain wishes you to remain calm and to assist in every possible way. Thank you for your cooperation."

Nikos picked up the telephone to the engine room. He did not like the chief engineer. Whenever he gave him an order he tried in some way to countermand it.

"Can't we go any faster?" he shouted.

"We cannot increase speed any more, Captain. The ship will not take it."

Idiot! He thought. I know what the ship will take, not you. "Do as I say!" he shouted.

The second officer handed him a message. The *Queen Elizabeth II* was also on her way to the rescue. Good. She was a much larger ship than the *Pericles* and could take on many more passengers. He looked at the radio report again. From her longitude and latitude they should arrive about the same time.

He picked up his binoculars and scanned the horizon. They were still too far away to see anything. The sailors were standing by their lifeboat stations and he had alerted the ship's doctor to have supplies ready to attend to the injured.

Each cruise they had a different doctor, an American, since most of the passengers were Americans in the Caribbean. He got a free two-week cruise with his wife to be on board and attend to anyone who was sick. This doctor, he had observed, was always the first off the ship when they docked. Now he would have something to do.

He rubbed his left jaw. His tooth was starting to ache again.

That was one of the problems with being at sea all the time, there was never the chance to have your teeth attended to properly. If it kept up he would have to have the tooth pulled, and he did not relish the idea of having it done on one of these islands. He took two more pain pills, and then he went in the chart room and spoke to the navigator. Instead of docking at Martinique early in the morning, they would probably arrive there sometime in the afternoon, depending on what happened with the *Verona.*

The steward brought him a cup of black coffee and he sipped it slowly. There would be no sleep tonight.

Alexa stood with some of the other passengers on the deck outside her chair. She could recognize Nikos' voice shouting orders in Greek over the ship's intercom to the members of the crew.

"This is exciting," a woman said. "I'll have lots to tell the folks in Grand Rapids when I get home."

"Look, there it is!" a man said.

Ahead, to the right, they saw flames shooting up into the dark sky. It was the burning ship.

Alexa saw Nikos stride out of the wheelhouse and look through his binoculars. Then he shouted again in Greek.

"I wish I could understand what the captain's saying," a fat woman complained.

Juanita's voice came over the intercom. "The captain has requested that the passengers please do not crowd around the lifeboats. We will be needing them for the rescue. Kindly go to a lower deck. Thank you."

Lukas came down from the bridge. "Please, everyone, go below." Reluctantly, the passengers started to move. Lukas smiled at Alexa and raised his eyebrows. "We need your cooperation, ladies and gentlemen. Thank you."

"There's another ship, a big one," a man said. He had a camera and was trying to focus it.

"Yes, it's the *Queen Elizabeth II.*" Lukas said. "Now please, sir, will you go below?"

They came closer, careful to avoid the rocks. Why had the Italian captain taken his ship through such a narrow channel?" Nikos wondered. Did he not have English maps? No wonder they ran aground. He would never have attempted to take the *Pericles* through that channel and his was a much smaller ship than the *Verona*. The fuel line under the ship must have ruptured when it scraped the rocks and started the fire. The *Verona* was an old ship with much wood paneling, making it burn all the faster.

He went into the radio room. "What is the situation?" he asked the chief radio operator. "You have made contact with the ship?"

"Yes, Captain. The *Queen Elizabeth II*. has picked up many of the passengers, and others got ashore on the island. But they do not have a complete count of all the passengers. There is at least one lifeboat missing and they want us to look for it."

Nikos went back to the bridge and picked up the megaphone. "Lower the lifeboats!" he shouted to the sailors and officers standing by each boat.

The first officer was looking out at the sea with his binoculars.

"Do you see anything?"

"No, sir."

The lifeboats from the *Pericles* were now in the water, circling around.

"Over here, Captain. I think I see something." He pointed to a speck. "It looks like a lifeboat."

Alexa looked out the porthole of her cabin at the burning ship. Flames and smoke filled the dawn sky. It was an awesome and frightening sight and she wondered how any of the passengers had been able to get off. Were some of them now trapped, unable to escape? She shuddered. Suppose that had happened to us? No, with Nikos in command it could not. I feel safe with him. He is the only man I have ever known who is everything a man should be.

Everything.

Over the ship's intercom she heard his voice shouting commands in Greek. What was going on?

Now Nikos could see the lifeboat and people in it, but it was burned and seemed to have no oars, drifting in a circle. One of their lifeboats had spotted it and was going toward it. He walked out of the wheelhouse and stood leaning over the rail, watching through his binoculars. He could make out the name on it now, *S.S. Verona, Genoa.* But why no oars?

The lifeboat from the *Pericles* had almost reached it. As he pulled up alongside, the officer in charge threw a rope to a person in the lifeboat. They were going to tow it. Nikos shouted through the megaphone but they were too far away to hear him. He could not see how many people were in the boat, but the stewards had prepared cots in the main lounge for survivors, the infirmary was ready also.

He rubbed his jaw. It was throbbing, in spite of the pain pills he had taken earlier. There was nothing he could do about it. *"Ola dexia!"* he shouted. The ship turned slowly to starboard.

The lifeboat from the *Verona* was now being towed to the *Pericles.* He made a quick count of the passengers as it came closer. There were over forty, including the crew members. He put down his binoculars and called to the engineer to stop the engines. There was no response. *"Krati!"* he shouted.

Sailors were lowering the gangway. Now he could see the faces of the passengers in the lifeboat and they looked bedraggled and frightened. Many of them were still in their nightclothes.

"It is all right," Nikos called down to them. "Do not worry. We will have you safely aboard in a few minutes." He turned to the second officer. "Where is the doctor?" he asked in Greek.

"I have not seen him, Captain."

"Then look for him. Some of those people may need him." He

ran down the stairs. I'd better not see that doctor first, he thought. What does he think he is here for? To dance in the discotheque, sun himself on the beaches?

The sailors were helping the survivors out of the *Verona's* life-boat and the first ones were climbing the gangway. Nikos stood at the top.

"Welcome aboard. I am Captain Meletis. We will give you every possible assistance."

One woman was hysterical. "I can't find my husband. We got separated. Where is my husband?" She looked around helplessly.

"We will locate him. He is probably in another lifeboat," Nikos said.

"No, he stayed behind to help some of the others." Then she screamed. "Oh, my God! Look!"

The blazing *Verona*, listing heavily to one side, rolled all the way over and, as water rushed in, her stern sank until only her bow and the bridge and one smokestack could be seen. But that was not for long. Suddenly her bow stood straight up and then, with a final shudder, she plunged beneath the sea. In only a few minutes the ship had completely disappeared.

"There go all the new clothes I bought for this cruise," one woman said.

"And my jewelry!" another cried.

"I hope that Italian captain went down with it," an angry man muttered. "If he hadn't been drinking so much and making time with the ladies we wouldn't be in this mess."

Nikos couldn't help hearing the last remarks. Better he does go down, he thought, than face what he will have to face for losing his ship. The nightmare of every sea captain. No matter what the reason, he was responsible.

He saw Juanita. "See that everyone from the *Verona* goes to the lounge," he told her, "so that we can get a count and their names."

"I do not think there are enough cots in the lounge for them all, Captain."

"We will put some with the passengers who have extra beds in their cabins. Will you ask those who have to please volunteer? It is only until we get to Martinique. And the sailors can bunk with the crew."

"Yes, Captain."

Alexa heard Juanita's announcement over the intercom. Hers was a double cabin, so she could share it with one of the women passengers from the *Verona*. As she opened her cabin door Nikos ran past her on his way up to the bridge. His face was haggard and he was holding his jaw. He threw her a quick glance but did not speak.

My poor love, she thought, how tired you look.

The lounge was pandemonium. The survivors were milling about with dazed expressions and drinking hot coffee served by the stewards. "Would you believe it?" Alexa heard one of them say. "They didn't even give the abandon ship instructions in English. They gave them in Italian and French."

Alexa was assigned the hysterical woman who had lost her husband. She was from Baltimore, she told Alexa, and it was her first cruise, a celebration of their fiftieth wedding anniversary.

"And now I don't know where my husband is." She started to sob.

Alexa put her arm around her. "We have an excellent captain on this ship. I'm sure he'll be able to locate your husband."

"Do you think so? He told me he'd send a radio message to see if my husband had been picked up by another ship."

"I heard that the *Queen Elizabeth II*. had taken a lot of the passengers."

The woman brightened. "Maybe he's on that."

"He probably is. Don't worry. Captain Meletis will take care of everything."

"What nationality is this ship?"

"It's Greek."

"I wish we'd booked this cruise instead. But the *Verona* was such a beautiful ship and my husband likes Italian food."

"Here we are." Alexa unlocked her cabin.

"Oh, it's small."

"But it's quite comfortable," Alexa said quickly. "Why don't you lie down and rest?"

"I am tired. But I don't think I could sleep wondering where Harold is." She took off her shoes and pulled the covers over her.

In a few minutes Alexa heard soft snoring.

I'll let her sleep, she thought, and get some breakfast. She tiptoed out of the cabin and closed the door quietly.

Fifteen

A steel band was playing on shore when they docked at Martinique in the early afternoon. Nikos held the walkie-talkie in one hand and clutched his jaw with the other. It was swollen and throbbing, but there was no way he could get to a dentist today. There was too much to do making arrangements for the survivors from the *Verona*. One man had a bad heart and should be put in the hospital for a few days, the doctor had reported, others had to get flights home. And he had long reports to write. He would just have to take some more pain pills and see a dentist on Grenada tomorrow.

If only that band would stop playing so loudly! The sound vibrated in his head. He would like to be lying down in his cabin now with his jaw packed in ice.

"*Anapotha!*" he shouted. The engines reversed. Men on the dock were catching the ropes and tying them to the posts. "Stop the engines!" he shouted. "*Krati!*" The ship came smoothly alongside inches from the pier and the sailors put down the gangway. He saw Alexa two decks below waiting to go ashore. For the passengers now a pleasant afternoon of sightseeing and swimming on Martinique. For him, the work was just beginning. He went back in the wheelhouse. The purser was waiting for him and also the ship's agent.

Alexa got her landing tag and went down the gangway. On the dock black women in colorful costumes carried baskets on their heads.

Taxis were lined up to take passengers on the tour of the island and passengers were haggling with the native drivers about the price.

Nikos walked past her with a black man in a white suit who was carrying a briefcase. They were both speaking French. If he saw her he did not appear to notice.

Juanita and Lukas were trying to get the passengers who had signed up for the tour to get started. They were to go four to a taxi, and since most of the drivers spoke little English, they were given a printed itinerary of what they would be seeing.

"Please, everyone," Juanita said. "We are late. Be sure to give the driver your ticket."

Alexa got in a cab with a middle-aged couple and an elderly woman and they started off. Climbing from the low part of the island where it was hot, the air suddenly turned much cooler, the vegetation more lush with large ferns and mahogany trees, bougainvillea and poinsettias, red anthurium. Streams where women were washing clothes, baby goats and lambs. The road was narrow and winding with small cars and trucks passing. They saw several schools for boys and girls, the children wearing bright blue uniforms.

They went through the ruins of Saint Pierre, where on May 8, 1902, Mont Pelée had erupted, wiping out the city and its thirty thousand inhabitants. His grandfather had lived in Saint Pierre, the driver said, but on that fated day he had gone to pick breadfruit in the hills. When he returned his house and everyone else was gone. The only other survivor was a prisoner who was occupying a dungeon cell.

"And now Mont Pelée is dormant?" Alexa asked.

"Yes. And I hope she sleeps forever," the driver laughed.

Alexa translated what he had said for the others.

They stopped at a beautiful deserted beach of black sand. Alexa picked up a handful and sifted the fine volcanic sand through her fingers, wondering where Nikos was now. If only they could come here together, forget the ship, the passengers, everything . . .

"Are there sharks in the ocean?" one of the women was asking the driver, who shrugged his shoulders and looked blank. "Big fish?" She demonstrated with her hands, clapping them together to indicate a shark biting off someone's leg.

"*Requins?*" Alexa asked.

He grinned broadly and shook his head. "*Pas ici.*"

"He said that there aren't any sharks here," Alexa told them.

"That sand looks dirty to me," the woman's husband said. "I'll take good old white sand any time."

They got back in the taxi. Alexa asked the driver about the plantation where Empress Josephine was born.

"*Trois-Ilets,*" he said.

How far was it? She would love to see it. Ah, it was too far, he told her, across the bay from Fort-de-France. She would have to come back another time. He would give her his card and she could ask for him when she did. He would be happy to drive her there.

"What is he saying?" the couple asked.

"We were talking about Josephine's house, but it's too far away."

They looked blank. "Josephine?"

"Napoleon's wife. She was born here."

"You don't say." The woman, who was named Esther, turned to her husband. "Did you know that, Irving?"

Irving looked as if he couldn't have cared less. "I thought we were going to stop at a rum factory," he grumbled.

"That's tomorrow on Grenada."

"Well I'd like a Planter's Punch when we get back on the boat."

"Ship, Irving. Don't let the captain hear you calling it a boat."

That evening a native troupe came on board to perform. The women wore colorful plaid cloth hats with points that turned up to indicate if you were married, single, or available and looking. Alexa bought two of them after the show to take home to Brooke and Cicily. She had not seen Nikos since she returned to the ship. Lukas came over and joined her.

"Did you like the show? I see you have bought the hats."

Then she saw Nikos standing at the door of the lounge. He was not in uniform but wearing slacks and a blue shirt. She hoped he would come over and join them but instead he just looked around the room and then went up the stairs.

Lukas noticed her glance. "The captain is not feeling well," he said. "And he has had much excitement with the rescue of the *Verona*." In a corner near the bar Sonia was sitting alone sipping a drink. "But then, there is always excitement around the captain, isn't that so?"

"It depends, Lukas, on what kind of excitement you are referring to."

Lukas smiled. "You always pretend you do not know what I am talking about."

Sonia got up and left the lounge, a sulky expression on her face. She was wearing a tight flowered dress with the back cut down to the waist.

"You like the captain," Lukas said.

She was walking on a crate of eggs, she must tread carefully. "Of course. Doesn't everyone?"

"It is part of his job to give the ladies a good time, a memorable cruise. If he flirts a little, it does not mean anything."

"Just what are you trying to say, Lukas?"

"You are not like Sonia and the others. You are a lady. I do not want to see you get hurt."

"Thank you for your advice, but I can take care of myself. And besides, you are imagining things."

"I do not think so. And I have noticed the way he looks at you. Or rather the way he tries to avoid looking at you." He paused. "The captain loves his sons very much. And Greek men do not get divorces."

"I think I'll turn in now, Lukas." She got up. "I'll see you tomorrow."

The letter from Katina had not contained good news. The Greek government wanted more money for taxes on the house. He did not know how he could pay it. He sent home everything he made, but it was not enough. Greek shipping owners were not known for paying high salaries to their captains. He took another pill. Always complaints from Katina in her letters. And then she would say how much his sons missed him. What was he to do? If he worked in the company office in Piraeus he would not make as much money as at sea. Whenever you left Greek waters your salary doubled.

Evangelos, now fifteen, needed a father around to guide and discipline him. At least Greece did not have the drug problem that the other countries had. Some of the American passengers would tell him of difficulties with their teenage children and ask him how he managed when he was away from home so much. He would like to be with his sons more. As for Katina . . .

He lay down on the bed. He had wanted to go over and sit with Alexa, to have her put her hand on his face and take away the pain. He wanted to hold her, to make love until all else faded, to murmur her name over and over again. She was like a princess to him, his golden one. And he must not hurt her. Even now, the officers were gossiping about them.

He dialed her cabin and his heart beat faster when he heard her voice.

"I've been worried about you," she said.

"I am all right."

"Will you promise me to see a dentist tomorrow on Grenada? I'll go with you."

"That will not be necessary. The ship's agent will go with me."

"I wish we could be together."

"I want you, *Alexa mou*. Tomorrow, when I am feeling better." There was a knock on his cabin door. "I must go."

It was time to sail.

The unchanging pattern of his life. Captain, you are wanted on the bridge.

Wearily, he got out of bed.

Sixteen

Grenada, isle of spices. Everywhere were natives selling baskets of nutmeg, saffron, cinnamon. Black boys were diving for coins near the ship thrown by the passengers. Alexa saw Nikos walking along the dock with the purser and another man who had come on the ship with the pilot boat.

The tour of the island included Government House, a stately white mansion with a balcony high on a hill. It had a somewhat unkempt look, as if the native woman governor had let it run down. Alexa could imagine it in the days when Grenada had a British governor and tea was served in the pergola at the end of a flower-bordered path. Looking down, she could see the *Pericles* anchored in the bay.

There was a beautiful drive through narrow roads and a stop at an 18th Century rum factory that was still operating, then a visit to two private homes. The first was that of an English couple who had built it to escape the chilly British winters. They said they spent four months a year on Grenada, served tea, and seemed desperate to talk to visitors. "Oh, must you go so soon?" they asked, disappointed when the group started to leave. In spite of the beautiful beaches, the spices, the mild weather, they appeared lonely. Maybe it wasn't such a paradise after all, Alexa thought.

The next house they visited was on a hill and owned by a woman, originally Polish, who had spent several years in a German concentration camp. From her terrace they watched the lights come on in the harbor and on the ship. Alexa wondered if Nikos was back on board.

If only we could live in a house like this, be together, swim on the beaches. Would the charm eventually wear off, would we finally get bored and long for company, the way these people did? And what about our children, his and mine? Where did they fit into the picture? They didn't.

They said goodbye to the Polish lady and returned to the ship.

He was standing outside the purser's office when she came on board with the others. She walked up to him and smiled.

"Did you enjoy the tour?" he asked.

"Yes. It's a beautiful island."

He took her arm. "Let us go out on the deck and sit down." He guided her to two empty deck chairs away from the other passengers.

"What did you do today?"

"The purser and I went to the hospital to visit the ship's carpenter, the one who was stabbed by the native on our last cruise."

"Yes, Lukas told me about it."

"It was terrible. And right on the dock near the ship. The man has two children. And he will not be able to return to Greece for at least a month." He wiped his mouth with a piece of gauze and there was blood on it.

"How is your tooth?"

"It was—how you say—" He searched for the word in English. "Infected. Ab—"

"Abscess?"

"Yes, abscess. I had it pulled. But it will not stop bleeding."

"Can't you lie down?"

"Lie down?" He laughed, then clutched his jaw. "Too much to do. On the ship I worry about everybody, but no one worries about me."

"I worry about you."

"I know. You are very sweet." He reached over and stroked her cheek. "Why do you care that I am unhappy?"

"Because I do."

He started to say something, but just then he saw three of the stewards walking toward him carrying a large silver cup.

"We won, Captain," they said in Greek, beaming as they handed it to him triumphantly.

"Whenever the ship is in port the members of the crew arrange a soccer game with another ship," he explained in English to Alexa. "It is for the men to get exercise. Today they won the match."

"Congratulations." She smiled at them and they grinned back.

Nikos said a few more words to them in Greek and then they left.

"They were so happy to give you the cup," Alexa said.

"Ah, they are good boys. Good boys." He put the silver cup on the table beside his deckchair and wiped the edge of his mouth again with the gauze. Two passengers were approaching. Even though he was not wearing his uniform, they recognized him.

"Good evening, Captain."

"Good evening." There was no place on the ship where they could talk quietly away from the others, except in his cabin or hers. And even that was not without risk. "I must go now and change," he said, picking up the silver cup. "Come up later. I will call you."

She stood on the bridge watching them leave Grenada, the lights around the harbor twinkling in the dark, a calypso band on the dock playing sensuous melodies, the warm evening breeze of the Caribbean and a sky filled with stars. Nikos, in his white uniform with the four gold stripes on the epaulets, his face serious, directing the ship.

When everyone had left the bridge, he beckoned her to come to his cabin. He locked the door and took her in his arms and held her close.

"Ah, *Alexa mou*," he whispered, "I need a woman to take care of me."

"I will take care of you."

"Do you love me?"

"You know I do."

He murmured something in Greek.

"What did you say?"

"It is a line from a poem of George Seferis."

"What does it mean in English?"

"So our life became one and it will be very difficult for it to separate again."

He led her toward the bed.

Later, back in her own cabin, she dreamed that she was on a ship, but the ship was sailing through cities, not oceans, as if the ship followed her through life when she was not on it. And she wandered all over it, this strange ship, looking for him. There was a different captain, one she had never seen before. "Where is Captain Meletis?" she asked. No one knew. They were all Greek, other Greeks, but not the one she wanted. He had vanished. And there was no way she could find him again.

When she awoke it took her a while to reorient herself. She was back on the *Pericles*, his ship, and he was on the bridge.

It was only a dream, she told herself. This was real.

Seventeen

In the morning she went out on deck to watch the docking at Port of Spain, Trinidad. A steel band was playing and there was much activity on shore. She saw Sonia in a brief green bikini drying her long blonde hair in the sun on an upper deck, obviously trying to attract attention from Nikos, who was busy docking the ship and appeared not to notice her. Or did he? Had he had an affair with Sonia on a previous cruise? The thought bothered her. I'm acting like a jealous wife, she told herself, and tried to push the idea out of her mind. After all, he can't help it if he's attractive and women throw themselves at him.

Next to the purser's office she saw Irving and Esther Silverstein, the couple she had shared the taxi with on the tour of Martinique. They were dressed in winter traveling clothes and had their luggage with them.

"Are you leaving the cruise?" Alexa asked.

"Yes, we're flying home as soon as we can get off the ship," Esther said. "It's my husband's business partner—"

"He died?"

"No, but he may!" Irving yelled. "The damned sonofabitch is liquidating my business. I got a cable last night. Just wait till I get my hands on him! 'Have a nice cruise, Irving,' he tells me. 'Don't worry about a thing, I'll take care of it all.' Bastard!" His face turned red and he started to shake with fury.

"Irving, remember your blood pressure," Esther admonished.

"Yes, I came on this cruise for a rest. Doctor's orders. A fine rest!"

"I'm so sorry," Alexa said. "I hope everything turns out all right."

The purser came up. "As soon as the ship is cleared you can leave," he said.

"When will that be?"

"In just a few minutes. The officials are with the captain now. Then you can get a cab right to the airport."

"Good."

"Oh, here is the captain now."

Nikos came over to them. "Everything is arranged," he said, shaking hands with the Silversteins. "I am sorry that you have to leave the cruise, but I hope you will come back and sail with us another time."

"Oh, thank you, Captain, we'd love to," Esther gushed. "Wouldn't we, Irving?"

"Yeah, well let's go now."

Nikos spoke in Greek to the stewards and they grabbed the bags and carried them off the ship followed by the Silversteins.

He turned to Alexa. "Did you sleep well?"

"Yes, Captain."

He smiled. "Come in the lounge and have a coffee with me."

They sat down in a corner and an officer came up with some papers for Nikos to sign. Alexa watched him as he signed with a flourish.

"Always something," he said when the officer had gone. He took a sip of the black coffee. "So, what do you do today? Are you going on the tour?"

"This afternoon. Unless you have other plans?"

"Me?" He shrugged. "I do not have plans. Always they have plans for me."

Sonia walked by on the deck outside and looked in the windows of the lounge, then continued strolling.

"I think your friend is looking for you," Alexa said.

"Who is that?"

"The girl in the green bikini."

He laughed. "Sonia? She has been on the ship before."

"So I gathered."

If I were not here, would he be with her? she wondered. "What are you going to do today?"

"I have reports to write, I must check about supplies for the ship, the chief engineer has a problem he wants to talk to me about." He leaned close to her. "It would be nice if we could go to a beach together, get away."

"That's what I was thinking too."

He sighed. "I am never free. Always they must know where I am. Always one foot in the prison."

"You have said that before."

"It is true." He finished his coffee. "And now I must go. Have a good day. I will see you later."

Her companions on the tour were a retired doctor and his wife. A kindly elderly man, he had become a gentleman farmer. "A doctor sees the end of life," he said. Now he wanted to see things grow, the beginnings of life instead of the end, the infirm with all their ailments.

After the tour the guide left them off in the town to shop. A carnival was going on and they stopped to watch it.

"What colorful costumes!" exclaimed the doctor's wife.

There was an orange-and-black butterfly float, a black Viking with a blond wig, three blacks carrying blue, silver and gold sailfish shuffling along to the calypso steel band, another man in a red foil lobster costume.

"Look, here comes the queen." The doctor pointed to a pretty young black woman in a red velvet robe sitting on a throne surrounded by girls in red-and-white costumes, silver hats with red pompoms and red obi ties around their waists. They carried red-and-silver poles with red flowers on the end and their faces were painted white.

But Alexa's glance was drawn beyond them to a stand where a man was taking pictures with a movie camera. Beside him sat a blonde girl. Nikos and Sonia. So that was the work he had to attend to, she thought.

He smiled and beckoned to them.

"Isn't that our captain?" the doctor's wife asked.

"Come," Nikos called. "There are some seats here."

"Yes, let's sit down," the doctor said. "We can get a better view over the crowds."

Nikos indicated a row of seats in back of him, as Sonia sulked. "I'm making some movies to take home to Greece," Nikos explained. "For my son. The little one."

"How nice," the doctor's wife said. "How old is your son, Captain?"

His eyes lit up. "Four years old. He will love to see these costumes."

The doctor was looking at Sonia who was wearing tight purple slacks and a white T-shirt with no bra.

"Did you enjoy the tour of Trinidad?" Nikos asked.

"Indeed we did," the doctor's wife said. "We went to a beautiful bird sanctuary on a large lake with islands."

"I got some great shots of a flock of egrets and a scarlet ibis," the doctor said.

Alexa noticed that Nikos did not appear to be listening, as if preoccupied with something. Suddenly their eyes met briefly and Sonia gave them an angry look.

"I must get back now to the ship," Nikos said. He stood up. "Please excuse me."

"And I have some shopping to do," Sonia said.

They went off in opposite directions. He seemed anxious to get rid of her, Alexa thought. Was it just a coincidence that they were together?

"The captain is so nice," the doctor's wife said. "And so hand-some."

"Not much of a conversationalist, though," the doctor said.

"I think he has difficulty with the English language. After all, he is Greek."

Yes, he is Greek, Alexa thought. He is Greek and he is married. And his sons are the most important things in the world to him. So where are we heading, Nikos and I? Do we go on like this, stealing moments on the ship, trying to hide our feelings in front of others, until . . . until finally we have to face reality, that there is no happy ending for us, can never be?

"You're looking very serious," the doctor said.

"Am I?" Were her thoughts that transparent? "It's nothing important," she said lightly.

"I did not invite her to come with me," Nikos said later when they were having a drink in his cabin. "She just appeared and joined me."

"You don't have to explain to me about Sonia," Alexa said.

"That is true. But I just want you to know that she means nothing to me."

"And what do I mean to you?"

"You know what you mean to me." He took her in his arms and his eyes were filled with agony. He buried his face in her hair. "*Alexa mou.* What are we going to do?"

"That is up to you."

"It is not up to me. I have no control over my life. And I have obligations, people I am responsible to. I do not wish to hurt them."

And if you did you would hate me, she thought. "We have three more days."

"Three days," he said bitterly. There was a knock on the cabin door. "They want me for something. Always."

Eighteen

*T*he storm came up without warning the next day.

They had gone ashore in bathing suits to swim and have a beach barbecue on the island of Tobago. Alexa went in on the first tender with Lukas and Nikos joined them later. It was a beautiful morning and the water was warm and clear. Some of the passengers went snorkeling on the other side of the island.

Alexa rubbed suntan oil on herself and lay back on the hot sand.

"This is the life, isn't it Captain?" Lukas said.

Nikos was watching one of the passengers, a fat man with white hair who was lying far down the beach letting the waves wash over him.

"What is he doing?" Nikos pointed.

"I think he's had too much rum punch," Lukas said. "He came ashore with us on the first tender and started drinking right away."

"He is drunk. Go get him out of the water."

Alexa opened her eyes and sat up. The man lay on the beach like a blob of whale blubber while the waves swept over him. Lukas ran to the edge of the water and pulled him out. The man was resisting, and no sooner had Lukas left than he was right back lying in the water again.

"I do not need to have a passenger drowned on this trip," Nikos said. "I will go speak to him. Where is his wife?"

Alexa pointed to a plump woman in a print shirt and shorts

eating a banana. Stewards from the ship were grilling chicken over hot coals. Lukas walked back, throwing up his hands in disgust.

Nikos ran down along the beach and dragged the man to his feet as a large wave was about to break over him. There was an argument and then the man waddled over to the table where his wife was sitting with some other people and took out his false teeth and put them on his plate. Then they fell under the table and had to be retrieved. His wife went to get coffee for him to try to sober him up. He promptly poured it all over his plate.

"Horace!" she exclaimed in dismay. "Look what you've done!"

"We have one like him on every cruise," Nikos said.

"Sometimes more than one," Lukas added.

They ate their lunch of barbecued chicken, salad, papaya, and tiny golden bananas.

"I used to have these bananas in Rio de Janeiro when I was a child," Alexa said.

At the next table Horace had finished his lunch and was back on rum punch. After a few minutes he wandered back to his favorite spot, drink in hand, and lay down. The waves were getting larger and larger.

"It looks like a storm," Nikos said. He looked down the beach and saw Horace lying at the water's edge. "Go get him," he told Lukas. "He must go back to the ship on the next tender. I will speak to his wife."

The unwilling Horace was finally persuaded by his wife and Nikos to get on the tender. They left with several other passengers who wanted to return to the ship.

"Now that he's gone we can enjoy ourselves, eh Captain? I will race you into the water," Lukas said.

Nikos laughed.

"You need to relax more. Doesn't he, Alexa?"

"I will have one more swim," Nikos said, "and then I will have to go back to the ship when the tender returns. Come, Alexa."

They drifted in the warm water, not wanting to leave.

"Ah, it is good," Nikos said.

Lukas swam off a ways to leave them alone, but soon other passengers surrounded them. Dark rain clouds were forming in the sky. And then they saw the tender returning with one lone person sitting in the stern.

"I do not believe it!" Nikos said.

"It's Horace. How on earth—"

"Why did they not keep him on the ship? Do I have to do everything myself?" He waded out of the water and dried himself with a towel. Alexa followed.

The tender came close to the shore and Nikos waded out to it. Alexa heard a shouting exchange in Greek between the officer in charge and Nikos. Then Nikos beckoned to Lukas and they got in. The tender started back to the *Pericles*, Nikos still shouting.

Well, so much for our swimming, Alexa thought. She went back and lay down on the beach.

In about half an hour the tender returned with Lukas. By now the sun was nearly hidden behind the clouds and the sea was getting very rough.

"The captain wants everyone to come back to the ship," Lukas announced. The tender bobbed around and a sailor tried to keep it steady. "There is a bad storm coming and the waves are getting rough. He wants all passengers on board. Are there any people around the other side of the island?"

A man said he thought there were five or six.

"Then send for them. As many as can, go on this tender."

Alexa rolled up her beach towel and put on her robe.

Lukas was watching the passengers as they got in the tender.

"Did you get Horace safely on board?"

Lukas rolled his eyes and muttered something in Greek. "I fell in the water trying to pull him out of the tender and I almost got crushed against the side of the ship. It is really rough out there. Even the captain almost fell off the gangway trying to help him."

The tender was almost full. Lukas got out. "I will stay here and round up the rest of the passengers." He said something in Greek to the officer and the sailor started the engine.

The waves threatened to come over the side as the tender pitched in the rough sea. Far out Alexa could see the *Pericles*. The distance seemed an eternity and several of the passengers looked frightened. It was the first time that she had ever felt fear of the sea. Salt water splashed in her face and a cool wind had come up. I'm glad I got on the first tender, she thought, as another tender from the ship passed them heading for the shore. It, too, was having difficulty navigating. Now the *Pericles* was closer and it was slowly turning in a tight circle.

"What is the captain doing?" a man asked.

"It is necessary to keep the ship turning," the officer explained. "The captain knows what to do."

"I sure hope so," remarked an elderly woman. "I've never seen such waves."

The closer they came to the ship, the rougher it was. It will be fun getting out of this tender and onto the gangway, Alexa thought. She saw sailors standing at the foot of the gangway waiting to help the passengers on.

The tender made several attempts to come alongside. A sailor on the *Pericles* threw them a rope and pulled them closer. The tender was bobbing up and down and the gangway was also, but they did not meet. The sailor in the boat handed a woman to a sailor on the gangway. She started to pull back.

"It's too far. I can't make it."

"You go now," he said firmly, and gave her a shove.

Passengers who had stayed on board were leaning over the rail watching.

Finally everyone was off the tender and it left to get more people.

Alexa went to her cabin to get out of her wet bathing suit. She was shivering from cold and yes, she admitted it, fright. She turned on the shower and felt the hot water run over her body. When she was dressed she went back up on deck. It was hard to walk without grabbing onto something. The second tender was discharging passengers and the sea was even rougher. Juanita was at the top of the gangway counting the passengers as they came back.

"Be sure to hang up your landing tags," Alexa heard her tell them.

The third tender could be seen starting out from the beach.

"This is a tricky operation," a man standing next to her said. "That Greek captain's doing a good job."

"Yes, he is."

She stood watching until Juanita announced over the intercom that everyone was safely back on the ship. There was applause from the passengers.

"The ship is now ready to sail," Juanita said.

Alexa saw Nikos standing on the bridge looking over the side as the anchor was being pulled up.

After the ship was underway he came in the bar for a few minutes and sat down. His face was strained.

"We almost did not make it with the last tender," he said, downing a Campari and soda. "It came within inches of being dashed against the ship. I hate it every time we have to use tenders to take the passengers ashore, especially when it is rough. They are not sailors and many of them are old. If anything were to happen . . ." He shuddered. "I do not like to think about it."

"You did a good job."

"It was lucky. I thought one lady was going to fall in the water getting out of the tender. She hesitated too long."

"I don't blame her. Some of those large waves can be pretty frightening."

"But when the sailors tell you to jump, you must. They know the sea, not the passengers. They wait until after the third wave and when they say to go you must go."

"Why until after the third wave?"

"Because there are always three rough waves in a row, and then the fourth one is calm."

"Always?"

"Always," he said, looking deep into her eyes. "It is a rule of the sea."

People were walking unsteadily into the lounge and grabbing on to tables and chairs to keep from falling.

"And now I must get back," Nikos said. "It will be a busy night on the bridge."

The ship pitched and rolled all through the night and there were creaking sounds and doors banging. The Greek show was postponed until the following evening after the Captain's farewell dinner.

Tomorrow Saint Lucia, she thought, then the next day Saint Thomas, and the cruise will be over.

Nineteen

*D*awn over the Caribbean, a full moon fading in a blue-gray sky. White and gray clouds slowly turning pink. The ship anchored, waves softly lapping the bow. Saint Lucia, its volcano outlined against the sky, jagged black peaks, green mountains.

The storm was over, but many of the passengers had been seasick during the night and still looked pale and drawn.

"Good morning, Captain," she heard a man say. "That was quite a night."

Nikos looked tired, his white uniform rumpled. "Yes, but we were out in the Atlantic. It is always rougher than when we are on the inside in the Caribbean."

He threw her a quick look. "How are you this morning?"

"I'm fine." She noticed that his eyes had deep shadows under them. "Did you get any sleep?"

"No. I will try to take a nap later."

The second officer came up to him and said something in Greek and they walked off together.

In a few days I will be back home, she thought. But that does not seem to be my real life anymore.

Only this, the ship, and him.

To drift from island to island on the ship, is it danger I am attracted to, or what? Where does it all end? No, do not tell me, I do not want to know.

Why do some lives cross, what is it that brings us together? A chance meeting, that is not really chance, but fate? Are we destined to give certain things to others, so that our lives become a tapestry woven of many strands?

I have seen him under all conditions. I have watched him under stress directing the rescue of a sinking ship, lowering the lifeboats, scanning the horizon for survivors. I watched his face when the crew brought him the cup they had won in the soccer match, the smile of pride as he fondled the cup, the affection of his men. He was in pain then, suffering but trying not to show it. I saw how they wanted to please him, how they would do anything for him, their captain.

He is a man unlike any other I have ever known. No matter what our destinies, no matter what fate may do to us, I will not ever regret the moments we have had together, she told herself.

She was seated at his table at the Captain's dinner next to a retired vice admiral. The admiral's wife was on Nikos' right. By now she knew the routine by heart. The guests seated at the table, then Nikos arriving and shaking hands with each one, the chief steward pouring wine, Nikos raising his glass and proposing a toast as they all drank.

The polite conversation, Nikos asking where everyone was from, how they had enjoyed the cruise. She discovered that the admiral had known her father and many of his friends.

"The Navy is a small club," he said.

Then the lights in the dining room went out and the stewards entered to applause bearing flaming desserts. And afterwards the steward adjusting the microphone for Nikos' height so he could give his speech. She knew that by heart, too.

Oh why couldn't you have been a short, stocky Greek captain? she thought, as she watched him, so tall and dashing in his white uniform with the four gold stripes.

He raised his glass filled with champagne. "And now I want to wish you a safe journey home. *Yiassou!*"

"*Yiassou,*" they all repeated.

The stewards passed out small Greek ceramic tiles with a colorful sailing ship, handcrafted on the island of Rhodes, a souvenir of the cruise from the Delphinaki Lines. Now she had two of them. Several of the guests asked the captain to autograph the back of their tiles.

"Don't you want yours signed?" the admiral asked Alexa.

"Oh, all right." She passed hers to Nikos. He had signed "Best wishes" on the other tiles. She turned hers over. "With love" was carefully printed and his signature. Their eyes met briefly across the table and then he stood up.

"Thank you for dining with me."

"Thank you, Captain."

He went up the stairs behind the dining room.

After dinner was the Greek show, with the stewards in costumes doing the different dances. Juanita explained the songs and dances and then the stewards invited the audience to join in by coming and grabbing different people. The long line wound around the room, everyone clapping and snapping fingers to the music.

"Aren't you going to dance, Captain?" a lady asked.

"No, I pulled something in my back. I will watch." He turned to Alexa. "I did it getting that man up the gangway yesterday. The drunk one."

Horace was whooping it up with the dancers, his face red, his walrus mustache flopping as he kicked his feet to the *syrtaki.*

"He seems to be feeling no pain tonight," Alexa said.

Nikos sat there watching, jingling his keys, the sign she had come to know of inner tension. At one point he threw his head back against the couch in a hopeless gesture and a passenger turned to look at him. His arm was flung out against the back of the couch.

"I will go up to my cabin now," Nikos said. "Wait a little while and then come up." He raised his voice. "Good night."

"Good night, Captain."

"Enjoy the dancing," he said and left.

*   *   *

"Ah, that was good," he said, holding her after making love. "If only—"

"I know." She put her fingers to his lips. "Do not say it."

"One more day. And then what? What happens?"

"I will come back."

"When?"

"I'm not sure."

"Two weeks together every nine months. Or longer. It is not very much."

"It is better than nothing."

"Nothing," he said bitterly. "That is my life. Nothing."

"Perhaps it would have been better if we had never met, since it makes you so unhappy."

He ran his hands over her body. "No, *Alexa mou*. Do not say that. I am glad that we met. It is just that it makes me feel so—" He groped for the English word.

"Trapped?"

"Yes, trapped. Like an animal in a cage. What can we do about it?"

The unanswered questions that had no answers.

"Why is love so complicated?" she murmured.

"Because it is life," he said. "And we cannot change it. The Greeks, they know that. They have always known it."

A seagull heralded their approach to Saint Thomas. The *Michelangelo*, flying the Italian flag, was in port, and next to her the *Empress of Canada*. Many yachts and small boats dotted the harbor.

Nikos gave a blast of the ship's horn.

Alexa glanced up at the bridge and then back at the harbor. The last day. Tomorrow San Juan, the end of the cruise.

She went back to her cabin. She had started to pack, but there were so many things she could not put in until the last minute. A sad Greek song was playing on the ship's radio. It was one she recognized, a ballad of love and parting. All Greek love songs are sad, he had told her. One more day and night before they must part for who knows how long? She felt like crying, but she must not.

The ship had docked. Now he must attend to all the details of the final day of the cruise. And tomorrow evening another cruise out of San Juan. And another and another.

Ah, *Alexa mou*, he thought bitterly, you see only the romantic part of it. You do not know what my life is really like.

The responsibility of the ship, the passengers. And my family in Greece. I cannot abandon them. My roots are there, my family name to be upheld. If I left them it would bring disgrace and dishonor. Katina would never give me a divorce. And my sons would turn against me if I asked for one. There are no happy lives. Only moments of happiness.

The passengers were returning to the ship talking about the jewelry they had bought on Saint Thomas, and crates of liquor were being carried aboard. He could never understand why to save a few dollars on a bottle of liquor they dragged it on a plane for an uncomfortable ride home, happy with their bargains. But did not the Greeks do the same thing with radios and tape recorders that they could get cheaper on Saint Thomas than Greece? Of course there was a big tax to pay. He knew that often the stewards asked passengers to carry something through customs in Piraeus for them because their suitcases were usually not opened. After the long months at sea they wanted to bring gifts home to their families. But still, it was a risk. The Greek Government did not like being cheated out of taxes. He always declared everything he bought. Once he had been given a car, a red Mustang, and he took it back on the ship to Greece but he could not keep it because the taxes were too high. He was forced to sell it.

With the colonels in power it did not take much for them to

find an excuse to throw you into jail. And if he were in jail, who would support his family? He had to walk a tight line, always looking over his shoulder to see who was watching.

"Good evening, Captain," a man said. "Did you go ashore?"

"For a little while."

"It's been a nice cruise."

"I am glad you have enjoyed it. I hope that you will come back on the ship another time."

He saw Alexa through the crowd wearing a white dress with a blue and green scarf and a deep pain went through him. Tomorrow morning she would be leaving the ship with the others and he did not know when he would see her again. In April the ship would be going back to Greece to start the Greek Island cruises. Would she come to Greece again? She had not said. Last year when he was in the Caribbean they had not yet met, now she was so much a part of his life that he could not imagine it without her.

But he could not imagine a life with her either, sharing the same house, waking up together in the morning. A normal life.

"Hello," she said, smiling. She was carrying several packages.

"I see you did some shopping."

"I wanted to get presents for my daughters."

"You will be happy to see your daughters again."

"Yes."

"I will miss you. The ship will be empty."

"You'll be so busy you won't realize I'm not here." She turned her face but not before he saw tears gathering in her eyes.

"*Alexa mou*," he said softly, and he wanted to reach out and take her in his arms. "I will see you later."

As the ship sped toward Puerto Rico and the moment of their parting, they clung to each other with desperation and their lovemaking was violent and reckless.

"I will say goodbye to you tonight and leave the ship quickly in the morning," she said. "If I look at you I am afraid I might cry in front of the other passengers."

"*Chryso mou.*" He covered her body with kisses. "How much I love you."

"We will be together again. Somehow, some way."

"You promise?"

"I promise."

And they made love together one more time and then she left his cabin and went back to hers. Only then did she cry. Finally, exhausted, she fell into a deep sleep . . .

She was on the island of Cyprus in the Church of Saint Barnabas watching a baby being baptized. Water was poured in a large brass font and the grandmother, a wrinkled Greek woman wearing a black dress and scarf, felt the water to see if it was the right temperature. The priest in gold robes was chanting from an open prayer book. Then the father approached bearing three lighted candles and put them in holders attached to the font.

The father was Nikos. Suddenly she realized it was their baby who was being baptized and the old grandmother was Nikos' mother.

But his mother was dead, she had died years ago.

A glass containing consecrated oil was poured into the font and the grandmother undressed the baby and she saw that he was a boy with light brown curly hair and dark brown eyes.

I would give you nice sons.

Nikos looked at her tenderly as the priest anointed the baby with holy oil and then dipped him three times in the water.

Our son. His name is Alexandros Nikolaos.

And he did not even cry when he was dipped in the font. Instead he smiled, an angelic smile.

Now the priest takes a brush and puts holy oil on the baby's forehead and in his ears. Then he wraps him in a white blanket and cuts a lock of his hair.

The grandmother hands the priest new clothes for the baby and he dresses him. Why is it that I, his mother, seem to have no part in this ceremony except as an onlooker?

There are other Greek relatives around but I do not know them. I am the only foreigner, the only non-Greek. But my son is Greek.

Now Nikos is holding Alexandros. He looks so proud. They are congratulating him. Do they congratulate only the father in Greece, not the mother? But I am the foreigner. He looks at me and our eyes caress each other. Together we have made a son. We start to walk out of the church.

Then we see someone. Katina.

She is dressed in black, her black hair uncoiled and streaming down her back. She stands at the entrance of the church barring the way. She screams at Nikos in Greek, words I do not understand. The priest steps in between and tries to calm her. It is no use. She is a madwoman.

She strikes out at Nikos trying to snatch the baby. Another priest comes and attempts to restrain her.

The torrent of Greek flows, as if from a play by Euripides, and I know the meaning even if I do not understand the words. I am a foreigner. I have taken her husband, I have destroyed her life. I have no right to the child.

The priest leads her away. The relatives are muttering, looking at me in horror, looking at Nikos. His eyes are tortured. We come out into the courtyard of the church. There are masses of yellow daisies and eucalyptus trees. In the fields beyond a shepherd is tending his lambs. It is such a beautiful sunny morning.

Then we hear planes. Many planes. We look up.

They are Turkish planes and the sky over Cyprus is black with them. They are dropping bombs.

We scream and the bombs are falling and exploding all around us. They are falling, falling . . .

She awoke. It was a dream. Only a dream, she told herself.

She had never even been to Cyprus.

They docked early in San Juan. She left the ship as soon as it was cleared and went through customs. As she was walking along the dock toward the taxis she looked up and saw Nikos standing, a lonely figure on the bridge of the ship. Like my father, she thought suddenly. The ship. The damned ship! She quickened her step along the pier. There were men like Nikos Meletis—and her father—whose love for the sea was greater than for any woman. She understood, but it did not help her pain. She was leaving him here in San Juan. She had been right long ago to vow never to fall in love with a man whose career was the sea. It was not his wife who was her rival, it was the sea, vast, endless, more powerful than any other force.

Never say never, she thought. I fell in the trap after all.

She glanced over her shoulder. He was watching her with a gentle, tender expression. He raised his hand and waved.

She waved back. She knew that she would never find any other man as exciting, and yet she must forget him. He had turned and was giving orders to the Greek sailors.

The ship, the damned ship!

The ship . . .

BOOK THREE

Twenty

*I*t was the first time Nikos had been to Copenhagen, and after he had finished his business with the ship's agent, he set out on foot to explore the city. He walked along slowly through the narrow cobbled streets past red-roofed houses and quaint shops. Over the door of a bakery hung a golden pretzel, a golden bull's head indicated a butcher, a red top hat a haberdasher, and an oak tree a savings bank. Never had he seen so many bicycles, even old people riding them. A housewife came out of a grocery store and put her purchases in a basket attached to the handlebars of her bicycle, another young mother was bicycling with her small daughter strapped to the back of the bicycle, her blonde hair blowing in the breeze, sound asleep.

She reminded him of Alexa. He had not seen her in over six months and she had given him no definite answer about when she would be on the ship again.

He arrived at the famous amusement park of Tivoli and bought a ticket at the entrance. There were many cafés, small lakes with boats, tow-headed children riding the carousel, which had not only wooden horses but all kinds of animals. A tall giraffe had a stepladder so you could sit on him and there was an elephant with a basket holding several laughing children.

How Fanis would love all this! Nikos thought. In three weeks, as soon as school was out in Greece, Katina would be coming on the ship with Evangelos and Fanis. He couldn't wait to bring Fanis to Tivoli. Surely there was no place like it in the world.

Even though he was separated so much of the time from his sons, when he was with them he was able to offer them exciting adventures. They would never forget the times on the ship with their father the captain, the visits to foreign ports. How many children had that? It was something for them to look forward to, and for him also. As for Katina . . .

She came with her problems of trouble at home, her complaints that he did not love her, her jealousy of every woman who passed. And he did not blame her. He had not given her much of a life. But he had given her sons. Wasn't that what every woman wanted?

He stopped in a café and had an open-faced sandwich and a glass of cold Tuborg beer and watched the pretty Danish girls. Several of them smiled at him. Was it his fault that he had always been attracted to blondes?

If only Alexa . . .

No, she was in Greenwich now with her daughters. But he would like her beside him here in this café, holding hands, laughing together.

He looked at his watch. Time to get back to the ship. The passengers would be arriving in a few hours for the first of the summer Scandinavian cruises and there was much to do.

Bells chimed in the old churches as he walked back. He looked up at the tower in the city square for the gold barometer girls. The one riding the bicycle was out, the other with the umbrella in.

Fair weather.

"And here is the statue of the Little Mermaid," said the Danish tour guide. "We will stop the bus for a few minutes for any of you who want to take a picture."

Alexa looked out the bus window. She was surprised that the famous statue was so small and she had not realized it was on a rock so close to shore. She felt restless and eager to get to the ship after the long flight from New York, but this tour of Copenhagen on the way to the pier was included. Their baggage had been taken by another bus and they were told that it would be in their cabins when they arrived.

Everyone got back in the bus and they started off again, the guide pointing out points of interest. And then she saw it, the familiar white ship with the blue and yellow smokestack and the Greek flag waving. As they came closer she saw Greek sailors standing around on the dock eyeing the pretty Danish girls passing and making remarks in Greek.

Where was he? Perhaps she should have let him know that she was coming on the cruise instead of surprising him this way, but she wanted to see his face when he saw her. Nikos, my love, she thought, I am here. For three weeks we will be together. She had tried to stay away, to forget, telling herself how futile the whole thing was, these brief frenzied meetings followed by long partings. She had dated other men and found them boring, she was filled with longing to see only Nikos, to have him hold her, make love to her . . .

A horrible thought crossed her mind. Would his wife be on the ship? That had not occurred to her until now. If Katina was on board it would ruin everything. Never mind. It was a chance she would have to take.

He could hardly believe his eyes. No, it was just an illusion coming toward him, it could not be . . .

And then she spoke. "Nikos."

He embraced her. "I was afraid to believe it was really you."

She smiled. "In the flesh."

He looked around nervously. "We must be careful." He was not in uniform, so the new passengers coming on would not know who he was, but out of the corner of his eye he saw the chief radio officer watching them. The chief radio officer had a fat ugly wife who knew Katina. "Come in the lounge and have a drink," he said. He raised his voice. "So, you are going to sail with us again. I am delighted to welcome you on board."

They sat on a couch in a corner of the lounge and he called a steward and ordered drinks.

"You did not let me know that you were coming," he said. "Why not?"

"I suppose I took a chance. Your wife could have been on the ship."

He frowned. "The next cruise. In three weeks she is coming with my sons."

She noticed that he said my sons, not our sons. Was that the way it was in Greece, the woman was not important? "I'm looking forward to seeing Norway and the fjords," she said. "I hear they are beautiful."

"They are. For the passengers."

"Not for you?"

"For me they are beautiful and dangerous." He smiled. "Like a woman. You are never sure of them. Do not worry, we take on two Norwegian pilots who are always with us in the fjords."

"I am never worried with you as captain."

Two ladies in their eighties, one wearing a hat and white gloves and another carrying a book, sat down at the next table and ordered sherry. At the word captain they glanced over.

"Are you taking the excursion to Moscow?" Nikos asked.

"Yes, I have my visa for it. That should be really interesting."

"I have never been there. I do not like the Communists. After the Greek Civil War they took many Greek children to Russia. They have never been seen again."

"You mean they just kidnapped them?"

"Yes, they took them from the villages."

"How awful!"

"War is awful." He finished his drink. "And now we have the Junta. People disappearing for no reason, tortured, killed."

She looked at him and saw in his dark eyes a tormented man, a man who was strong and tender, a man of intelligence and simple tastes, a man she loved and admired.

"Our lives have been very different, *Alexa mou.*" He reached out and fingered a pearl and diamond pin she wore on the lapel of her jacket. "I come from a very poor family, I have worked hard all my life, while you . . ." He paused. "I think you are very rich."

"No, I am not. And what does it matter?"

"Ah, it matters."

"What cabin are you in?"

"A-21."

"I will call you later." He got up. "I have now many things to do." He smiled and there was tenderness in his eyes. "I am glad you are here."

The ladies she had seen in the lounge were seated at her table for dinner. They were diplomatic widows and lived in Washington. The one who earlier had been wearing a hat and white gloves introduced herself as Henrietta Treadwell. Her husband was once ambassador to Cuba. "Years ago," she said, "when Havana was the most delightful place, with casinos and charming parties. You can't imagine what it was like then, the Paris of our hemisphere." Her friend, Priscilla Morris, had lived in Moscow when her husband was attached to the American embassy there. "Priscilla is reading *War and Peace* in Russian," Mrs. Treadwell told the others.

Between them they had seen most of the world. I wonder if I'd have the energy at eighty-plus to take a cruise like this with an excursion to Moscow, Alexa wondered. I doubt it. More power to them. Across the room she noticed a distinguished-looking man dining at a table alone. He had a black patch over one eye. The stewards were paying him a lot of attention. I must ask Nikos who he is, she thought. As usual, the first night out, the captain dined in his cabin.

There was a German tour group on board, most of them middle-aged to elderly and fat. Looking around she realized that she was about the youngest passenger on board, except for two teenagers with their parents. Perhaps she should have brought Brooke and Cicily, but then she would have no time to be alone with Nikos. They were at summer camp in Maine, a beautiful spot on Lake Sebago, and they had been eager to see all their friends again and go sailing and hiking. She was going up to visit them when she returned from the cruise.

I think you are very rich, Nikos had said, and it seemed to bother him. She tried to imagine Nikos as a small boy on Corfu, but she could only see him as he was now, towering over everyone, so handsome in his uniform with the four gold stripes, in total command. There had been only a hint of the small boy staring hungrily in a shop window when he fingered her pin, one that had been left to her by her grandmother. Did he wonder how he could ever buy her anything like that? But it did not matter. She did not care what he could give her. She only wanted him.

If only life were that simple. But for now, she wanted to believe it. She had to believe it. She was in love and that was all that mattered.

He came to her cabin later, and when he took her in his arms the long months in between never existed, it was only now, her body next to his, his voice murmuring her name, the exquisite feeling of being one for all eternity.

After he left she fell into a deep sleep, rocked gently by the motion of the ship, as if in a cradle.

She dreamt that she walked into the ship's lounge and there sitting at a table were Nikos and her father. Both were in uniform, two captains, one American, one Greek. Her father looked the way he did when she was a child. He was not a tall man, nor handsome, but he had strong features and a deep booming voice.

They were talking about her, but they did not see her. She walked closer. Still they did not notice her, as if she were a ghost.

She awoke, half in, half out of the dream. I am glad they have met, Nikos and Daddy, she thought. They are both men of the sea, strong men and courageous.

Much later she would recall that dream and realize its significance.

Twenty-One

As they came into Stockholm harbor, Alexa noticed the man with the eye patch whom she had seen dining alone. He was on the bridge with binoculars, or rather half a binocular made specially to accommodate his good eye. She wondered again who he was. She must ask Nikos. Now he was busy with the ship, shouting orders, running back and forth from the wheelhouse, throwing her only a passing glance.

As soon as they docked she was going on the morning tour of the city, then this afternoon the group that had signed up and obtained visas were departing from the Stockholm Airport for Moscow. They would join the *Pericles* two days later in Leningrad.

One hour before the scheduled departure the Norwegian cruise director called a special meeting of the group going on "the Moscow Execution." Alexa hurried to the lounge. There were thirty-three of them, all Americans, plus Dagmar, their Danish tour guide.

Olaf had ordered drinks for all of them. "I have an announcement to make," he said, "but first drink your martinis."

Then he told them that the Russians had changed the plane at the last minute to a smaller plane which would not accommodate all those who had signed up, so they were to draw lots to decide who would go. There was more bad news. The Kremlin would be closed Thursday, their only day in Moscow.

"I have taken many groups to Moscow," Dagmar said, "and every time there is some problem."

When her number was not drawn, Alexa tried to be philosophical. After all, I have another forty or fifty years to see Moscow, she told herself, while for most of these elderly passengers it's now or never. Still, she couldn't help being disappointed.

Going up the stairs to her cabin she ran into Nikos.

"Who is the man with the patch over his eye who was on the bridge with you this morning?" she asked.

"Ah, you noticed him. He was a German admiral who lost his eye in a sea battle with the British at Narvik. Now he works for the Delphinaki Lines in their Hamburg office. I will introduce him to you when you get back from the excursion to Moscow."

"I'm not going. I got bumped."

"Bumped?" He looked puzzled.

"They couldn't take everyone, so we had to draw lots and I lost."

"That is too bad. But you will still see Leningrad."

"Yes, I hear that's a much more beautiful city. But I'd like to see Moscow. Once."

"I must go now," he said. "I will see you later."

She went back to her cabin. Suddenly there was an announcement over the ship's intercom. The Soviets had a change of mind, had bumped another tour group, so all thirty-three could go as originally scheduled.

"Please pick up your passports from the purser's office and be in the bus to go to the airport in ten minutes," Olaf said.

Every seat on the Aeroflot flight was taken. The plane had a gray interior with blue seats and narrow aisles, the signs printed in Russian and English. Next to Alexa's seat was an exit and a sign: ESCAPE ROPE. Her seat belt was too large, no matter how tight she pulled it. It was very warm and she wondered if the plane was air-conditioned. A blonde stewardess gave a speech in Russian, which she repeated in English. Another brown-haired stewardess passed hard candies. They were about to take off.

The engines started and they taxied out on the field. She had heard bad things about Aeroflot, but the take-off was smoother than she expected. Once in the air, she looked down. Below lay the Swedish countryside dotted with small lakes. The flight to Leningrad was supposed to take an hour and a half, then they would go through customs and change to another Aeroflot plane for the flight to Moscow.

The air-conditioning was turned on and the stewardess passed out damask tablecloths in plastic bags with AEROFLOT written in blue on the bags. They were served box dinners of cold roast beef, green beans, and potato salad, with a choice of white wine or lemonade. What good food for a Russian plane, she thought, and then noticed on the box that it had been catered by Scandinavian Airlines. Oranges and bananas were passed and then steaming hot tea and coffee and small packets of Russian cigarettes.

Suddenly there was an excited announcement in Russian. What has gone wrong? Alexa wondered, looking nervously at the sign: ESCAPE ROPE.

"We are now flying over the Soviet Union," the stewardess said in English. "We will be landing in Leningrad in twenty-five minutes."

Alexa looked down and saw what looked like flat countryside, green with patches of brown. It gave her a strange feeling of being in enemy territory. Below was a long winding road that ended at a lake, a few scattered houses, a river curving through green forests.

The stewardess passed out candies again. The NO SMOKING signs came on and Alexa was aware of a sharp pressure in her ears as they descended, banking steeply. More forests and ploughed fields with small lakes, clusters of houses, a group of apartment buildings, factories. The landing gear went down. Their descent was steep, over the railroad tracks, fields of wheat, a highway, and then a fast rough landing, the plane rattled and shook as if it wasn't going to be able to stop, but finally it did. She breathed a sigh of relief.

She saw only Aeroflot planes on the field and many officials in uniform. Their Danish tour guide was met by a dark-haired Intourist girl carrying red and white gladioli. The airport was suffocating. They went through passport control and customs. They were told that the current July heat wave was most unusual. Russians carrying bundles pushed and shoved them as they waited in line. Bas relief white stucco scenes of workers decorated the walls and there was a large photograph of a statue of Pushkin. On another wall was a huge map of the Soviet Union with cities and air routes marked.

After a short wait, their Intourist guide led them out onto the field to board another Aeroflot plane for Moscow, this also full. The windows were fogged up, so it was hard to see out. The engines started, stopped, then started again. There was a long announcement in Russian from the stewardess with no English translation, then they raced down the field and took off. It was almost nine in the evening and still light.

On this flight they were served a sickening carbonated lemon drink in gray plastic cups. There was a white new moon in the sky as they approached Moscow. Now they turned and banked steeply. All she could see were pink clouds against indigo blue. They banked again. The sun had disappeared suddenly and the horizon was a deep rose beyond the silver wing of the plane.

There was an excited announcement in Russian and the signs went on. They were ready to land. She could dimly make out a winding river. An unsmiling red-haired stewardess passed caramel candies. It was almost dark outside. Now she could see lights, the new moon was a golden crescent. The landing gear went down.

They were in Moscow.

On the drive into Moscow from the airport their Intourist guide pointed out three white crosses that marked where the Germans were driven back in World War II., which the Soviets called "The Great Patriotic War." The feeling against the Germans was still strong and she could see why none of the Germans on the cruise had elected to take the trip to Moscow.

They drove down a wide tree-lined boulevard with apartment buildings and large stores that took them right to the Kremlin walls and their hotel, the Intourist. They had expected to stay at the Hotel Rossia, the largest hotel in the world with six thousand rooms, but the change was not told until they arrived. No reason was given.

"I hear they always change your hotel," the elderly woman sitting next to Alexa whispered. "Then if you have any Russian friends who might contact you, they don't know where to find you."

The Intourist Hotel was where members of the press had stayed on President Nixon's recent Moscow trip. The rooms were plain and functional, and her bathroom had a large tub and heated towel racks. She was surprised to find toilet paper and a small cake of pink soap, things they had been told to bring with them from the ship. The hotel was not air-conditioned. She pulled back the curtains and after much pushing and straining she was able to open one of the windows about two inches. The other window would not budge. Across the street she could see large stores and around the corner the Kremlin walls with the red stars shining.

Finally I am in Moscow, she thought. I only wish we could see the Kremlin. After coming all this distance, it didn't seem fair that it was closed their only day there.

Dawn came early. At four the room was flooded with light. She put on a sleepshade she had brought with her and went back to bed. Suddenly she was awakened by loud marching music. She jumped out of bed and ran to the window expecting to see a parade. Then she realized it was only the radio going on. It was six in the morning and the room was like a sauna.

Breakfast took nearly two hours. They sat at long tables and finally were served bread, strawberry jam, and small cups of coffee. One couple said they couldn't open their windows at all and the only way they could sleep in the stifling room was to wrap themselves in wet sheets.

"Those double windows are geared for Russian winters, not this heat," a man said.

She made an attempt to change some dollars into rubles before starting out on the morning tour, but the line was so long she gave up.

Their group had been divided into two buses and they had another Intourist guide. Her name was Tamara and she was quite pretty, though on the stocky side. She wore a white knit suit and red sandals and her reddish-gold hair was tucked in a white visor cap. Alexa was surprised to see that she was wearing eye liner and blue shadow, also pale lipstick and polish on both her fingers and toes.

Tamara told them that Moscow had eight million people. The Russian women they saw on the streets were all fat, wore print house dresses and no make-up, had frizzy hair and thick muscular legs. They looked strong and they saw women driving streetcars, carrying bricks, and cleaning sidewalks. They all had unhappy expressions. In a few dreary-looking apartment buildings were feeble attempts at window boxes with straggly grass and pathetic flowers. Tamara started to tell her captive audience about all the improvements since "The Great October Socialist Revolution."

"What's that long line of people waiting for?" a man asked Tamara.

"They are waiting to get into the Lenin Mausoleum." She pointed out the Lenin Library. "It is the second largest in the world, after the Library of Congress."

They crossed the bridge over the Moscow River. Opposite the river loomed the gold cupolas of the Kremlin. Tamara told the bus driver to stop. She pointed out the Assumption Cathedral, where all the Czars were crowned, also the Annunciation Cathedral, the home church of the Czars. She indicated the Armory, a large yellow building with a green roof which houses the collection of weapons, ambassadorial gifts, and carriages.

Mrs. Treadwell raised a white-gloved hand. "Is there any chance of getting in to see the Kremlin?"

"No, it is closed today."

"How long has it been closed on Thursdays?" Mrs. Morris asked.

Tamara ignored her.

"But this is the only day we have in Moscow and we had so looked forward to visiting the Kremlin," Mrs. Treadwell said.

"Impossible!" Tamara snapped. She pointed out the belfry with two cupolas, the highest building. "Since it is not an active church," she said, "its many bells no longer ring out."

"Are there any active churches in the Soviet Union?" a judge from Kentucky asked.

"Some, but most are now museums." Anxious to get away from the subject of religion, Tamara started a long recitation about the cabinet of ministers, while the bus driver read a copy of *Pravda* with a bored expression. "Now, we will have a quiz to see how many of them you can name."

Alexa felt like a child being herded around by an unpleasant governess.

"Not all Russians are Communists," Tamara said. "That is a privilege that must be earned, and the Communist Party members are the most honorable citizens."

They got back in the bus and drove to Red Square, while Tamara continued with her propaganda speeches. No cars were allowed in Red Square, so the bus had to park in a special place. Tamara pointed to Saint Basil's Cathedral with its colorful painted cupolas. "It was built in the 16th Century during the reign of Ivan the Terrible," she said.

"May we go inside?" Alexa asked.

Tamara gave her a cold look. "It is not on the tour."

Back in the bus, they continued their scheduled tour, past the Bolshoi Theatre, a beautiful building with white columns and the sculpture of a chariot and prancing horses over the entrance, also the theatre founded by Stanislavsky, and a children's theatre. They turned on Gorky Street, the administrative and shopping center.

"Why are the streets of Moscow so much wider than those of other European cities?" a woman in the back of the bus asked.

This question pleased Tamara. "The streets of Moscow were

once paved with cobblestones," she said, "but after the Great October Socialist Revolution they were widened."

"I don't see many cars on the streets," a lawyer said.

"That is because public transportation is so cheap that most Soviet citizens do not need cars."

All medical services are free, Tamara informed them and there are many women doctors in the Soviet Union. Most people live in apartments, which you apply for through your office. No, you cannot own a house in the Soviet Union, nor land. That is all owned by the State, except for possibly a few houses in the country.

Behind a yellow wall they saw some beautiful houses.

"What are those?" the lawyer asked.

"I do not know," Tamara said.

"They look like houses to me."

"You want to know everything, don't you?" A long pause. Finally she said, "Those are houses for guests of our government."

They drove out to the Lenin Hills to see the university.

"Moscow University was founded in 1755," Tamara said, "and all education in the Soviet Union is free."

There were more propaganda speeches and then they stopped for luncheon in one of Moscow's best restaurants. They were served a greasy soup with barley and a hunk of mutton floating in it, a tough meat that no one was able to identify, overcooked vegetables, and a choice of vodka or kvass to drink.

"What is kvass?" one of the women asked.

"It is the drink you see them selling from stands on the streets," Tamara said. "It is made from pumpernickel bread."

"I'll have vodka," the lawyer said.

Most of the group joined him, but Alexa and a few of the others decided to try the kvass.

Alexa took a sip.

"How do you like it?" Tamara asked.

"It's different," she said tactfully, trying not to gag.

They were served oranges for dessert. Oranges were very rare in the Soviet Union, they were told, and these oranges had come from North Africa.

After lunch they visited the Pushkin Museum to see the French Impressionist collection.

"These paintings were privately owned before the Great October Socialist Revolution," Tamara said. "Now all the people can enjoy them."

A ride on the famous Moscow subway was next on the itinerary. Everyone was looking forward to that, but they had not counted on rush hour. The longest and fastest escalator Alexa had ever been on led down to the trains and Russians shoved past them to fight their way into the packed cars. The elderly members of the group looked apprehensive.

"We will go three stops and get off, then back two stops and get off," Tamara said. "And please stay together. We will have to jump on and off very quickly."

The station had marble walls and mosaics depicting Soviet scenes, planes, tractors, husky factory workers. A train came roaring up to the platform, doors opened and they were shoved in by the crowd. The Russians sitting on the packed train stared at the Americans, especially their shoes. At the next stop more people got on, they were pushed around and had to fight for air. Manners seemed to be lacking in the new society, also deodorants. The doors opened and Mrs. Treadwell headed for them.

"*Nyet!*" Tamara yelled. "Not here. The next stop."

"But I thought you said—"

Tamara grabbed her just before the doors closed. The Russians in print dresses and greasy work clothes looked with amusement at the tall thin lady wearing white gloves and a hat.

The other stations all had similar scenes of workers and tanks. What did I expect, paintings like the Sistine Chapel? Alexa wondered, as they came up the long escalator and out into the hot Moscow air. She was eager to get back to the hotel and have a bath. Some of the group were going to visit the GUM department store, but later reported that it smelled of fish and there was nothing interesting to buy.

An early dinner had been arranged at the hotel as they were going to the theatre before taking the night train to Leningrad. First there was a fashion show, the clothes way out of date. No wonder the people on the subway had stared at their clothes. This was followed by a performance of the Pyatnitsky State Academic Russian Folk Song Choir. Everyone was fanning himself with his program because of the heat and body odor, but the songs and dances were marvelous with colorful costumes. This was Russia at its best, Alexa thought, but they were the songs and dances of old Russia, of the villages and the land, and they had a haunting sadness.

They returned to Red Square to walk around it at night. Saint Basil's looked like something out of a Russian fairytale, and Alexa asked if they could go inside.

"No," Tamara said. "It is closed."

Alexa looked over at the Kremlin walls with its guards. Suddenly she was overcome with a desire to get out of this country with its atheist society where the churches were now museums. And yet she felt sorry for the people, plodding through their drab lives day after day, all joy and laughter missing from their existence, all free will, all incentive taken away from them by the State. And the Intourist guides, dedicated Communists all, were like computers fed certain information, so that they could only answer what they were programmed for. She shuddered.

"Come, everyone," Tamara said. "Back to the buses."

At the train station groups of small boys surrounded them asking for chewing gum. Tamara handed out tickets to everyone and then boarded the train herself. She was going to escort them to Leningrad and deliver them to another Intourist guide, then fly back to Moscow.

Alexa was surprised to find that the Red Arrow Express was quite comfortable. She shared a compartment with another woman in the group, Ada McBride, an elderly widow. A hefty woman porter was in a small room at the end of the car. Alexa was thirsty and asked her for some water, but she didn't seem to understand.

"We've got some Scotch," a man in the next compartment said. "Come join us for a drink."

"No, thank you." She was tired after the long day, and decided to turn in. She lay there listening to the voices and laughter in the next compartment and the sound of the train wheels, wondering what Nikos was doing on the ship. Finally, she fell asleep.

Twenty-Two

*H*e had sailed into Leningrad harbor before as a sailor in the Greek Royal Navy, but never as the captain of a ship. Nikos looked through his binoculars as they approached. There were many Russian freighters and cargo ships in port and a Norwegian cruise ship, the *Sagafjord*, was docked next to where they were heading. Luckily the *Pericles* was not a very large ship. He did not have a lot of space and would have to maneuver very carefully. He gave orders to the engineer to slow speed.

The hammer and sickle made him shudder whenever he saw it and he saw it everywhere here.

The former German admiral, Karl von Schleinitz, was on the bridge looking at the Russian ships through his half binocular. He wondered what he was thinking now. He had heard that the admiral's only son had been killed on the Russian front. Von Schleinitz was seventy-five but you would never guess it to look at him. His bearing was trim and erect, he spoke five languages fluently, played the piano.

An interesting man, Nikos thought. We come from totally different backgrounds, we were enemies during the war, but we both love ships and the sea. The fact that Von Schleinitz worked for a shipping line after his retirement proved that he couldn't stay away. Will I be like that at his age? Or will I, like the old Greek men, sit in the Athens park clicking worry beads, watching the girls, dreaming of my days at sea?

Passengers were standing around on the lower decks for their first glimpse of Leningrad. Slowly, skillfully, he edged the ship against the dock, the Russian pilot standing beside him. It was going to be a tight squeeze and he must not scratch the paint on the sides. The Delphinaki Lines had paid seventy thousand dollars to have the ship painted before they left Piraeus, and the owners did not like to spend money. Sailors tossed the guy ropes and the men on the pier caught them and slipped them over the stanchions. Now carefully, just a few more minutes. The Russian officials were waiting and watching and next to them were the uniformed guards who would stand at the gang-way and check each passenger's visa as he or she came on or off.

Finally they were docked. There was applause from the passengers and Von Schleinitz nodded in approval. Over the intercom Olaf was giving an announcement telling everyone not to rush to the exit, first the ship had to be cleared by the Russians. When it was, they would be summoned to the lounge. There was plenty of time.

When the formalities were completed, the ship's agent told him that there was a man who wanted to see him. A Greek. If he could spare a few minutes . . .

"Of course," Nikos said.

The man was in his early thirties, short and stocky, with intense black eyes. "I am Andreas Linardos," he said. "Can we talk in your cabin, Captain?"

"If you prefer."

They went up the stairs. He had heard of Andreas Linardos from other captains who had sailed into Leningrad. He came from a mountain village in Epiros, and during the Greek Civil War the Communists had taken him along with many other Greek children and sent them behind the Iron Curtain, where they were never seen by their families again. The *pedomasoma* it was called, the gathering up of all children between the ages of three and fourteen. Andreas was eleven years old when he last saw his country, and every time a Greek ship was in port he came on board to talk to Greeks and get news of relatives. The Russians would not let him leave, and Nikos suspected that he was very carefully watched. What did he want? Nikos closed the door of his cabin and poured two drinks.

"I have something to ask you, Captain." Andreas said, looking around nervously as if the walls might be bugged. "As a Greek to a fellow Greek. A great favor."

Nikos shifted uncomfortably. "If there is something that it is possible for me to do." He paused. "A message that you want me to take back to Greece?"

"No, Captain. I want you to take me back to Greece."

"But how? It is not possible. No, I would like to help, but that is out of the question. There are Russian guards on the ship, they will be looking out for Russians trying to defect—"

"But I am Greek! They have tried to make a Soviet citizen out of me, but my blood is Greek, my heart is in Greece."

"I sympathize, but—"

"For more than twenty years I have lived in this country of snow, this country of slaves, dreaming of the Greek sun, the special blue of the Greek sky. And now my mother is dying. I want to see her once more. You are my only chance."

"You have asked other ship's captains?"

"They have refused. They are afraid."

"And with good reason."

"But I think that you, Captain, are not afraid of anything. At least, that is what I have heard."

"And where have you heard that?"

"From other Greeks who come on ships here to Leningrad."

"They exaggerate."

"I do not think so." Andreas offered him a cigarette.

Nikos shook his head.

"I do not blame you. These Russian cigarettes are terrible."

"I have quit smoking," Nikos said.

Andreas inhaled slowly, then looked at Nikos. "They say that you escaped from the Germans during the war. After you had been captured and sentenced to die."

"That is true."

"So I thought that you would understand how I feel."

On the screen of memory he saw again the cell where he waited with the others who were to be shot. The young German guard he made friends with, who let him go out to work in the fields, and then, once out in the open, he ran, expecting any minute a bullet in the back, he was young and in good shape, he got away, they did not catch him. And a second time he was captured, this time in Northern Greece, and again he was lucky, he escaped. But if it had not been for the German guard . . .

Andreas was watching him. Yes, it was dangerous. But life was dangerous. Someone had helped him, a stranger and an enemy made it possible for him to escape, to be alive today. Now it was his turn to help someone. "I will think of a way," he said.

"Thank you, Captain."

"We are only here overnight. We sail tomorrow afternoon."

"I have it all figured out," Andreas said. "Here are the plans . . ."

Twenty-Three

*T*he Red Arrow Express sped toward Leningrad. Alexa pulled up the shade and looked out the train window. The sun was shining through a forest of slim birch trees and an occasional small house dotted the landscape. They passed a haystack, a stocky woman wearing a kerchief, two men in work clothes walking along the railroad tracks, a factory.

"It's nearly eight," Ada McBride said. "Didn't we leave a wake-up call for seven-thirty?"

"Maybe the train is late."

Just then there was a loud knock on the compartment door. Alexa opened it. The unsmiling woman porter stood there with tall glasses of tea in ornate silver holders that looked as if they had been left over from the time of the Czars.

"Thank you," Alexa said. "Can you tell me if the train is on time?"

"Of course. We arrive in Leningrad in half an hour."

"Then I'd better get dressed quickly," Ada McBride said.

Alexa sipped the lukewarm tea, wishing she could have hot coffee instead. The porter came back with more custom declarations for them to fill out. Now there were buildings and many train tracks, a woman in a hard hat working in the rail yard, two women laying bricks.

At the Leningrad station they were met by their new Intourist guide, a slender young man named Vladimir. Stocky women in print dresses were hurrying to trains, all with grim faces. Before starting their tour of the city they dropped Tamara off at the airport to fly back to Moscow.

Driving down Nevsky Prospekt they saw women washing windows. All the Russian women had great muscular legs and none wore stockings. Vladimir pointed out the Winter Palace, green with white columns and bronze statues on top. He told about the "abdication" of the Czar and how the workers started to fight for a better life. They passed a large department store. "That belonged to a wealthy merchant before the Great October Socialist Revolution," Vladimir said. Now it was a shabby mess. Vladimir told them that students were a privileged group in their country. He said that the workers used to live several families in one room before the Great October Socialist Revolution, then they occupied the flats of the bourgeois who "left our country."

How interesting the way they rearrange history, Alexa thought.

A truckload of soldiers passed. They came to the Square of Victory with all modern apartment buildings. "They are going to put a monument here to honor those who fell in the siege of Leningrad," Vladimir said.

Now they were on the outskirts of Leningrad. They passed farmlands and haystacks, a red truck. Vladimir explained how land, houses, apartments, are all owned by the State. They turned at a statue of Pushkin. "This area was all occupied by the Germans during the war," he told them, as they entered the Egyptian gate to the town of Pushkin.

"We are now at the Summer Palace," Vladimir said.

Parks surrounded the palace. During the war the Germans used part of the palace as a barracks. Old shabbily-dressed women handed them felt slippers to tie on over their shoes to preserve the wood floors. They shuffled through elegant rooms which were in the process of being restored. On the walls they saw photographs of the way the palace used to look before the war and the fire.

"Only skilled artists are allowed to work on the restoration," said Vladimir.

It is strange how they keep all these things of the past that they have such contempt for, Alexa thought. Such a contrast to come out of this elegant relic of yesterday, where once gracious, beautifully-gowned ladies swept down the staircases and waltzed in ballrooms with chandeliers, to see the typical Russian women of today, most of whom are fat, sloppy, ugly-looking.

As they headed back to Leningrad, they saw hardly any children on the streets. Vladimir said they were in the country for the summer. In other words, being raised by the State. Nothing belongs to you in the Soviet Union, Alexa thought, not your land, not your house, nor even your children. If I were a Russian woman I would be working in a factory and Brooke and Cicily would be wards of the State. She shuddered.

They were on their way back now to join the ship and the others, who had been sailing around to some islands in the Baltic while they were on their Moscow excursion. She had only been in the Soviet Union two days, but already the feeling of oppression clung to her like a smothering fog, she wanted to breathe free air, to shout, to laugh, to be able to express her opinions freely, without fear. This is what it is like, she thought, to live in an atheist society in a country where the churches are now museums. No wonder so many of them wanted to escape!

He was putting his life on the line, Nikos thought, but it was not the first time, and if he was careful the plan should work. Andreas Linardos had left, but he would be back later. He would have to enlist the aid of his cabin steward and possibly another member of the crew and hope they would not talk. But they were all Greeks, helping a fellow Greek.

And if anything went wrong, he, Nikos Meletis, would take full responsibility. As always.

But nothing must go wrong.

*   *   *

As she was unlocking her cabin door, she saw Nikos coming down the corridor, and she noticed that he looked worried.

"Hello," she said. "I'm back."

He seemed startled. "Oh, I did not see you. How was Moscow?"

"Interesting. And grim. It was quite an experience."

He appeared to have something on his mind and was only half listening. "Good. I will talk to you later."

What is wrong? She wondered, as she watched him go down the stairs. She went in her cabin and washed up. After lunch they were going to visit Petrodvorets. It had been a choice of that or the Fortress of Peter and Paul, and she preferred to see the castle of Peter the Great on the Baltic with its fountains. And tonight they were going to attend a performance of the Kirov Ballet. Then tomorrow morning the Hermitage Museum, which she was looking forward to seeing.

Tomorrow afternoon they would sail for Helsinki. As eager as she was to see all these places, it would be a relief to leave Russia.

The drunken singing was coming from the end of the pier.

The Russian guard on the gangway saw two Greek sailors staggering with the weight of a third man who was slung over their shoulders. And then he saw the captain appear on the bridge. The Russian smiled, the first time he had permitted himself a smile since the *Pericles* had docked in Leningrad. They thought only Russians got drunk on vodka, but look at these foreigners who couldn't hold their liquor. The captain was in a rage. He shouted something in Greek and ran down the three flights from the bridge deck. The Greek sailors were too drunk to notice. They approached the ship singing and a few passengers getting out of a bus after a performance of the Kirov ballet stared. Among them was the beautiful blonde woman he had observed earlier. He wondered if she was an actress when he looked at the photograph on her visa, but he did not recognize her name.

The captain brushed past the guard and ran down the gangway. Now the sailors recognized the captain and the singing stopped. A few days in the ship's brig, the Russian thought, watching the scene.

The captain was shouting. He grabbed the one who was being carried. The Russian blinked. There was something familiar about him, but he was dressed in blue jeans and had a navy jersey with *Pericles* on it. His hair fell across his face. The captain came up the gangway, the sailor slung over his shoulder like a dufflebag, the other two drunken sailors following.

"I apologize for this," the captain called in English as he went past. "These men will be dealt with, you may be sure."

He saw the blonde woman coming up the gangway with the others and he wanted to ask her how she had enjoyed the ballet but they were not allowed to have any unnecessary conversation with the passengers. He took the number she handed him and gave her back her visa.

She looked at him and smiled. "Thank you," she said, and walked on.

Nikos unlocked the door to his cabin, deposited the drunken sailor on his bunk, and then locked the door.

Suddenly the sailor was sober. "We made it," Andreas Linardos said.

"We have not yet sailed. Until we are out of Russian waters I will not be able to breathe freely. And that is not until late tomorrow afternoon. If they discover that you are missing—"

"They will not. Relax, Captain. You worry too much. Let us have a toast to freedom."

Nikos poured two glasses of ouzo. *"Yiassou,"* he said.

Andreas raised his glass. *"Yia tin eleftheria."*

Yes, to freedom, Nikos thought. That will be when we dock in Finland. Two days from now. He would have to get Andreas Linardos to the Greek consulate in Helsinki and have them arrange for his passage back to Greece. There would be a lot of paperwork. And if the

Russians found out, the next time he came to Leningrad they could arrest him for helping in the escape.

But they must not find out.

"Yia tin eleftheria," Nikos said.

Twenty-Four

*H*e did not get much sleep that night. He had given Andreas the bed in his cabin and slept on the sofa that made up into a bunk in his outer cabin. It was safer that way. They sailed at five in the afternoon. He would just have to hope that nothing went wrong between now and then. He had done what any Greek would do for a fellow Greek. In the past he had been lucky, he had faced danger and death many times, and always he had come through. All of a sudden he felt a strong desire for a cigarette. But he had quit. And when he made up his mind about something, that was it.

On the wall above his desk the photographs of his sons looked down at him. How would they manage if anything happened to him? Especially Fanis, who always looked at him with such trust. A feeling of guilt swept over him. Until Alexa, other women had never been a threat to his family, he could take them or leave them, and a Greek man was not expected to be faithful, they all had their little side adventures and the wives understood.

With Alexa it was different. He was in love with her and he did not want her to be hurt. But he did not want to give her up either, and he was tormented by the terrible idea that one day he would have to. How could he explain to his sons that he loved another woman, that he was leaving? They would never forgive him, they would hate him. And he did not want to hurt Katina, because even though he did not love her, she had been a good wife and mother to his sons and he felt tied to her in a way he could not explain. What was the solution? He ran his hands through his hair.

He heard Andreas Linardos stirring. Suddenly there was a knock on his cabin door and it made him jump.

"Who is it?" he called, his palms beginning to sweat.

"Can I see you for a minute, Captain?" It was the first officer's voice.

Nikos unlocked the door and opened it a crack. He yawned. "It is that important to disturb me at this hour?"

"I am sorry, Captain. We have trouble with the radar. Both of them are out."

"Both of them?" Nothing must delay their departure with Andreas Linardos aboard. "You are sure?"

"Yes, Captain."

"I will check them myself. Just give me a minute to get dressed."

The officer turned and started to leave.

"And get a weather report for the next twenty-four hours from the chief radio operator."

"Yes, Captain."

"I will meet you on the bridge." He closed the door and locked it again. Once before they had to sail with the radar not working and fix it at the next port. They had been lucky then, but it was not an experience he was eager to repeat. So long as there was not bad weather and fog it was all right.

If not . . .

But he could not risk any delays. And he did not trust the Russians to fix it properly. A few hours delay, the discovery that Andreas Linardos was missing—it was all they would need. No, he would have to have it repaired when they docked at Helsinki if it could not be fixed before sailing time. For the fjords the radar would be necessary.

Hastily he threw on his uniform.

As she got in the bus with the others for the tour of the Hermitage, Alexa wondered what was bothering Nikos. He had seemed distant ever since she returned from the Moscow excursion, and he had not suggested coming down to her cabin last night. She waited and then she called him. His voice had been cold, impersonal. Or was it guarded? "I am very tired," he said. "I will talk to you tomorrow."

Was someone with him in his cabin so that he could not talk freely? But at that hour? A twinge of jealousy went through her. And this morning she had caught only a brief glimpse of him standing on the bridge with the first officer. He had not even noticed her.

Had she done or said something to offend him? Sometimes the language barrier got in the way and he misunderstood what she had said. Or he replied something entirely different to a question she had asked, which made her realize he had not understood. But why did he not say so? She had never once heard him admit he did not understand something. Was it his pride? What was that word that the ancient Greeks used?

Hubris. That was the word she was looking for. But it meant excessive pride leading to downfall.

He told her that his family had been very poor and that he had to work hard all his life. Underneath was he still insecure, needing the image of always being in control of everything? At times there seemed to be a wall around him that she could not penetrate.

The Intourist guide had her microphone and was telling them about the paintings they would see at the Hermitage.

"And because there will be many different groups there, we must all stay together. No one is to wander off."

In a way, Nikos was no more free than these Russians, with someone constantly watching them, Alexa thought. Will he ever be? How lucky were lovers who could spend all their time together. But was it precisely this uncertainty that lent excitement to their love affair? There was never a chance for boredom to creep in. Away from his ship and all his duties, would he find himself restless as her father did? The sea had been his mistress for so long, could he abandon her and be content on shore?

"We have now arrived at the Hermitage Museum," announced the Intourist guide. "Please form a line outside the bus and follow me."

"There is a Russian spy ship watching us, Captain," the first officer said.

Nikos felt his heart skip a beat. "So I see." He put down his binoculars. Did they suspect anything? Three more hours until sailing time and the radar was still not repaired.

"What do you think they are looking for?"

"Probably defectors. I imagine they watch every foreign ship in the harbor."

"They seem especially interested in us."

Would they come on board and search his ship before they sailed? A chill went through him. "It is probably of no consequence," he said. "But keep me informed."

"Yes, Captain."

He went back to his cabin. Andreas Linardos was lying on the bunk reading a paperback novel.

"Good, you found something to read," Nikos said.

"You have a fine collection of books, Captain. I see you are quite a reader."

"When I have time. And passengers who have been on the ship send me books."

Andreas pointed to the photographs on the wall of the outer cabin. "Those are your sons?"

Nikos nodded.

"Fine-looking boys. When I get back to Greece maybe I will find myself a Greek woman to marry and start a family. I always wanted children, but I did not want anything that would tie me to the Soviet Union."

"You do not have a girlfriend in Leningrad?"

Andreas grinned. "Several. You know how we Greeks are."

"I mean a special one who will wonder what has happened to you and make inquiries of the authorities?"

"There was one for a long time, but we broke up." He noticed that Nikos had a very serious expression. "Why? Is something the matter?"

"I hope not. But there is a Russian spy ship in the harbor that is observing us closely."

"They do that all the time. They do not wish anyone to leave this land of freedom and opportunity."

"Nevertheless, I will be glad when we are out of Russian waters." Again he felt a craving for a cigarette, but he controlled it. Since early morning he had had nothing but black coffee and there was a pain in his stomach. He had better eat something or the ulcer would start up again, and that he did not need. "I will have my cabin boy bring us some food. What would you like?"

"Anything so that it is not Russian food."

Nikos smiled. "How about fish, moussaka, and a Greek salad?"

"Perfect."

"And baklava for dessert."

"But won't all that food cause suspicion?"

"No, I often invite guests to my cabin for lunch when we are in port. And my cabin boy will not talk." Or would he? Sometimes it was those you trusted the most who betrayed you, not even meaning to, by an innocent remark, a slip of the tongue, wanting to appear important, knowing something that the others did not. No, Yiannis was a good boy, he had been with him for many cruises, he could always count on him to be discreet. He picked up the phone and started talking rapidly in Greek.

Twenty-Five

Nikos looked at his watch. Half an hour until sailing time. The passengers who had been on the Leningrad excursions were arriving back at the dock and from the bridge he could watch the Russian guards checking their visas and handing them back their passports as they started up the gangway. Alexa got out of the second bus and glanced up at the ship. He turned away. Soon the Russian pilot would be coming on board to guide the ship out of the harbor. Nervously he paced back and forth. The weather report was good and there was no fog on the Baltic, which was fortunate, since the radar was still not working properly. It would have to be repaired at Helsinki.

Please do not let anything go wrong, he prayed.

The German admiral was climbing the stairs to the bridge. He walked forward to greet him.

"Will you join me for a drink, Captain, after we sail?" Von Schleinitz asked.

"I will be glad to." He looked at his watch again. "I am just waiting for the pilot."

Von Schleinitz leaned on the rail and stared out at the harbor.

"Did you go ashore, Admiral?" Nikos asked.

"Yes, I took the excursion to Petrodvorets."

"Petrodvorets?"

"The palace built by Peter the Great with the famous golden

fountains, his Russian Versailles. It was a summer residence of the Czars. During the war in the fighting around Leningrad much of it was destroyed, but it has been completely restored."

"I would like to see it," Nikos said. "On another trip." He looked nervously down at the dock. There was some kind of a disturbance going on. Several Russian soldiers were arguing with a passenger.

"There is someone I would like you to introduce me to," Von Schleinitz said. "An American lady who was on the excursion to Petrodvorets. She appears to be traveling alone."

"Of course." Then he saw Alexa climbing the stairs to the bridge. She would be wondering why he had been ignoring her. As soon as he got Andreas Linardos safely off the ship he would explain everything.

"There she is," Von Schleinitz said. "The beautiful blonde lady."

Alexa. That was the woman the admiral wanted to meet. The old goat. He was seventy-five years old, there were plenty of lonely women on board closer to his age. "I admire your taste, Admiral," he said. Von Schleinitz smiled. Nikos held out his hand to Alexa, keeping his voice impersonal. "Did you enjoy the excursion?"

Her expression was guarded. "Yes, Captain. The palace was beautiful."

"Mrs. Hollister, Admiral von Schleinitz."

"How do you do. I have noticed you on the bridge."

He bowed slightly. "I have invited the captain to have a drink with me as soon as we sail, and I would be honored if you would join us."

"Thank you. I would be happy to."

The Russian soldiers were not allowing the passenger to board the ship. Nikos recognized the senator from New Hampshire. What was going on? He did not need any trouble just as they were about to sail. Every minute was precious. They could delay the ship, discover that Andreas Linardos was missing, then the game would be up.

Olaf's voice came over the intercom. "Any passengers who still have rubles are kindly requested to turn them in immediately to the chief purser's office. It is illegal to take rubles out of the Soviet Union."

"Excuse me," Nikos said. "I had better see what the disturbance is about. Why don't you both go down to the main lounge and order a drink and I will join you shortly."

"That is an excellent idea." Von Schleinitz offered Alexa his arm. "I visited your country once when I was a cadet on a training cruise," Nikos heard him saying as they walked away. "Our ship docked at Long Beach and they took us to Paramount Studios where Marlene Dietrich was making a film . . ."

"Nyet!" the Russian soldier kept saying, still holding the senator, while his wife stood by helplessly.

Nikos walked up to them. "I am Captain Meletis and we are ready to sail. What is the problem?"

"They won't let my husband board the ship," the senator's wife said. "Please do something, Captain."

"Why are you holding one of my passengers?"

There was a flow of Russian.

"Is there someone in charge who speaks English?" Nikos asked.

One of the soldiers beckoned to an officer, who quickly came over.

"This is an American passenger on my ship," Nikos said, "and your men will not let him reboard. Why?"

The officer did not smile. "He has committed a serious offense."

"What is that?"

"He has been observed talking with Soviet citizens and we saw one of them give him something."

"That is not true," the senator said. "A man stopped me and tried to get me to take a message to someone, but I refused."

Nikos saw the first officer walking toward him in a great hurry. "Captain," he called, "the pilot is now on board and wishes to see you."

"I must go," Nikos said. "We are about to sail, and I warn you that there will be grave international consequences if you do not let this passenger go at once."

The officer said something in Russian to his men who released their grip on the senator. "Possibly our men made a mistake," he said in English. "If they did not, you will hear from us the next time you are in Leningrad. Have a good trip, Captain."

Did they suspect something else? He thought uneasily of Andreas Linardos in his cabin.

"Let us get back to the ship," Nikos said to the senator and his wife, "before they change their minds. I do not wish to include Siberia on our itinerary."

The Russian pilot was waiting for him in the wheelhouse. He was a tall man with a gruff expression and the bloodshot eyes of a heavy drinker.

"I am sorry I was not here," Nikos said, shaking hands with him. "May I offer you something to drink?"

"Vodka," the pilot said, looking in the direction of the captain's cabin.

Nikos turned to the chief steward. "One vodka and a Campari and soda."

"Right away, Captain."

They walked to the rail and looked down at the dock. The sailors were getting ready to take up the gangway.

"All visitors are kindly requested to go ashore now," came Olaf's voice over the intercom. "The ship is ready to sail."

Did there seem to be an unusual number of military men standing around or was it just his imagination? The Russian spy ship was still in the harbor as well as many freighters and tankers with the hammer and sickle.

The chief steward appeared with the drinks and the pilot drained his in a few gulps. Nikos took a sip of his Campari and soda and put it down. He did not like to drink much and only did it with a guest as a courtesy. He checked the time. Only a few more minutes now. His hands were wet with perspiration. The second officer brought the walkie-talkie out to the bridge and the longshoremen were waiting for the order to cast off the ropes.

Now the gangway had been rolled up. The minutes seemed to drag. Nikos looked at his watch, then at the pilot.

He nodded. "All right, Captain."

Nikos took the walkie-talkie. *"Mola ola prima,"* he commanded.

The men on the dock unloosened the ropes holding the ship.

Andreas Linardos felt the ship moving and heaved a sigh of relief. Soon he would be back home in his beloved Greece, the country he had not seen since he was a child. Even with the colonels in power, it would not be as bad as the country he was now leaving. No place could be that bad.

He heard the cabin door being unlocked and then the captain came in.

"The pilot boat has just picked up the pilot," he said. "Before long we will be out of Russian waters."

"Safe."

"Yes, safe."

"I do not know how to thank you, Captain."

Nikos waved his hand. "Forget it. We are both Greeks, are we not? You would do the same for me." He picked up the phone by his bed and dialed the main lounge. "This is the captain. Tell Admiral von Schleinitz and Mrs. Hollister that I will be down to join them in a few minutes."

"Here comes the captain now," Admiral von Schleinitz said.

Alexa saw his tall figure striding across the lounge, smiling at passengers on the way to their table.

"I am sorry I was delayed," Nikos said, sitting down.

"What will you have to drink, Captain?" Von Schleinitz asked, as a steward appeared.

"Campari and soda."

"The admiral has been telling me about the time he came to Leningrad when he was on a submarine," Alexa said.

"A very long time ago," Von Schleinitz said. "When I was a young officer."

"So you were also on submarines," Nikos said. "Did you like them?"

"Not too much," the admiral said. "We were all required to serve on them for a period, but they gave me claustrophobia."

"I think it must be awful to be trapped in a submarine," Alexa said. "When I was a child my father showed me one in the Brookline Navy Yard that had stuck underseas. A friend of his had been on it. They finally got it up, but by then everyone on it was dead." She shuddered.

"That can happen," Nikos said. "We had things go wrong with the ship I was on. At the time I was not afraid, but when I thought about it afterwards . . ."

"It takes a special breed of man for submarine duty," Von Schleinitz said. "For me, I do not like closed in places where I cannot breathe fresh air."

"I agree," Nikos said.

"Yet I am glad I had the experience."

It seemed strange to her to hear these former enemies chatting pleasantly together, but then she had heard her father express admiration for the skill of Japanese admirals he had fought. Their great bond was the sea and mastery of it.

"But we must not bore the young lady with our sea tales," Von Schleinitz said.

"No, I find it interesting," Alexa said quickly. "Were you born near the sea?"

"Lübeck. It is in Northern Germany, a very old town forty miles from Hamburg. My family had lived there for several generations."

Just then the bell rang for the first seating of dinner.

"Will you both join me at my table for dinner?" Von Schleinitz asked.

Nikos hesitated.

"I'd love to," Alexa said.

"I would like to very much," Nikos said, "But I have work to do and I had planned to eat in my cabin."

"I understand. Another time, then?"

"Yes, another time." Nikos stood up. "Thank you for the drink."

Something is wrong, Alexa thought, and I wish I knew what it is. After dinner she had gone back into the lounge for a brief time, but Nikos had not come down again. She did not feel like calling his cabin and getting another rebuff. Was he not feeling well? During cocktails with the admiral he had been pleasant, but impersonal. But that was how he always behaved with her in front of others. Was it because his wife was coming on the next cruise and he did not want gossip around the ship? No, there was something else bothering him.

And now she had the elderly German admiral trailing her around, making things even more difficult.

She looked at the telephone by her bed. No, I won't call him. He knows where to find me.

Then the phone rang. Eagerly she picked it up. "Nikos?"

There was a pause. "Excuse, please. I must have dialed the wrong cabin." The voice had a German accent.

She dreamed that she was back in Rio de Janeiro, a child once more, and her hated German governess Bertha was punishing her for getting out of bed when she was supposed to be taking her nap. She put out her hands to ward off the blows, but it was no use. Bertha had pulled up her nightgown and was striking her blow after blow with a sharp whip.

"Bertha, please, I promise I won't do it again."

"You are a bad girl. And a liar as well."

"I want my father. He'll make you stop."

"Your father is not here. He is on his ship. And he is not coming back. Not for a long time. A long time . . ."

Twenty-Six

*T*he sun was shining brightly as they docked at Helsinki and greeting them were smiling Finnish faces. What a contrast after Russia! Alexa thought. She glanced up at the bridge. Nikos was coming down with two men who appeared to be Greek, at least they were all speaking Greek and they were in a hurry. He barely nodded at her in passing.

What is going on? She wondered. She stood by the rail looking down at the dock. In a few minutes Nikos and the two Greeks walked off the gangway and got into a waiting car.

She looked at her watch. The tour of the city would be starting soon and she had better get her landing tag. She checked in her purse to be sure she had her excursion ticket and then went down to the deck where the gangway was attached. Two fat German women shoved past her and got ahead of some other passengers waiting in line, who gave them nasty looks.

Nikos, she thought, already the days are going so fast. I don't care about the sightseeing, I just want to be with you. She noticed the chief purser smiling at her. "Have a nice excursion," he said.

It was done. Andreas Linardos was safely off the ship, the arrangements had been made to fly him back to Greece. Nikos gave a sigh of relief. He felt as if a heavy burden had been lifted off his back. Now he just hoped that there would be no repercussions when he returned to Leningrad on the next cruise. It was a chance he had to take.

He had seen Alexa looking at him with a puzzled expression, as if she wondered why he did not come to her cabin or suggest that she come to his. How could he explain to her the reasons? As ship's captain he walked a tightrope, his personal considerations did not matter, only the safety of the passengers and the ship. The ship. He had endangered his own life many times, but never the ship.

It was something his wife did not understand, it was something no woman could ever understand.

Even Alexa, whose father had been a captain. What was it she had told him once, lying in his arms? "I swore that I would never fall in love with a man whose life was the sea."

"But you did," he reminded her.

"Yes," she said. "One should never say never."

Women and the sea were rivals, so it had been since men first set sail in ships, so it would be forever.

And the sea was in his blood.

Later he saw her coming back on the ship. He walked up to her. "Let us go have a drink," he said.

She smiled and pushed her hair out of her eyes. "I thought you'd never ask, Captain."

"There was a good reason."

"I was beginning to think you had a woman in your cabin."

"There was someone, but not a woman." He took her arm. "Come. We will go to the top deck where there are no passengers." He saw several German ladies approaching. "No, let us go up to my cabin and I will have the steward bring us something there."

He said something in Greek to a steward and started to leave, but the German ladies surrounded him.

"Captain, could you tell us something?" asked a tall thin woman who spoke English with only a faint German accent.

"If it is possible."

/

"We have been told that the Greeks consider Tuesday to be an unlucky day and that most Greeks will not start a new business or a long trip on a Tuesday. Is that true?"

"It is so."

"Why is that?"

"It is because the fall of Constantinople took place on a Tuesday."

The woman nodded. "But suppose you have to start a cruise on a Tuesday?"

He shrugged and smiled. "Then I cross my fingers."

They laughed and the woman translated in German for her companions.

"Excuse me," Nikos said, taking Alexa by the arm, "I must go now."

They started up the stairs but were interrupted by the first officer. He said something in Greek, Nikos answered, gesturing impatiently, the conversation continued while Alexa waited. Then the first officer left.

"What was that?" she asked.

"The radar. We had trouble with it at Leningrad. It is now operating."

When they were alone in his cabin, he told her about Andreas Linardos.

Her face went pale. "Wasn't that very dangerous?"

"Of course."

"Are you going to put that in the ship's log?"

"There are many things I do not record in the ship's log."

"Like us?"

"Yes, like us, *Alexa mou.*" And he took her in his arms and kissed her.

Later that night after the ship had sailed, he came to her cabin and they made love again and again with a violence and passion that seemed to devour them both.

"Do not leave me ever, my Alexa," he murmured. "There is no life for me without you."

For two days they sailed the Baltic Sea. At Oslo a long letter was waiting from Katina, bringing him back to reality. In less than two weeks she would be flying from Athens to Copenhagen to join the ship, bringing Fanis and Evangelos.

"I know you will be happy to have your family on board, Captain," an elderly lady had said to him in the lounge the night before, giving Alexa a cool look.

"Very happy."

"And how long will they stay?'

"The rest of the summer."

"It must be difficult being away from them so much."

"Of course." He noticed that Alexa was looking uncomfortable. He turned to her. "Would you care to dance?"

"Thank you, Captain."

Ah, for how long this charade! He put Katina's letter back in the envelope. He must now go check the supplies the ship was taking on at Oslo. And then there were the two Norwegian pilots who came on board early this morning. They would remain on the ship through the fjords. He must see that they were comfortable, had everything they needed.

There was a knock on his cabin door.

"Yes, I am coming," he said.

The train pulled out of the Oslo station.

"I took this trip from Oslo to Bergen when I was a child and I've never forgotten it," Mrs. Treadwell said. "It is one of the most beautiful train rides in the world."

"So I've heard," Alexa replied. They were to spend the night at a hotel in Bergen and join the ship the following afternoon. She looked out the window. If only Nikos could be with me, she thought.

I am tied to the ship, I am never free. Always they must know where I am.

Soon the outskirts of the city with its tall apartment buildings fell behind them and they were in the country with fields of purple and yellow flowers and a lake bordered by pine trees. The train blew its whistle, then they were climbing high up through forests of pine and birch, she saw a few small yellow and red houses, a stream, a pond with water lilies.

"Can't you just hear the music of Grieg?" Mrs. Treadwell said. "How well he captured his beautiful Norway!"

Across the aisle several members of the group were reading newspapers, paying no attention to the scenery. One man was going over the stock market quotations with a frown while his wife was engrossed in a John McDonald mystery. Three women who were traveling together were complaining that their married children never wrote to them. Another woman was discussing trivia at home.

They passed a deep blue lake with an island in the middle, tall pines, a red farm, stacks of logs, red houses trimmed in white. A small girl with a black-and-white collie waved to them and Alexa waved back.

Do not leave me ever, my Alexa. There is no life for me without you. The words kept repeating themselves in her head. Oh, Nikos, my love . . .

Now they were on a covered bridge with open wood slats on the sides through which she could catch glimpses of the landscape. It was very rocky with no trees and patches of snow on the ground. At a yellow station the train stopped and four hikers with backpacks got on. Across from the station she saw a red hotel on a lake. It was eight in the evening and the sun was still shining brightly.

They went through a series of tunnels and then the train started down the mountain. The landscape was green again with deep gorges and mountain streams, farmlands, sheep, cows, hay stacked in a long line, red and yellow houses, darkness falling now and lights going on.

In a little over an hour they would be in Bergen.

Nikos stood on the bridge, one of the Norwegian pilots at his side. The sea was rough and the ship pitched in the high waves and rain beat against the glass of the wheelhouse windows.

"I hope it clears by the time we get to Bergen," he said to the pilot.

"You have not been to Norway before, Captain?"

"It is the first time. I have always wanted to see the fjords."

"You will find them very beautiful. I was born in a small town on the Sognefjord."

An enormous wave slapped the bow and the ship rolled.

"We have some of the most beautiful scenery in the world," the pilot continued, "but also much rain. Almost every day. It is the reason we Norwegians are such sun worshippers."

"You must come to Greece," Nikos said.

The other Norwegian pilot came into the wheelhouse. Nikos looked at his watch. Midnight. They worked in four-hour shifts and it was time to change. One pilot slept while the other was on duty.

"I will turn in now," Nikos said. "See you in the morning."

"Goodnight, Captain."

He went to his cabin and took off his uniform. Alexa would be in Bergen now. He lay down on the bed and stared at the ceiling, thoughts going through his head, alternatives with no solution. On the ship he had control, in his personal life it was a different story. Like the ancient myth, he was caught between Scylla and Charybdis. He was eager to see his sons, they were part of him, his blood flowing through them, his hopes going into the future. But Alexa was his heart. Their souls were one. Oh, *Alexa mou*, what are we to do? He did not see how he could stand the whole summer with Katina on the ship. She would be poking into everything, going through his drawers, questioning him, causing scenes . . .

He struck the wall with his fist. Who was not controlled by fate? Even when he thought he held destiny in his hands, what life was not battered by storms, as the ship was now, and all one could do was wait it out, hoping for the best.

He closed his eyes. The ancient Greeks were right. _To moraion phigin adinato._ It is impossible to escape your fate.

She saw him up on the bridge talking to the handsome blond Norwegian pilot. She climbed the stairs and he walked over to her.

"You are back on the ship," he said.

"Did you miss me?"

"Yes."

"Much?"

"Very much."

She was aware of the pilot watching them. "I hear I missed some rough weather."

"That is right. We had a bad storm. How was the train ride?"

"It was lovely. And I bought some Norwegian sweaters this morning." She indicated the one she was wearing.

"I like it." One of the officers was approaching. "I will come by your cabin later," he said, lowering his voice.

She heard shouting in Greek outside her cabin and she recognized Nikos' voice in an argument with someone. A few minutes later there was a knock on the door.

Cautiously she opened it.

"I am here," Nikos said. He glanced around to be sure that the corridor was empty of stewards or passengers, then quickly stepped inside, locked the cabin door, and took her in his arms. "_Alexa mou,_" he murmured, pressing her body against his. "How much I have wanted you."

"I've wanted you too. Last night in Bergen, lying in my hotel room—"

"Then what are we waiting for?" He unbuttoned her sweater and led her over to the bed.

*   *   *

At Narvik two new pilots came on board to replace the other ones. It was a bitter cold morning, seven degrees centigrade, as they sailed up the North Cape, and Nikos rubbed his hands together to keep them warm. He had on a heavy overcoat and a navy knitted cap, but gloves got in his way, so he could not wear them.

"There's a reindeer, Captain," said the Norwegian pilot.

"Where?"

"Up on that mountain."

Nikos looked through his binoculars. "Ah yes, I see."

They were approaching Hammerfest, the top of the world. A desolate place, he thought, as he gazed at the town in the distance. There were a few stores, cafés, a church, houses painted blue, yellow or white.

The local pilot came alongside in the pilot boat and climbed up the rope ladder. Nikos went to meet him.

"I am Captain Meletis," he said, holding out his hand. "Welcome on board."

Alexa leaned over the rail looking at the town. She was wearing a red Norwegian coat with a fur hood, boots and mittens, and still she felt cold. Nearby several fat German women lay wrapped in blankets on deck chairs snoozing off the food.

Nikos came down from the bridge. "Are you going ashore?" he asked.

"I thought I'd walk around the town."

"Good, I will join you. I need to stretch my legs. Let us go." He took her arm and they went down the gangway.

Suddenly she stopped. "I forgot my landing tag."

"Do not worry." He smiled. "I will see that you get back on board."

They walked past blue and yellow houses with gaily patterned curtains in the windows. Though it was late June, here spring flowers were just starting to bloom.

"I don't think I'd like living in Hammerfest," she said. "It must be awful in the winter."

"It would be quiet. Sometimes I think that is what I would like. To get away where no one could find me. To fish, to read, have no responsibilities."

"I think you'd be bored after a short time."

"You are probably right." He noticed some passengers from the ship approaching. "Let us go down this road."

They came to a church and a small cemetery. She read some of the names on the tombstones and the dates.

"I wonder about their lives, if they were happy."

He shrugged. "Like most people, for a little while."

"And then?"

"And then it is over and they lie here."

"That's a depressing thought."

"Not necessarily. Have you ever seen the tomb of our great Greek writer, Nikos Kazantzakis? He is buried on Crete, outside Heraklion."

"No, I haven't."

"But you have heard of him?"

"He wrote *Zorba the Greek*."

"That and many other books. His grave is all alone on a hill overlooking the town. There is a tall wooden cross and a plain white tombstone, and on it is written: 'I wish for nothing, I fear nothing, I am free.'"

It was starting to rain. She shivered.

"Come," he said. "You are cold. Let us find a café and have some coffee."

She could not sleep that night after he left her. And when finally she did, she dreamt that she was again in the small cemetery in Hammerfest. She was alone in the rain putting flowers on one of the graves. On the tombstone was carved: CAPTAIN NIKOS MELETIS: I WISH FOR NOTHING, I FEAR NOTHING, I AM FREE.

Only the dates were blurred.

Twenty-Seven

Now the white nights are almost over, only four more days remain of the cruise. They are sailing down the fjord to Hellesylt and Nikos is not yet on the bridge. Finally, as the village is in view, he appears wearing navy slacks and a sweater and looking haggard. It is cold and rainy and many of the passengers have colds. After they anchor he comes over and stands beside Alexa.

"How are you?" he asks.

"I'm fine. You did not take the ship out last night. Were you sick?"

"Ah, I caught cold."

"Are you all right now?"

"Oh . . ." A shrug. "It is better."

"You should wear your heavy coat."

"I cannot move in it."

I know him so well, I love him so much and I know he loves me, but this game we must continue to play—for how long? Sometimes I think I will go crazy from wanting him. In a few days I will be off the ship. Can we be together tonight, or will the one-eyed admiral be watching him or the German passengers clumping about?

"You are not taking the excursion?" he asks.

"No. I am going to go ashore after lunch and walk around."

The bell rings for lunch.

"Do not leave yet, there is no hurry."

They stand side by side watching the passengers getting in the boats to go ashore. Admiral von Schleinitz is among them.

"I wonder how he feels coming back to Norway after what happened to him here."

"He is very taken with you," Nikos says. "Not that I blame him."

"Are you jealous?"

"I cannot afford to be jealous."

"I don't care anything about these men who are following me around on the ship. I want only you."

"Ah, *Alexa mou.*" He stares off into space. The last bell rings for lunch. "I had better not keep you or you will not get anything to eat. I am going to take a nap, and if I feel better, I will come by tonight."

She was late getting down to the dining room, so the only place left was at the French table next to a lady lawyer from Paris, who said her husband was sick and in the cabin with a fever. She showed everyone at the table the photographs of her dogs—two Labradors and a German shepherd who was blond with a black muzzle.

"I am glad the cruise is almost finished," she said. "I miss them, and they will be so happy to see me."

"How do you keep such large dogs in a Paris apartment?" Alexa asked. "It must be difficult."

"Not at all. Every day after work I take them for an hour's walk in the Bois de Boulogne."

She even had photographs of former dogs she had owned. For her, they were her children.

"I saw you up on the bridge with the commandant," the lady lawyer said. "I had a long talk with him the other day. We discussed philosophy, many things. He is charming."

"Yes, he is very nice."

"I must have the steward bring some soup to my husband in the cabin," she said calling him over. The steward seemed to have some difficulty understanding what it was she wanted.

Alexa spoke to him in Greek, he grinned and nodded.

"*Amesos*," he said.

"He will bring it right away."

"You speak Greek?" the lady lawyer asked in amazement.

"Some."

"You are unusual for an American. I mean that as a compliment. Usually Americans do not speak other languages. So, you also speak Greek. You did not learn it just on this cruise?"

"No."

"Ah, I see. You have sailed with the commandant before?"

"Yes, several times."

She smiled archly. "I do not blame you. Why not? He is a very handsome man. If I did not have my husband . . ."

Are we that obvious to everyone? Alexa wondered.

"Do not look embarrassed. We French are all for romance." She pushed back her chair. "Now I must see how my husband is doing. Men, when they are sick, they like to be pampered. In fact, all the time." She smiled and left.

That night it happened, what he had feared.

It was after the Greek show and he and Alexa had left the lounge separately. First he had gone to the chart room to check something with the navigator and then, as he opened the door to Alexa's cabin, the chief radio operator suddenly was standing beside him. Alexa was sitting on the bed still in her evening gown with a startled expression.

"This is the chief radio operator," he said, trying to explain, though no explanation was really possible. "He thought this was the radio room."

She said nothing.

"He is a good friend of mine," he said pointedly, turning to the chief radio operator. "So what is it you want?"

"A message, Captain—"

"Give it to me." He grabbed it and put it in his pocket.

The radio operator left and Nikos closed the door and locked it.

"How could he have mistaken my cabin for the radio room?"

"It is right down the hall. Do not worry, he will not say anything." He sat down on the bed beside her and stared moodily ahead.

"Nikos?"

He did not reply.

"It is all so complicated." She paused. "Perhaps you were happier before."

"Before? What do you mean?"

"Before I came into your life, before we were important to one another."

"Ah, *Alexa mou.*" He took her in his arms. "I can no longer imagine life without you." He stroked her face. "And in four days it ends."

"It will never end. We will be together again."

"Each time I think I will never see you again, that it will be the last time."

"We belong together. Nothing can separate us."

He felt the ebb and flow of her breath, the scent of her perfume, her body soft and yielding against his, the motion of the ship beneath them, it was suddenly unbearable that time, time that waited for no man and crept on with relentless feet, would soon take her away . . .

"Hold me," she said. "Hold me close. Never let me go."

The Captain's Farewell Dinner. She was seated directly across from Nikos, with Mrs. Treadwell on his right and the French lady lawyer on his left. Admiral von Schleinitz was at one end of the table talking in German to a pretty young woman from Heidelberg who was on her honeymoon.

"My wife was complaining to the captain that the ship was too cold," the young husband told Alexa. "And the captain said, 'Cold? On your honeymoon? You have this boy to keep you warm. Snuggle up to him.'"

"Of course," Nikos said. Their eyes met and there was pain in them. Then he looked away.

"The captain is a romantic," said the French lady lawyer. "*Vive l'amour!*"

"And now I would like to propose a toast to the captain," Mrs. Treadwell said. "Such a delightful cruise." She raised her glass.

The others joined in. "To the captain!"

Nikos looked embarrassed. "Thank you very much. I hope you will all come back again and sail on the *Pericles*."

"With pleasure," the lady lawyer said. Her husband appeared less than enthusiastic.

Admiral von Schleinitz remarked that he was going to visit his married daughter and his grandchildren in Darmstadt after the cruise.

"I understand your family will be coming on board tomorrow, Captain," said Mrs. Morris.

"That is right."

The lady lawyer was watching Alexa with a knowing look. A shipboard romance. Over now. We French take these things in our stride.

Just then the lights went out and the stewards entered bearing flaming desserts. There was the usual applause, the lights went on again, champagne was poured, and Nikos was handed the microphone to give his farewell speech. The familiar details, so painful now, another parting, a long separation, to meet again she knew not when. Tomorrow, she thought, different passengers would be on the ship. And his wife.

"And now I wish you a safe journey home," Nikos said. He glanced at her briefly, then sat down and started talking to Mrs. Treadwell.

Tomorrow I will get off the ship as early as I can, she thought, so I do not risk running into his wife. I do not want to see him with her, with his sons, pretending to play the happy family man. I will get the first taxi I can to the airport . . .

"You should spend some time visiting Germany," her dinner partner was saying. "There are so many beautiful places to see."

"I'd like to," Alexa said. "But I have to get home. Perhaps another trip."

"I will give you our address in Heidelberg. You must get in touch with us when you do."

Addresses exchanged on parting were seldom followed up. She saw Nikos watching her with a sad expression. Then he pushed his chair away from the table.

"Thank you very much for dining with me."

"Thank you, Captain."

Carrying their ceramic tiles as a memento of the cruise, they went into the main lounge.

Nikos did not come down again to join them.

He called her cabin later that evening.

"Do you want me to come up?" she asked.

"It is not possible." There was a long pause. "And tomorrow . . ."

"I know."

"Are you going to stay in Copenhagen?"

"No, I have a morning flight." She could hear voices in the background.

He shouted something in Greek. "I must go now," he said. "Until next time, then. Take care of yourself."

As the ship approached Copenhagen harbor, he could see Katina waiting on the dock with Evangelos and Fanis. They were waving and he waved back. The Danish pilot was beside him on the bridge. Alexa was nowhere in sight.

She sat in her cabin beside her overnight case, her coat on the bed, waiting for the announcement that the ship had been cleared. Through the porthole she could see his wife and sons waving to him and a pain went through her that was almost unbearable. She checked in her purse to see that she had everything. Her passport, picked up from the purser's office yesterday, her plane ticket, enough Danish money for cab fare. Tonight she would be in New York and tomorrow on her way to Maine to visit Brooke and Cicily at camp. She had her life and he had his. Concentrate on that, she told herself. They came from different worlds and their two worlds did not meet. Only in bed. She bit her lip to keep back the tears.

Stewards were running up and down the corridors, eager to get everything cleaned up and get their mail, a letter from a loved one in Greece. At the open doors of their cabins, passengers waited to leave the ship.

The waiting seemed interminable, and then finally it came, the announcement.

"All passengers may now proceed ashore."

She put on her dark glasses, grabbed her things, and ran as fast as she could. I hope I don't pass him with his wife on the stairs, she thought. At the exit there was a long line. Let me by, she wanted to say, I must get off, but she had to wait her turn.

Then she saw him. He was giving orders to one of the officers, and Katina and his sons were nowhere in sight. They must have gone up to the cabin, his cabin, where so many times they had made love. I cannot stand it, if this line doesn't move faster I will start crying uncontrollably. She knew that he saw her too. Oh, my love, how will I live without you until we meet again? Are the few weeks we have together from time to time worth all this pain?

The line was moving now. All she wanted was to get as fast as she could to the airport.

It was two hours later that he heard the news.

"There has been a bad plane crash at the Copenhagen Airport, Captain," the chief purser said. "A jetliner was taking off—"

"And what happened?"

"It was having difficulty in climbing, like it was having engine trouble. And then it caught fire and crashed into the bay. They do not expect to find any survivors."

Suddenly he was half-mad with fear. Which flight was she taking, which line? He had not asked. Whenever she left he tried to block out the fact that she was leaving and that he might never see her again. Never see her again. But not dead. Even if she was alive somewhere in the world there was always the chance that they would be together again. He tried to control his voice. "Which plane was it""

"I do not know, Captain."

"Then find out!" He grabbed the purser by the shoulders. "There could have been passengers from the ship on it."

"I will make further inquiries."

"And let me know as soon as you can."

"Yes, Captain."

He could not go himself, he had to attend to the duties of the ship. Katina came down the stairs, followed by Fanis and Evangelos. She noticed his face.

"What is wrong, Nikos?"

"A plane crash. Possibly passengers from the ship."

"That is too bad. I—"

"Please, take the boys and go in the lounge. I will join you later."

"I have never seen the captain so upset," observed the second officer. "What is it?"

"A plane crash at the airport," the radio officer said.

"You think she was on it?"

"It is possible. He has sent the chief purser to the airport to find out."

"It is awkward, with the wife—"

"Careful, here he comes."

What was taking the purser so long? He paced back and forth. There were many planes, it was a busy airport, the chances were that she was on another flight. But he had to know. He could not rest until he found out. *Alexa mou*, he thought, and he could smell her perfume and feel the softness of her skin, and the possibility that she was dead was more than he could bear.

Then he saw the purser approaching. He rushed up to him.

"It was an S.A.S. plane, Captain. They are searching for bodies."

"Where was it bound for?"

"New York."

"My God!"

"I do not think any of the ship's passengers were on it. The Germans were flying on Lufthansa—"

"If it went into the bay there could be survivors."

"I do not think so, Captain, but they are looking anyway. The plane hit with such impact that it broke in several pieces."

Sometimes people survived, had miraculous escapes . . .

"Do you want me to check the flight she was taking?"

"Who?"

"The American lady. Mrs. Hollister."

"Yes. Yes, find out." He pulled himself together. Once more he was the captain, cool and calm in a crisis, giving orders. "I want to be sure that none of the ship's passengers were on it."

"Yes, Captain."

She was not on the plane. She had taken another flight that had left just before the one that had crashed. By now she would be halfway to New York. He checked his watch. It was time to sail.

Another cruise, new passengers. The endless routine, existing till they saw each other again. If she had been on that plane that crashed he did not know how he could have gone on living. But she was alive. She was speeding in the opposite direction, but she was alive.

The harbor pilot was on board now, the second officer had adjusted the walkie-talkie on the dock side. Katina and Evangelos were leaning over the rail watching the activity on the pier below and Fanis was playing with one of the stewards. Sailors had rolled back the gangway and locked it in place.

Nikos picked up the walkie-talkie. *"Mola ola prima."* He said.

The men on shore let the ropes go, and slowly the *Pericles* moved out to sea.

BOOK FOUR

BOOK FOUR

Twenty-Eight

March 1974. Athens in the rain. She got a taxi in front of the airport and a porter put her luggage in the trunk. "To Piraeus," she said in Greek. "The *Pericles*."

"You speak Greek," the driver said. "You are Greek-American?"

"No."

He looked dubiously at her blonde hair and blue eyes. "I did not think so. Then how you speak Greek?"

"I have studied it. And I have visited Greece many times."

He smiled. "You like Greece?"

"Very much." And a certain Greek man, she thought. When a woman falls in love with a country it is almost always because of a man.

"You speak very good Greek."

Then he started pouring out his troubles. He was a student, but he had not enough money for books at the university and work in Athens was hard to get. So to continue his studies he drove a cab. She noticed a picture of the Virgin Mary with Jesus hanging from his mirror, also a picture of a bearded Greek priest in black robes, and a wooden cross with a silver figure of Christ. At one point, when he gave forth with a torrent of angry Greek, most of which she couldn't understand, he grabbed the cross. Each time he passed a car or bus he crossed himself, a good idea, she thought, the way he was weaving in and out of traffic.

"I'm not in a hurry. There is plenty of time."

He gave no sign of having heard her as he continued to rave and rant. All Greeks seem to be unhappy and frustrated, she thought. Perhaps because they have to be careful what they say and they can't sit in tavernas and argue politics any more under the current military government.

He turned around. "You have perhaps noticed that we are not a very calm people?"

She nodded. An understatement.

He swerved suddenly and jammed on his brakes to avoid hitting two fat Greek women crossing the street.

"Careful!" she screamed. "Please go slower."

"Do not worry. I have never had an accident."

She breathed a sigh of relief when finally he pulled up at the pier where the *Pericles* was docked.

"So you are here at last," Nikos said. "When the January and February cruises were canceled, I was afraid that you might not come."

"Everyone at home told me I was crazy to take a cruise to the Middle East," she said, laughing.

"I will try to see that it is not dull."

"It is never dull sailing with you, Captain."

He smiled. "When did you arrive in Athens."

"A few hours ago. I came straight from the airport to the ship."

He saw the chief engineer looking for him. "I must go now. Meet me in the main lounge for a drink after we sail."

"We are to sail early," he told the chief engineer.

"Not at seven?"

"No. I have just talked to the owners. They want us to sail at five."

"But what about all the passengers?"

"The ship has been overbooked. That is why the *Ulysses* is ready to take on the rest. The company does not want to lose money."

"I have talked to some of the crew of the *Ulysses*. They thought they were going to get several week's vacation after returning from the Caribbean before starting the Greek Island cruises. The captain has a new baby he has not seen. They are very angry."

Nikos shrugged. "Company orders."

"And the *Ulysses* is a very old ship. Will not the passengers who have booked the *Pericles* be angry?"

"Probably. But there will be nothing they can do about it. And there is something else."

"Yes, Captain?"

"You know that there are two Palestinian guerrillas being held in the Athens jail? The P.L.O. has made threats to take a Greek ship as hostage and hold all the passengers until the guerrillas are freed."

"That is not good news."

"No, but the company has lost a lot of money by being forced to cancel the January and February cruises, so they are sending the two ships on this cruise to make up for it. And at each of the ports they are paying the harbor master to plant depth charges around the ships at night—"

"Depth charges?"

"Yes, to go off every fifteen minutes, so that frogmen will not be able to swim underneath and attach a bomb to the hull."

"What about the daytime?"

"They are not worried about that. It is only at night when they could not see them."

"It should be an interesting cruise."

"Are all the crew back on board?"

"I will check."

"If not, we will have to sail without them. I have strict orders to sail at five."

Alexa took off her raincoat and hung it in the closet. It had been freezing when she left New York, but here it was warm. She had never been to Greece before in March. After the cruise she was flying to the island of Mykonos for a week. Then when the ship was there she and Nikos could be alone together in her cottage at the Rhenia Hotel.

The steward appeared with her large suitcase and put it on the other bed. "You are sailing with us again? I am very happy." He grinned.

"Thank you." Suddenly she could feel the ship moving. She looked at her watch. It was only five. "Aren't we supposed to sail at seven?"

He looked blank.

She repeated it in Greek.

"I do not know. Captain must have orders."

She looked out the porthole. She could see passengers waiting on the dock beside their luggage and a small boat with the chief steward and several of the crew was trying to catch up with the *Pericles*.

"I wonder what's going on? Look."

"It is Panayiotis." He laughed. *"Grigora, grigora!"* he called.

"The captain won't sail without the chief steward, will he?"

As if to answer her question, the ship slowed speed and the small boat came alongside. Panayiotis and the two crew members scrambled aboard.

Passengers were walking up and down the corridors looking for the bar.

"In here, Harry!" someone called. "We still have the booze we got last night in Athens. Come join us."

She closed her door and started to unpack. She was tired after the ten-hour flight from New York, but exhilarated to be back on the ship again.

My ship, she thought. His and mine.

"Ah, *Alexa mou*, how I have missed you," he murmured, pressing her naked body against his. Now, as they lay in each other's arms, it was as if the long months apart had never been. "I do not want you to leave me ever again. I want you with me always."

"But—"

He covered her mouth with his. "There are no buts. You belong to me. I will manage to work things out." He could not bring himself to say the word: divorce. "Somehow."

"I want to be with you, my love."

"And we will be. When I thought you were on that plane I almost went mad."

"Which plane?"

"The one that crashed at the Copenhagen Airport."

"I was booked on it, but I changed to an earlier flight."

"Thank God! But I was afraid . . . you cannot imagine what torture I went through."

"But I am here. We are together. Nothing will ever separate us."

And as she spoke those words he felt a chill go through him. "No, never," he said.

As they approached Alexandria, an announcement came over the ship's intercom. "From now on it is forbidden to take pictures of the harbor."

She thought, it does not look like Lawrence Durrell's description of a city under water, poetic, shimmering in the sun, but instead gray with smoke towers blowing white and gray smoke, an ordinary port. On the right was a lighthouse with seagulls circling, to the left an Egyptian freighter passing. Nikos came out of the wheelhouse wearing a white turtleneck sweater, the Egyptian pilot beside him, and put on his glasses to look at the horizon. It was forbidden, even to the captain, to use binoculars.

The town looked very flat, the buildings now appeared sand-colored. They were entering the breakwater. Storage tanks, a submarine net, a Russian freighter, an Egyptian destroyer. Never had she seen so many ships in one port. The *Pericles* blasted its horn.

A band wearing black uniforms greeted them, and among the brass bugles she heard the odd sound of a bagpipe. Old men were selling wares on the dock. A man in a long black robe and white turban with what looked like a brown rug thrown over his shoulder, a silver bracelet on one arm. Another man along the rail tracks carrying a basket of oranges on his shoulders, and a man in a shabby gray suit, open blue shirt, blue skull cap, trying without success to sell newspapers to passengers getting off the ship. The *Ulysses* had caught up with them during the night and was docking behind them. A boy of around twelve in a dirty blue suit and green turban with filthy bare feet called to the passengers to throw down money. She shuddered. "A dirty city, Alexandria," Nikos had said. It was depressing, all the filth and poverty.

"Why are we sending Egypt guns and planes?" said a man standing beside her. "Brooms are what they need!"

During dinner the depth charges started and each time the ship shook. As the passengers looked nervously around thinking perhaps that they were being bombed, an announcement came over the ship's intercom.

"Ladies and gentlemen, please do not be alarmed. Due to the recent hostilities between Egypt and Israel, the ship's company has arranged with the harbor master to set off depth charges at intervals around the ship. This is for our protection. The depth charges will go off only at night. Thank you."

"Well, I'm jolly glad that was explained," an Englishman sitting at Alexa's table said. "I was beginning to think I was back in London during the blitz."

There were three English, two Australians, and an American couple from St. Louis at Alexa's table. She looked across the room to where Nikos usually sat, but his table was empty.

"Are you taking the excursion to Cairo in the morning?" one of the Australian ladies asked Alexa.

"Yes, I've signed up for it."

"Good, so have we."

The English couple were going to fly in the morning to Luxor and Karnak.

"I wish there was time to do both," Alexa said. "But this is my

first visit to Egypt and I wanted to see the pyramids and the Sphinx."
She also was leery of flying Air Egypt, but she did not say so. Some
passengers had left the ship as soon as they docked to take the train
to Luxor. "I wonder what the train is like?"

"Filthy, from what friends have told us," the Englishman said.
"And so ancient they thought it was going to come off the rails the
way it rattled."

"That doesn't sound very pleasant," remarked the lady from
St. Louis. "We had friends who took the cruise up the Nile. I understand those ships are quite comfortable."

Another depth charge went off.

"I hope we can get to sleep tonight with those going off," one
of the English ladies said.

"I think we're going to turn in early," said the lady from
Melbourne, getting up with her companion.

"See you in the morning," the Englishman said. "Cheerio."

"I've never made love before accompanied by depth charges,"
Alexa said. "Is this going to happen at each port."

"Is necessary." Nikos smiled. "I promised you this cruise would
not be dull."

"So you did, my love." She ran her fingers across his chest. "And
thus far, it isn't."

Twenty-Nine

*A*t seven-thirty the next morning they were in the buses for the four-hour ride to Cairo. On the way they had a brief tour of Alexandria, driving through the shopping area, which was filthy, past apartments with clothes hanging from balconies, until finally they came to a better section where there was a beautiful hospital. Their guide pointed out the university where she had learned English and said how much Mrs. Sadat had done for Egyptian women. Education in Egypt was free, she told them, but unfortunately there were not enough schools for everyone.

Leaving Alexandria behind, they saw tiny donkeys pulling carts piled high with carrots, clusters of mud huts with straw roofs, a small mosque, irrigation ditches, people working in the fields, a lone brick hut with a camel outside. The guide pointed to some bales of cotton. "Cotton is Egypt's main crop," she said. "Before the revolution of 1952 there was feudalism. There were many foreigners who owned land here, but when they left in 1956 they gave their land to us." She switched to French and repeated everything for the benefit of an elderly French couple seated at the front of the bus.

"What are those sails we see in the fields?" a woman asked the guide.

"They are feluccas, small fishing boats on the Nile."

"But where is the Nile?"

"We are going along the green delta that is by the Nile, but we cannot yet see it. Later on we will."

This green strip was the only part where things could be grown, the rest was desert, their guide said, but there were plans by Germans to build another canal closer to Libya to have electricity.

They passed three women walking with baskets on their heads. A man dressed in black with a white turban riding a donkey and leading a cow. An Islamic cemetery with palm trees. A funeral procession, people in black, the body covered by a yellow cloth. In Arab countries one is buried in the ground without a coffin, the guide told them, then a round mound of stone is placed above to mark the place.

Now they could see the Nile just on the other side of the railroad tracks, and feluccas, their sails tied back to the masts. A train passed. A gray Mercedes with six Egyptian men honked and zoomed by their bus. Alexa noticed that a man in the back seat was reading a newspaper. A young boy riding a white donkey waved. They crossed the Nile, now wide with a low bridge, so the feluccas had to lower their sales to pass under. A market place packed with Arabs in white. A post with soldiers. A village where they made tiles. Everywhere there was squalor and dirt.

The rest stop was coming up, the guide announced, and beyond the rest stop they could not take any more photos. This was very serious, she warned, and if violated the bus would be stopped, cameras taken, the trip annulled.

The rest stop was at Tanta, half-way to Cairo. As they got out of the bus, ragged children swarmed around them and they were warned to hang on to their purses and not to put anything down. The toilets were filthy and you had to roll up your slacks and wade through pools of urine and excrement.

"Have you ever seen anything like this?" the woman from St. Louis said, holding her nose. "Ugh!"

"Have you ever been to India?" asked the Englishwoman.

"No, and I don't think I'd care to if it's like this."

"Let us go now," the guide said. "We have two more hours to Cairo."

They got back in the buses. They passed military installations and covered fighter planes. A town, some boys playing soccer in a field, a woman with the lower half of her face veiled. Again they crossed the Nile. It was very wide now with an island in the middle and people washing their clothes by the side.

As they approached Cairo they saw people selling oranges by the road, stacked high in baskets. The first stop was at the National Museum. It was very dark inside and they were installing electric lights for the first time. The guide told them that many of the treasures from the tombs of the Pharaohs were currently on tour in Russia.

They visited a mosque and a souvenir shop.

"When are we going to eat?" a man asked.

"We have luncheon planned at the Mena Hotel next to the pyramids," the guide said. "I am sorry we are a little late, but the museum took longer than expected."

"If she hadn't had to repeat everything in French, we'd be eating now," the man complained, glaring at the French couple.

It was almost three o'clock before they were served at the Mena Hotel, a greasy lamb and rice dish and a salad. Soft drinks or beer were charged extra. Alexa observed the French couple eating the salad, but after all the filth she had seen she was afraid to risk it. She ordered a Coca-Cola and poked around at the rice casserole.

After luncheon they went to visit the pyramids and the Sphinx. Somehow, thought Alexa, they were kind of disappointing, not like seeing the Acropolis or Venice for the first time. She rode a camel to the pyramids and had her picture taken on it to show to Brooke and Cicily.

"This is the same camel Nixon rode when he was here," the man leading the camel told her.

Oddly she enjoyed the camel ride more than any of the trip and she didn't get the seasick feeling that she heard often accompanied it.

As soon as the sun went down it became very chilly and she was glad she had brought a sweater for the long drive back to Alexandria and the ship.

Nikos was sitting in the lounge with the captain of the *Ulysses* when she walked in and they seemed to be having a serious discussion.

Later he came to her cabin, and again they made love to the sound of depth charges exploding around the ship.

"Oh, Nikos," she said, as she lay in his arms afterward, "hold me close. Never let me go."

And he caressed her, murmuring her name over and over. "*S'agapo, chryso mou,*" he said. "*S'agapo.*"

The Palestinian in the frogman's suit swam through the murky waters, the bomb held carefully between his teeth. He had timed the depth charges carefully. Fifteen minutes. That was all he had.

The officer on watch stood on deck looking out at the city. Alexandria looked better at night, he thought, like Istanbul. The dirt did not show.

A depth charge went off. He looked at his watch. They continued until the cycle was finished. He started to go back into the wheelhouse. Then he stopped. What was that outlined in the water just below the surface? It was coming rapidly toward the ship like a small black whale, except that there were no whales in the Mediterranean.

The water rippled. There were a lot of stars shining and a crescent moon in the sky. The ship was quiet. Most of the passengers were already in their cabins, exhausted after the long excursion to Cairo.

The officer picked up his binoculars. The object was still moving, swimming around to the other side of the ship from the harbor.

Quickly the officer crossed and peered down into the water. He could no longer see the object. Should he call the captain? The captain had told him to report anything unusual. Surely no frogman would try to get near the ship with the depth charges exploding every fifteen minutes. Unless it was a suicide mission.

He heard a splash. "Who is there?" he called.

Better get the captain. He walked back in the wheelhouse and down the corridor to the captain's cabin and knocked on the door. He waited, then knocked again. "Captain?" No answer. He turned the door handle. "Captain?" he called, and walked in. The cabin was vacant, he could see the empty bed turned down. It had not been slept in. Where was the captain?

Rapidly he returned to the wheelhouse and called over the ship's intercom. Wherever the captain was on the ship, he would hear the announcement.

There was no time to lose.

"Captain, come to the bridge immediately. It is most urgent!" shouted the voice in Greek over the loudspeaker in the corridor outside Alexa's cabin.

Nikos sprang out of bed and started to pull on his clothes.

Alexa half rose on one elbow. "What is it?" She had never seen him dress so hastily.

"I do not know. An emergency of some kind." He pulled on his trousers and grabbed his jacket.

And before she could say anything else, he was gone.

He ran in the wheelhouse, buttoning his jacket. His hair was disheveled. The second officer had a smirk on his face. Let him think what he wished. "What is it?" Nikos yelled.

"Captain, you told me to report anything unusual—"

"Yes?"

"There is something in the water swimming around the ship—"

"Where?" He grabbed his binoculars.

"Come with me, Captain."

They started for the port side when there was a sudden explosion that rocked the ship.

"Those depth charges are coming pretty close," Nikos said, looking over the rail. Then he saw something. There was a bright red stain spreading over the dark water reflected in the ship's lights and then a leg floated by.

A body. The depth charges had hit someone.

"Do you think it is a frogman, Captain?"

"Possibly."

"Then there could be others?"

"There is a chance. We must get a message to the captain of the *Ulysses*."

"Yes, Captain."

"I will stay on watch. Do not say anything to anyone else. We do not want to alarm the passengers."

It was what he had feared, but it must be kept quiet. It would ruin the cruise, the passengers would want to fly home, the company would have to refund their money. He would telephone the owners in Athens in the morning.

Had the frogman been able to attach a bomb to the hull of the ship before he was blown apart by the depth charges? He did not think there had been enough time. They would just have to wait and see if there was a ransom note. If there was, the ship would have to be evacuated, a bomb disposal unit called in . . .

The officer was watching him. "Get me the chief radio officer," Nikos said.

Thirty

*A*t eight-thirty the next morning he went to the office of the ship's agent and telephoned the owners of the Delphinaki Lines in Piraeus. They had received no ransom note.

"Then it is possible that he did not have time to plant a bomb before he was blown up," Nikos said with relief.

"Let us hope so, but we will get in touch with the harbor master and have divers check the ship just to be certain. What time do you sail?"

"At two this afternoon."

"We will order the depth charges increased in Beirut and Haifa to every ten minutes."

"Very good."

"Say nothing to alarm the passengers."

"That goes without saying."

"Thank you for your report, Captain. We know we can rely on you."

He walked out of the agent's office and back to the ship. Say nothing to alarm the passengers. He would have to think of a good excuse as to why they were increasing the frequency of the depth charges. The ship could be blown up but the cruise would not be canceled. Too much money lost. He would like to have some of that money for all his years of hard work, being on call twenty-four hours a day, giving up vacations. Greek shipowners were demanding, they required everything of their captains, but they did not like to pay them. In Beirut the company expected him to give a luncheon on board for the Greek Ambassador to Lebanon and other dignitaries, so he would have that to concern himself with as well as everything else to do with the ship. In what other job, he wondered, could they get so much work out of one person for so little pay?

And Katina wanted Fanis to go to a private school next year. On a Greek sea captain's salary? Fanis had just turned seven. It was hard to believe. He smiled. Ah, for Fanis he would do anything. He would approach the owners for a raise when he returned from the cruise.

What a dirty city Alexandria was! Once there had been many Greeks living here, but now most of them had left. He saw a couple approaching him. They looked Greek.

"Hello, Captain," the man said.

"Hello." He tried to place them. "You live here in Alexandria?"

"No, we are on the ship. We have sailed with you before. Tony Papadopoulos. I own a Greek restaurant in Yonkers, New York. And this is my wife Agmeni."

"Ah, yes. Now I remember." He did not, but he had to pretend to. So many passengers, and they all remembered him. "This is your first trip to Egypt?"

"For me, yes. My wife lived here as a child."

Agmeni smiled. She was in her forties, plump and plain. "Captain," she said, "what was all the commotion last night?"

"Commotion?"

"My husband and I were taking a late stroll around the deck and we noticed you and one of the officers looking into the bay as if someone had fallen overboard."

"Ah, that." He must think quickly. He had not seen any passengers about, but then he had been very busy. "We were checking the depth charges. To see that they were far enough away from the ship."

"Are we going to have depth charges in the other ports as well? It is not easy to sleep at night with them going off."

"That I regret, but is necessary. It is for the protection of the passengers while we are in the Middle East."

"In Famagusta as well, Captain?" Tony asked. "After all, that is a Greek port."

"No, not in Famagusta. Cyprus is calm. For the moment. If the Turks do not start anything."

"How well I know," Tony said. "My parents came from Cyprus. There were always problems with the Turks. They are never satisfied. They want the whole island."

"True." If they started discussing the situation on Cyprus with the Greeks and the Turks he would be here all day. "I must get back now," he said. "I will see you on the ship." He would ask the chief steward to have them seated at his table one evening.

He continued walking. Papadopoulos. He frowned. The same name as the hated colonel. Could he be a relative? But Papadopoulos was a very common Greek name, there was probably no connection. Nevertheless, he must be on his guard. One wrong remark falling into the wrong ears and you could be thrown into prison without knowing who your accusers were or what crime you were guilty of. He had seen it happen to friends. As long as the Junta was in power no Greek was able to speak freely.

Now he could see the ship and he walked more rapidly. He strode through the customs house past vendors selling their wares and then he saw the first officer pacing back and forth by the gangway. He was looking for someone and flipping worry beads nervously.

"Captain, I am glad you are back."

"Yes? What is it?" Nikos asked. Could he not leave the ship for a moment without a problem?

"They have found the body. It washed up on shore. Or what was left of it."

"A Palestinian?"

"They do not know." The officer flipped the worry beads faster. "Was there a ransom note?"

"None. At least not yet. But divers will be here soon to go over the ship for a bomb. And the owners want the depth charges increased to ten minutes apart in both Beirut and Haifa."

"It was a mistake to keep those two Palestinian terrorists in the Athens prison. They should have executed them or else sent them somewhere else."

"It is now too late to think of that," Nikos said. "And what country wants them?"

"There must be someplace other than Greece. We have enough troubles as it is."

Nikos looked over his shoulder cautiously to see if anyone was listening. I am on edge myself, he thought. Years of walking the tightrope. But it would not look good to see the captain with worry beads.

"Put those beads in your pocket," he told the first officer. "They make the passengers nervous."

He was in the chart room with the navigator when he got the news. The divers had found a bomb. It had been timed to go off as soon as the ship passed the breakwater. Luckily the bomb experts had been able to defuse it. But would there be others? Obviously the Palestinians knew the cruise itinerary. Should he change it? It was up to the captain's discretion, but it would complicate matters if he did. All the tours would have to be rearranged, others canceled completely. He ran his fingers through his hair. What to do? Beirut was the next port and he had heard that there were many Palestinian guerrillas living in Lebanon.

"We are still going to Beirut, Captain?" the navigator asked.

The officers wanted to go to the Casino du Liban, the passengers also. It had one of the most spectacular floorshows in the world. He had not seen it, but people who had told him it was better than anything in Las Vegas.

If the depth charges were increased and they took extra pre-cautions . . .

Every decision he made affected so many. When he was a young sailor having fun in the different ports, he did not realize how well off he was. This morning he had noticed a few more gray hairs. "The captain is so young," the passengers always used to say when they met him for the first time. "I will get older," he said, and he was. Rapidly.

The navigator was still waiting for his answer.

"I am not sure," Nikos said slowly. "I must weigh the options."

"We sail in three hours."

The flip of a coin. He could ask no one's advice. For the captain there was no higher authority other than God. He looked at his watch. "We will sail for Beirut as scheduled," he said.

"What did you do today?" he asked. They were sitting in a corner of the lounge having a drink together.

"I took the tour of Alexandria," Alexa said. "We went to see King Farouk's palace. It was really beautiful. Have you been there?"

"Me?" He laughed. "When would I get the time?"

"It overlooks the bay of Alexandria and all the rooms are very ornate. Finally we came to a room with some things preserved in a glass case. They had the jewelry that belonged to the queen and the dolls of the princesses and also a book that the queen was reading just before she left. Do you know what it was?"

"I cannot guess."

"*Lady Chatterly's Lover* in French."

From his expression she could not tell if he had never heard of the book or if his mind was on other things.

"Something is bothering you," she said. "What is it?"

He shrugged and threw out his hands in a hopeless gesture. "My wife is coming to join the ship at Cyprus. On Saturday." He downed the rest of his drink.

"I see." Her voice was tinged with anger. "Why didn't you tell me before?"

"There was nothing I could do about it. She has never been to the Holy Land. I promised her the trip before I knew you were coming on the cruise."

I thought we had two whole weeks together, now we have only one before his wife joins the cruise. "Why didn't she come at the beginning?" she asked.

"Because she is bringing Fanis and he is still in school. Saturday starts his spring vacation." He signaled a steward to bring them more drinks.

"This is Wednesday. We have only three more nights to be together."

"*Alexa mou,*" he said softly, his eyes filled with agony. "I do not know what to do."

Nor do I, she thought. We have been together off and on, for four years now. I am thirty-nine, next year I will be forty. Do I want to continue following a Greek ship around, snatching intervals of love whenever we can? But I can't give him up either. Should I force a decision? But if I back him against the wall . . .

"I do not want to hurt anyone," he said. "People I have responsibilities to."

The chief engineer was approaching. Was it he, the one with the fat ugly wife, who had informed Katina that she was on the ship again?

"I must go now," Nikos said. "They want me for something. I will see you tonight. Around eleven."

He got up quickly and went to meet the chief engineer.

That night there were no depth charges exploding, only the wave rocking them gently as they sailed toward Lebanon. They clung to each other fiercely, as if they could melt into one and nothing could separate them.

"I have made a decision," he said. "I cannot live without you, *chryso mou*. I want you with me always. Is that what you want too?"

"Yes, my love," she whispered.

He sat up in bed and ran his fingers through his hair. "I will ask Katina for a divorce. Evangelos starts at the university in September, and Fanis is now seven years old, I can have him with me part of the time . . ."

"Would she agree to a divorce?" She saw his nude body outlined by the moonlight coming through the porthole, gleaming on the gold wedding ring on his right hand.

"I can no more go on like this. It is tearing me apart."

He took her in his arms and they made love again.

And like all lovers, they allowed themselves to dream of a future free from problems and only eternal bliss and happiness.

Thirty-One

*B*eirut, with its elegant shops and nightclubs, the Paris of the Middle East. Beirut, with its seething hatred between Moslems and Christians, fringed by Palestinian camps of ragged refugees. The *Pericles* docked in the early afternoon. A tour of the city was planned and that evening dinner at the Casino du Liban. The passengers were informed that the casino was very dressy and long gowns and furs were in order for the ladies, black tie for the gentlemen.

As she was leaving the ship for the casino, she saw Nikos, brow furrowed, talking to the chief engineer. The depth charges had started again and one of the passengers remarked that they seemed closer together than in Alexandria. Nikos looked up as she passed, their eyes met, then he looked away. Something was troubling him.

She got in the bus for the drive to the Casino du Liban. Some of the ship's officers were also in the bus, sitting way in the back. But not Nikos. He had stayed on the ship. She looked out the bus window at the lights of Beirut as they drove up the hill to the casino.

"Are you taking the excursion to Damascus tomorrow?" asked the Englishman sitting next to her.

"No, I'm going to Baalbeck instead," Alexa said.

"Too bad. You could join us. That's my wife across the aisle and her sister. I say, it's very brave of you to go on this Middle East cruise all by yourself."

I'm not by myself, I'm with Nikos. That is until his wife comes on the ship. "I like to travel alone," she said. "Then I can do exactly as I please."

"You've got a point there. The three of us don't always agree on which tour to take."

"It is difficult to decide sometimes. I'd like to take all the excursions in Israel, but it would be too exhausting, so I've settled for Bethlehem and Jerusalem. I've always wanted to see them."

"I was last in Israel as a major in the British Army. In 1946. It was called Palestine then."

"You'll probably see many changes."

"No doubt. But what we're really looking forward to is Cyprus. We have some British friends there." He paused and then said wistfully, "One time I thought Cyprus was where I wanted to retire. We even rented a house in Kyrenia for a year, but Maude missed England."

His wife leaned across the aisle. "You missed England, too, Cyril," she said.

He smiled and patted her hand. "Guess you're right at that, old girl."

The Lebanese tour guide stood up in the front of the bus and took the microphone in her hand. "Ladies and gentlemen, we have now arrived at the Casino du Liban. Please stay close to me and do not wander off on your own. Thank you."

He sat down at the desk in his cabin and started writing in the ship's log. Outside he could hear the depth charges going off every ten minutes. He found his mind wandering as he made the notations. All his life he had worked so hard, living for others, did he not have a right to happiness like normal men? Time was passing. He was fifty-one, no longer young, even if he did not look that age. If he was going to change his life, now was the time.

From the wall above his desk the photographs of Katina and his sons stared down at him and he felt a sudden guilt at what he proposed to do. You give with one hand and destroy with the other.

He had meant to speak to Katina before this, but each time he looked at her he found it impossible to broach the subject. Like plunging into icy water, jump, and the shock is not as great as going in inch by inch. He could still see his sons, have them with him. And Katina he would like as a sister, a friend. He saw her blazing eyes when she was angry, heard her shouting, and knew that would not be possible. Her love for him would turn to hate, like Medea, she would want revenge. He did not blame her. But she would get over it.

He closed the ship's log. He had tried to forget Alexa, but it was not possible. He loved her, he would love her always. They belonged together.

He put the ship's log back on the shelf and went down to the lounge.

"How was the show at the casino?" Nikos asked her when she returned.

"It was fantastic! I've never seen anything like it in my life."

"Good. I am glad you had a good time." Passengers were coming in the lounge and he hoped they would not notice him. No such luck. A middle-aged woman who had been drinking too much called out, "Captain, you missed a great show."

He forced a smile. "So I hear."

A depth charge exploded and Alexa put her hands over her ears. "Those things are driving me crazy!"

"Come let us go to your cabin. You go ahead and I will follow in ten minutes." He stood up and shook hands with her formally, raising his voice as a steward passed. "Good night. Thank you for having a drink with me."

"Good night, Captain."

Out of the corner of his eye he saw the steward smile at another. We are fooling no one, he thought.

It was during the luncheon for the Greek Ambassador that the message came. The ship was under siege. One false move and they would all be held hostage. Palestinian guerrillas had machine guns trained on them, and they would be held until the two guerrillas in the Athens prison were released.

Most of the passengers had left the ship to go on the excursions. He looked at his watch. They were due to sail at ten this evening. Nine hours. He excused himself from the table and went to the chief purser's office and called the owners in Piraeus. They had received a ransom note.

"Do you think they are bluffing, Captain?"

"No, they mean business. And they have chosen a time when the Greek Ambassador and other dignitaries are on board. They must have had information from someone."

"What do you think we should do?"

"The ransom will have to be paid. I see no other solution."

There was a sharp intake of breath at the other end of the phone. "But even so, the Greek government will not release the guerrillas from prison. They are adamant."

Nikos paused. "I will see if their leader will come on board and discuss it with me."

"They want a plane ready to leave Athens for Beirut with the two guerrillas by six o'clock this evening. And the money."

"Somehow, we will have to comply. Otherwise . . ."

"We will rely on you, Captain."

The messenger was waiting beside the gangway, talking to the Lebanese guard. Nikos relayed the message from the ship's owners.

"The owners of the company are ready to comply. If your leader will come to the ship, we can make arrangements—"

The Palestinian shoved a gun between Nikos' ribs. "You come with me, Captain," he said in heavily-accented English.

"I am not leaving my ship."

"You have courage, Captain, but I am the one holding the gun."

"What good would it do to shoot me? If you did, you would not get your men back, nor the money."

The Palestinian pulled the gun back but still trained on Nikos in case he made a quick move.

"Bring your leader here," Nikos said calmly, "and I will meet him. By then, all arrangements will be made by the ship's owners."

"You had better not try any tricks, Captain," he said with an evil smile. "Or you will not live to regret it."

And he left.

Nikos returned to the table. The stewards were serving dessert.

"I am so sorry to be absent so long," he told his guests. "Urgent business,"

"Is everything all right, Captain?" the Greek Ambassador asked.

"Yes, all is under control."

"Good. It is a delicious lunch. But you have hardly eaten anything." The steward came over with a warmed plate of food and Nikos waved it away. "That is no doubt how you stay so trim." The ambassador patted his fat stomach and smiled.

The stewards poured champagne and Nikos raised his glass. "I would like to propose a toast to all my honored guests. Thank you for dining with me on my ship."

They drank and then the Greek Ambassador lifted his glass. "To Captain Meletis. It is a pleasure to be here."

"You are most kind," Nikos said. "And now let us go to the Dionysus Lounge for coffee."

"If you will forgive me, Captain, I must get back to the embassy," the ambassador said.

Nikos hesitated. "I am afraid there is a slight problem. Palestinian guerrillas have surrounded the ship. But I am sure it will all be straightened out very soon. I am waiting for their leader now to make the arrangements."

The ambassador turned pale. "You mean that we are being held hostage?"

"It looks like it. For the moment," Nikos added quickly.

The ambassador regained his diplomatic aplomb. "In that case, I will have coffee. Strong. Let us adjourn to the lounge. After you, Captain."

The afternoon wore on. Nikos looked at his watch. Soon it would be time for the passengers on excursions to return, but they would not be able to get on the ship. What had gone wrong? Had the owners refused to pay the ransom? He knew how reluctant they were to part with money. His guests were getting restless and conversation was strained.

Then the second officer appeared. He spoke quickly in Greek to Nikos. Nikos stood up. "Excuse me," he said.

The leader was an unshaven man of medium height with piercing black eyes, wearing a rumpled khaki uniform and a white Arab headcloth.

"You are the captain? Good, let us go to your cabin."

Nikos looked at him warily. He towered over the man, but he also observed the revolver in his holster. He had better play along and not try anything. "This way," he said. The Palestinian followed.

"Would you like something to drink?" Nikos asked, when they were seated facing each other in his cabin.

"I do not drink," he said, looking around the cabin and taking in the photographs of Katina and Evangelos and Fanis. "You have a family, I see. You would not want anything to happen to them, I am certain. I also have a family."

Nikos watched him. What was the man up to?

"So. The owners of the Delphinaki Lines have not been very cooperative."

"They assured me—"

The Palestinian waved his hand. "They think they can fool us. Give us fake money. Did they not think we would check it first?" His eyes blazed with fury.

So that was what had happened. He kept his face impassive, waiting.

"Now, Captain, you are going to telephone Piraeus and tell them not to stall any longer. Do you understand?" His fingers brushed the revolver. "I will be beside you to hear what you say."

"I understand."

"Good. Then let us proceed."

Thirty-Two

Alexa knew something was wrong when the buses pulled up to the dock and she saw armed soldiers surrounding the ship. Nikos, she thought in terror, have they done something to him? A man was approaching their bus dressed in khaki shirt and trousers and a white Arab headcloth.

"What is going on?" a woman asked the guide.

"I do not know."

The bus driver opened the door and the man said something to the guide in a language Alexa could not understand. The guide nodded.

"Ladies and gentlemen," the guide said, "we are requested to remain in the bus for the time being."

"How long will that be?" a man grumbled. "I want to get back on the ship and have a shower and a drink. That was a long trip to Baalbeck."

"I am very sorry," the guide replied, "but instructions must be obeyed." She appeared somewhat nervous.

Alexa looked out the bus window but she could see no sign of Nikos. Black limousines were lined up alongside the ship and she suddenly remembered that Nikos was entertaining the Greek Ambassador and Lebanese officials for luncheon. But it was now five-thirty and they were supposed to sail at seven.

Then she saw Nikos. He was standing at the top of the gang-way talking to the man in the Arab headcloth. The man had a gun trained on him.

"There's the captain," someone said. "It looks like he's being held hostage."

A cold fear ran through her. She recalled that when terrorists took over a plane they sometimes threatened to shoot people one by one until their demands were met. There was the co-pilot of a Lufthansa plane who had been shot as a warning and his body thrown out of the cockpit. Was that what they planned to do with Nikos?

Her hands were perspiring and her throat was dry. No, this can't be happening, she told herself, her eyes frozen on the scene at the top of the gangway.

The guide started to tell them stories about the history of Lebanon, but no one in the bus was listening.

Then a jeep pulled up to the gangway and two soldiers got out. More terrorists? Were they going to take Nikos away, put him in prison?

One of the soldiers gave a message to the Arab leader, who read it hastily, still holding the gun on Nikos. Then he put the revolver in his holster. The two of them went back inside the ship.

A few minutes later a portly man in a dark business suit was escorted to one of the waiting limousines. Several others followed and drove off. She could see Nikos near the exit shaking hands with each as they departed. Then the man in the Arab headcloth came down the gangway and walked over to the bus. He said something to the guide and she nodded and smiled.

"You may all go back on the ship now," she said.

"It's about time," said the man who wanted a shower and drink, as they all scrambled for the exit.

Nikos heaved a sigh of relief. The ransom was paid, the plane had left the Athens airport with the two Palestinian guerrillas carrying them to Tunis. But it had been a close call and he would not stop worrying until the ship had sailed from Beirut.

He did not approve of hijackings or terrorist acts, but he saw no end to them until the Palestinian question was settled. In forming

Israel had they not taken their land? They would only become more bitter and violent until they finally had a homeland.

As a Greek he could appreciate their feelings. To him Istanbul would always be Constantinople, taken from them by the Turks.

"All visitors are kindly requested to go ashore," came over the intercom. "The ship is about to sail."

God willing, he thought as he went up the stairs to the bridge. The second officer had the walkie-talkie ready, the Lebanese pilot was on board and drinking coffee brought to him by the steward. "Good evening, Captain," he said.

"Good evening." Nikos was relieved to note that it was the same pilot as yesterday and not a terrorist in disguise. He looked down at the dock. The sailors had taken up the gangway. He checked his watch, then nodded to the pilot.

"Go ahead, Captain."

Nikos picked up the walkie-talkie. *"Mola ola prima,"* he ordered, and the men on shore untied the ropes.

She leaned against the railing watching the lights of Beirut disappear into the distance. The Lebanese pilot had been picked up by the pilot boat and they were out at sea now headed toward Cyprus. Cyprus, she thought with a shudder, where his wife comes aboard. Their last night alone together. The second officer had put away the walkie-talkie and gone inside the wheelhouse, the sailor had taken down the flags, only she and Nikos remained on the bridge. It was a night full of stars and sadness.

Nikos walked over and stood beside her and they remained silent looking out at the sea.

Then, out of nowhere, she heard herself saying, "When I was four years old my favorite uncle jumped from a ship and drowned."

He appeared startled. "I am sorry. You never told me before."

"I hadn't thought about it in a long time." Why had she thought about it now? She looked down at the churning sea and wondered what it would be like to drown. A quick death and painless, slipping beneath the dark waters? Or was it? "They lied to me about the way he died," she said.

"What did they tell you?"

"My mother said that his cabin had been freshly painted and he opened the porthole to get some fresh air and fell overboard. To this day she insists that's what really happened."

"How do you know that it wasn't an accident?"

"Because a passenger who had been on board talked to my grandmother afterwards. He said he had noticed my uncle on deck earlier that evening because he was one of the handsomest men he had ever seen and that he had the saddest expression he had ever seen. So that when it was announced he was missing he was not surprised. The man was a priest and he had tried to talk to my uncle, but said he obviously wanted to be alone."

"He was your mother's brother?"

"Yes. He was a year younger than my mother and they were very close."

Was that why her mother couldn't face the truth? The accidental death by drowning, the way other suicides were covered up by a convenient heart attack. Keith. She shivered. She was guilty of the same thing. She had never told her own children the entire facts. How could she? Their father a transvestite? No, better the accident with a gun than have them know the ugly way it really ended.

Her uncle had left a large amount of money and his jewelry and paintings to a close male friend. Was there something he was trying to hide, was he a closet homosexual? He was very handsome and charming and had never married. Suddenly she felt goose bumps on her arms.

"You are shivering, my darling," Nikos said, putting his arms around her. "It is cold on the bridge. Let us go to my cabin."

"Where will you be staying on Mykonos?" he asked her later. "The Leto?"

"No, the Hotel Rhenia. It is on the hill away from the town."

"Ah, yes. Opposite Tourlos Bay. It is new?"

"Fairly new, I think. It has individual white cottages covered with bougainvillea. It looks charming."

"You go to Mykonos as soon as the ship docks?"

"Yes, Saturday. A week from tomorrow."

He nodded.

Tomorrow your wife comes on the ship, she thought, watching his tortured face in the moonlight. I will take all the excursions, stay out of her way. We will only be able to exchange glances when she is not around. Why did she have to come on this cruise when we have little enough time together as it is? Tomorrow night his wife will be in this cabin.

He sighed. "It is getting late. We dock at Famagusta at seven in the morning."

"I will get dressed." She reached for her clothes that she had tossed over a chair. When she was dressed she hastily put on lipstick and ran a comb through her hair.

"I will see that no one is around," he said. Cautiously he opened his cabin door, looked up and down the corridor, then beckoned. "It is clear."

These cat-and-mouse games, soon they will be over, she told herself, soon we won't have to hide, we can be together openly. "Goodnight, my love," she whispered.

Already his mind seemed to be on the docking at Cyprus, his wife arriving. "Good night," he replied absently.

Thirty-Three

A cold breeze was blowing the flags of the *Pericles* as they approached Famagusta. Cyprus, she thought with a shiver, where his wife comes aboard. Will she be waiting when we dock? Or will her plane arrive later in the morning? He had not said. He was on the bridge looking through his binoculars. To the right were white buildings, blue hills to the left. Seagulls circled overhead. The ship's horn gave several sharp blasts. She saw the small gray pilot boat coming out flying the Cypriot gray-and-white flag. Nikos put down his binoculars, glanced over his shoulder, and their eyes met for a brief moment. His face was strained.

How I love everything about him, she thought. He has such a sense of command, such strength. I watch him directing the ship and I think of how he is with me. There is, there can be no other man. He is the one I have dreamed of always, and now that fate has crossed our lives, nothing can keep us apart. Nothing.

The pilot came up the stairs and Nikos walked forward to greet him. Then they went in the wheelhouse. A sailor climbed the mast with the flag indicating the pilot was on board.

Cyprus looked very green. A few ships were in the harbor, mostly freighters. A freighter passed on their starboard side and another was approaching to port. Nikos and the pilot came out of the wheelhouse. They were drinking coffee and discussing the docking in Greek.

I'd better not be on the bridge in case Katina is waiting at the pier when we arrive, she thought, and went down to a lower deck. She would be taking the tour of the island as soon as they docked at Famagusta. She would keep herself busy every minute, act as if she was just another passenger, so that the rest of the cruise would pass quickly and then she would see him on Mykonos. They would be able to be alone together away from the ship in her romantic little cottage at the Rhenia Hotel. By then he would have spoken to Katina, asked her for his freedom.

They could plan for their future.

Cyprus was covered with yellow, red, and white wildflowers. A bird trilling above the ancient ruins of Salamis, faded paintings under an arch, vines growing from the moss-covered stones and dandelions waiting to be blown away in the breeze.

Strange, she thought, how all civilizations make the same mistakes and end the same. Now, among the Corinthian columns of the gymnasium, birds fly, tourists walk over the mosaic tiles, gaze into the empty baths.

"Since 1400 B.C. Cyprus has been predominantly Greek-speaking with a small Turkish minority," the guide told them. "However until 1960 we never had a Greek-speaking leader. In antiquity Cyprus was ruled by Phoenicia, Persia, the Ptolemies and the Romans. Later came the Byzantine, Venetian and Ottoman rule, succeeded by the British."

As the guide rambled on about the history of Cyprus, Alexa found her mind wandering back to the ship and Nikos. Katina had not been waiting on the dock, so that meant she was arriving later in the day.

"Now let us get back in the bus," the guide said. "We are going to visit the Church of Saint Barnabas."

They drove through a pretty countryside with masses of yellow daisies and saw a shepherd tending his lambs.

"The eucalyptus trees here were imported from Australia by

the British," said the guide. "Cyprus used to be very swampy with much malaria. There have also been many earthquakes on the island."

At the Church of Saint Barnabas a baby was being baptized. A priest in gold robes was chanting from an open prayer book, then the baby was undressed, anointed with oil and dipped three times in the water. I have been here before, Alexa thought, and then she remembered the dream. It was in this very same church and the baby was hers and Nikos'. But why on Cyprus?

"Come everyone, please," the guide said. "We are going to look at the mosaics and we are behind schedule."

Leaving the church, they came to the village of Trikoma. Blue-and-white flags were everywhere and *ENOSIS* was written on a wall in white paint.

"What does that word mean?" a man asked.

"*Enosis?*" The guide paused. "It means union with Greece. Tomorrow, March 25th, is Greek Independence Day and that is why you see all the flags."

They started to climb high into the mountains and as they neared the top they could see the Kyrenia part of the island with the coastline and sea far below.

"Now we are coming to the castle of Kantara," the guide said. "The bus cannot go all the way up to the castle, so we will park just below and walk. It is a steep rocky path, so if anyone has heart trouble or difficulty in walking, I would advise you to remain in the bus."

Two very fat women decided to stay in the bus, but the others followed the guide to the top. The view was worth it.

"During the war the castle was used as a lookout post," said the guide.

Looking out at the sea and the Turkish coast in the distance, Alexa suddenly felt a cold fear grip her, a nameless terror that she could not shake off. It seemed that she could hear guns above the birds' singing, see men lying dead on the beaches. The guide was telling them the history of the castle, but she was not listening to what she said. All she wanted to do was get back on the ship and Nikos, to sail away from Cyprus.

But his wife was on the ship now. She would be with him on the bridge tonight when they sailed and tomorrow when they docked at Haifa. "She has a temper like a Turk," Nikos had said of Katina. Alexa shuddered. A Turk. What worse comparison could a Greek make? But soon Katina would be out of the picture. She and Nikos would be together. She would be his wife, not Katina.

Nikos and Katina climbed up the outside stairs to the bridge, a steward following them carrying her suitcases. The second officer was standing near the railing looking out at the harbor of Famagusta. He turned when he saw them. *"Ti kanete?"* he asked Katina.

"Kala," she replied, her eyes sweeping the deck below for any young pretty lady passengers.

"You go on in to the cabin," Nikos told Katina. "I'll be there shortly."

The passengers were starting to return from the excursions, but he did not see Alexa anywhere. He just hoped that he could avoid her coming face to face with Katina.

"Everything all right?" he asked the second officer.

"Yes, Captain."

"Good." That was unusual. But he had enough on his hands with both Katina and Alexa on the ship at the same time. He ran his hands through his hair. Katina seemed in an explosive mood. He would have to handle her carefully. He walked over to the railing and looked down at the dock. And then he saw Alexa. She was getting out of one of the tour buses. He turned quickly and walked back inside the wheelhouse. He must go to the chart room and see the navigator, then check the weather reports.

When he returned to the cabin Katina had unpacked and changed her clothes.

"Let us have a drink in the Dionysus Lounge," she said.

Usually Katina avoided the lounge when she came on the ship

because her English was poor and she did not like to mingle with the passengers. "But I thought . . ." he hesitated.

"Are you afraid I will run into the woman you are having an affair with?"

Had someone said something to her. The chief engineer? "I do not know what you are talking about," he said angrily. "And besides, I have many things to do before we sail."

"Very well. I will just walk around the ship." She smiled but there was venom in her eyes.

"You are free to do whatever you wish, Katina," he said, and walked out of the cabin. Better not have any scenes with her. It was too risky.

Alexa was standing on a lower deck watching the sunset over Cyprus when she noticed a woman staring at her. The woman was obviously Greek with black hair pulled back in a coil and dressed in a purple wool dress with gold jewelry and black boots. Her nails were painted a deep red but she wore no lipstick. And then Alexa realized who it was. Katina.

Not far away a steward was watching both of them with interest. A Greek drama about to unfold. And he had a ringside seat.

"Ah, there you are. Maude and I were just talking about you." It was the Englishman who had thought of moving to Cyprus. "Beautiful sunset, what?"

"Lovely." She could feel Katina's eyes boring into her.

"We wanted you to have a drink with us. Maude is waiting in the lounge. Figured you'd be out on deck. Or else up on the bridge with the captain."

She didn't really want to go in the lounge. She wanted to stay on the deck alone with her thoughts, the breeze blowing in her face as they sailed. Nikos walked out on the bridge followed by the pilot. Katina was watching them both.

"I'd love to join you for a drink," she said. "Let's go."

Thirty-Four

*K*atina had taken the pins out of her hair and was sitting on the bed brushing it. "Evangelos has a new girlfriend," she said.

"So? That is normal." Nikos wondered what Katina was leading up to. "He cannot study all the time."

Katina's eyes narrowed. "I do not like her. You must speak to him when you come home."

"What is wrong with her, Katina?"

"For one thing, she is not Greek."

A long time ago he had heard those words. His parents. Patricia. And finally, he had married a Greek woman. To please the family? Or because it was expected of him?

"How did he meet her?"

"With some friends. She is Danish. She came to Greece with a study group. And now she is going to stay."

"She is pretty?"

"What does that matter? Is that all men think of? This affair has gotten much too serious. And I had other plans for Evangelos. I want him to marry the niece of Soula Vassilakis. She is a good Greek girl, from a fine family. She will have a large dowry. It will be a suitable marriage."

"But Evangelos is only eighteen. First he must do his military service, then he has to finish the university—"

"I am not talking of next week, but of Evangelos' future. It is up to the family to arrange these things. And he thinks he is in love with this Danish girl. He is neglecting his studies to be with her."

Carefully he put his jacket on a hanger, his back turned to Katina.

"Our family is Greek and it will remain Greek," Katina continued. "With no foreigners."

He tried to get the conversation on a lighter tone. "I am surprised that you have not yet selected a bride for Fanis. Already he is seven—"

"I do not think you are being amusing." Katina's eyes flashed. "And speaking of Fanis, he was sent home from school last week for misbehaving. If you could spend more time with him perhaps he would be more obedient. He does not listen to me."

"How can I spend any more time with him than I do? I am on the ship."

"That is exactly my point. You could retire."

"And how would I support my family?"

"I do not mean that you should stop working. But the company could give you a position in the office in Piraeus, so that you would not have to be at sea all the time."

"Katina, we have discussed this before." And there is another matter I want to discuss with you, but now is not the time. "I am very tired, Katina. Let us go to bed."

She held out her arms to him. "Come here, Nikos."

"I am sleeping on the couch in the other room. I have to be up early for the docking at Haifa." Had he ever desired her as a woman? But that was not important in a Greek marriage. Theirs had been arranged by the families as now she wanted to arrange the marriage of Evangelos. The typical Greek mother. Now, he thought, I will choose the woman I wish to marry: Alexa. "Goodnight, Katina," he said and turned out the light.

At Haifa the Israeli officials kept the passports and handed out landing cards to the debarking passengers. Like in Russia, Alexa thought, tucking her landing card in her purse. In the customs house their purses were opened and inspected before they could board the buses.

"Why are they so suspicious?" she asked the purser, who was standing nearby.

"Because we are a Greek ship coming from Arab countries," he replied.

Just then she saw Nikos and Katina coming down the gangway. Let them not be on the same bus, she thought, hurrying outside where the buses were waiting.

The young people were very attractive, she noted, both men and girls, and everyone greeted each other with *"Shalom."* An old man wearing a black skull cap and carrying a basket, an Israeli policeman on a motorcycle, another man with white hair riding a bicycle. Refugees from where, what have their lives been? she wondered. A middle-aged man, hands in his pockets, was whistling *"Torna a Surriento."* They looked at everyone with suspicion.

She observed trucks filled with bags of cement, many cars and taxis, white houses with red roofs, tall buildings on the hill in back of the port. Suddenly two jet fighter planes streaked overhead.

"Everyone taking the tour to Jerusalem and Bethlehem, please board the buses now," the guide said.

Nikos and Katina were coming out of the customs house. Quickly she boarded the closest bus, which was almost filled, and out the window she saw Nikos and Katina heading for another bus. Had they seen her? She could not be sure. When they stopped it would be difficult to avoid running into them, but she was going to try her best.

Why, oh why did Katina have to come on this cruise?

The bus started off and the guide introduced himself. He was a smiling middle-aged man who told them that he had a son and daughter, both soldiers in the Israeli Army.

On the way to Bethlehem they stopped at a souvenir shop. She had wanted to buy a bible with a mother-of-pearl cover from the Holy

Land, but there was only jewelry for sale and tourist junk. The shop owner was obviously a friend of the guide and he got a cut of the sales. She finally selected some bookmarks with pressed wildflowers from the Holy Land.

When they came out of the shop she was glad to see that the other bus with Nikos and Katina had gone somewhere else to buy souvenirs. And at Bethlehem and Jerusalem, if they were there at the same time, there would be so many other tourists that the chance of coming face to face with Nikos and Katina would be remote. Or so she hoped.

From the time when she was a child and used to sing, "O Little Town of Bethlehem," at school Christmas pageants, she had wanted to visit Bethlehem, and now her thoughts were only on Nikos and Katina and how she could get through the rest of this terrible week.

Katina seemed in a better mood today, Nikos observed. She held on to his arm chatting happily about the sights, and smiled pleasantly at the passengers who greeted him.

"How nice to have your wife able to join you, Captain," an elderly woman said. "Is this the first time you have seen the Holy Land, Mrs. Meletis?"

Nikos translated the question into Greek for Katina, who nodded and smiled. "Yes, the first time. But now I come more often with my husband."

Her English was improving. Had she been studying in his absence? Nikos wondered. Several years ago he would have been pleased if she had been able to converse with the passengers in English. Now it no longer mattered.

He did not know how he was going to approach the subject of divorce. Apparently Katina had no idea how unhappy he was. Or had she and was now trying to make amends?

Just then he saw another bus from the ship pull up and park outside the walls of the old part of Jerusalem and the passengers got out. Alexa was among them. He turned quickly but not before Katina had noticed. Her eyes narrowed but she said nothing. I hope they are not going to join our group, he thought nervously.

"Are you looking for someone?" she asked him in Greek.

He did not answer.

"The blonde lady who has been on the ship before?"

"There have been many blonde ladies who have been on the ship, Katina. I cannot remember them all."

"And now we are going to walk through the walled city and along the Via Dolorosa," their guide said. "There are many tour groups today, so let us all stay together so that you do not end up in the wrong bus." Someone laughed. "You may laugh, but it has happened before. Now, please follow me."

Alexa had seen Nikos with Katina clinging possessively to him and it gave her a strange feeling. The Greek wife, unwilling to let go. She had heard that sometimes they threw acid in a rival's face. And Nikos had been smiling, acting as if everything was fine, the captain with his wife enjoying the sights, she the outsider, just another passenger. She had noticed him turn away quickly when he saw her get out of the bus. By now she should be used to it, but she wasn't. Katina did not look as if she intended to give him up without a fight. And she had his sons. Surely that would weigh in his decision.

But he loves me, she told herself. And I love him. Everything will work out all right.

During the next two days she took tours to Tiberias on the shore of the Sea of Galilee, saw Tel Aviv, and visited an Israeli kibbutz. At Antalya, Turkey, the ship anchored in the bay and the passengers went ashore in lifeboats to visit the ancient cities of Perge and Aspendos. Nikos and Katina remained on the ship.

It is almost over, she thought. Thursday Rhodes, that evening the Captain's Dinner, and then Piraeus, the end of the cruise.

It was one of the few times she was not at the captain's table for the farewell dinner, but how could she be with Katina on the ship?

Katina was seated opposite Nikos, with the purser on one side of her and a man she had heard speaking Greek. From her place two tables away, Alexa faced Nikos. Their eyes met at one point and he looked anguished. Then he stood, gave his usual speech wishing them all a safe journey home, and he and Katina left the table.

She went directly to her cabin and started to pack. As soon as the ship docked at Piraeus in the morning she would get a cab to the airport and her plane for Mykonos.

Mykonos, where she and Nikos could be alone together, away from the ship, without Katina.

Thirty-Five

Mykonos at night. The sound of waves lapping the shore. Red hollyhocks and hedges of pink oleander. A crow cawed. Standing on the terrace of her cottage, she could see the white town in the distance with lights going on and cruise ships anchored in the harbor. In two days his ship would be here.

The red roof of a tiny white church down the hill. A small girl singing a Greek song. A golden sliver of a new moon in the sky and a single star. A black-and-white kitten crawled along a stone wall. More lights going on in the town, pink and green, and the lights of the cruise ships. The air was cool and it was still, so still. Then she heard a man's voice speaking Greek and the child called *"Baba!"*

And she thought, Is the world so different after all?

The wind was blowing across Mykonos, making ripples in the water of the harbor. Only one cruise ship was anchored now. Tomorrow he will be here, she thought.

She was sitting at a little taverna eating an omelet, tomatoes, and coarse Greek peasant bread. A simple lunch, but good. A Greek man at the table in front of her was swinging red glass worry beads and explaining to two American tourists about winter on Mykonos and how quiet it was. A blue motor cart filled with onions roared up a narrow white cobblestone street. A Greek military man passed, a reminder that even here the Junta was in control. A tiny white-and-caramel kitten crawled under her table and she reached down to stroke it. A plump Greek woman in a print dress strolled by holding a little boy by the hand. He wore short olive pants, a dark green sweater, and carried a red carnation. Suddenly he pointed to the kitten and cried "*Gata!*"

How adorable Greek children are with their large brown eyes, she thought. If Nikos and I had a child I wonder what he or she would look like? "I would give you nice sons," he had said. Were daughters not important to a Greek man, only sons?

The sea was turquoise and deep sapphire. A tender was going out to the cruise ship. What would it be like to live on an island, to never get away? she wondered. The women work so hard, no wonder they get old young.

Another Greek man twirling worry beads. Four small Greek boys walked by. She noticed that one had blond hair but brown eyes. Petros, the famous pelican of Mykonos, was standing on a ramp stretching his wings and looking out over the harbor. A priest with a gray beard and long black robe and hat passed, then two Greek women, one young, the other old and dressed in black with a black shawl.

Mykonos. How far away I am, she thought, and yet I feel at home among these people. They are simple and real. But could I change my life enough to become a Greek wife? For him, loving me means scandal, dishonor, hurting those who love him. Is the price too high?

The dream versus the reality. Oh, Nikos, my love, what are we to do?

A gray naval ship is entering the harbor, it looks like a destroyer, but I can't be sure from here. On the terrace the blue-and-white Greek flag waves in the breeze, not as strong as it was yesterday. Little white houses with blue doors and windows, blue geraniums, a white kind of lily I have never seen before.

This afternoon his ship will be here.

*   *   *

She sat at a table along the waterfront and waited. The *Pericles* was anchored in the bay next to the *Statendam* and tenders were bringing the passengers ashore. The meltemi was still blowing and a lock of hair blew across her face. She brushed it out of her eyes, and then she saw him. He was walking toward her in long strides wearing gray slacks and a black turtleneck sweater. His face was tired and strained. I am waiting like all the Navy wives I once swore I would never be, she thought, and she called his name.

He smiled. "Ah, there you are." He sat down in the chair next to her and she noticed that he had brown worry beads in one hand which he flipped back and forth over his fingers.

"How have things gone?" she asked. Had he spoken to Katina? And if so, how had she reacted?

"Ah, such a trip! I lost one of the anchors at Delos. I had to leave it, otherwise we could not sail. Then at Istanbul we were quarantined. Cholera. We cannot dock. The authorities come on board and inoculate everybody. The passengers are angry. They want to see Istanbul. We come back and anchor at Rhodes at one o'clock in the morning. At three we leave." He stared ahead fingering his worry beads.

"I thought you didn't use worry beads." She smiled. "Did you have to have an inoculation?"

"Me? No, I have already had one." He ordered coffee. Some of the sailors from the *Pericles* walked by. "So, how is Mykonos?"

"I've been exploring the island. It's been too chilly to go swimming. I didn't realize the wind blew so much here."

"The meltemi, yes, it blows very often. Especially in August. Then the sea is very rough."

She decided to broach the subject. "Did you speak to Katina?"

"About what?"

She was startled. "About us."

"There was no opportunity. Always my son was around."

"I see."

"No, you do not see. You do not know how difficult it is." There was agony in his eyes.

"Have you changed your mind?"

"I have not changed my mind. But Katina and I have been married many years. I do not want to hurt her. I must find the right time." Passengers from the ship were passing. "Let us get away from here," he said. "There are too many people."

They walked through the town and along the narrow road leading to the Rhenia Hotel. The sun was starting to set and from the hills came the bleating of a lamb.

"I am going to take the *Naïas* back from Mykonos Friday," She said. "I didn't like that little plane they flew us over in. It was really buffeted around by the winds."

"Then you will be in Athens that night?"

"Yes, at the King George Hotel."

"We dock at Piraeus Saturday morning. I will speak to Katina then and come to see you afterwards at the hotel before I sail."

Sunday I fly back to New York, she thought. And he will be off on another cruise. And another.

"You could find a job for me?" he asked.

"In New York?"

"Yes, or in Greenwich. With a travel agency, perhaps?"

Now the reality was facing her. Because of course he could not remain in Greece. And his roots were in Greece. The only work he had done was on the sea. "I can ask my friends," she said. "I'm sure you could find a job."

They walked hand in hand up the rocky path to the Rhenia Hotel. The horizon was shaded from pink to mauve to blue and lights were going on in the town, twinkling across the bay. She unlocked the door to her cottage and as soon as they were inside he took her in his arms and pressed her against him.

"I have missed you, *chryso mou*," he said. "I want you always."

"And I want you always."

They lay down on the wide bed and she thought: We've never

made love away from the ship. The ship had confined their lives, defined it. The ship. To hell with the ship!

And they made love passionately, wildly, forgetting everything else.

Later he said, "We forgot to eat dinner. And now it is too late. I must get back to the ship."

"What time do you sail?"

"Eleven-thirty." He sat up and started to put on his clothes.

Even here we cannot spend the entire night together, she thought as she watched him dress. But soon . . .

"I will stand on my terrace and watch your ship sail," she said. "It will be dark and you will not be able to see me, but you will know that I am there waving to you."

He grabbed her quickly and kissed her. "I will see you in Athens," he said and left.

Thirty-Six

*S*he was sitting at a sidewalk table in front of the King George Hotel watching the parade pass by. It was too early to hear from Nikos and she was bored waiting in her room. A Greek family strolled by, the woman young but already losing her figure, dressed in a tan skirt, green sweater, black hair pulled back, sad expression, carrying a baby. A little boy walked along with the husband, both nicely dressed. The husband looked around happily, out for a Saturday stroll with his family. Later, she thought, he will sit in a café with other men, flirt with women, while the drab wife sits home.

And she wondered if she could adjust to the Greek way of life, where the woman was nothing but a cook and bearer of sons. But she would not have to. Nikos was going to come to the United States, get a job there.

People were constantly getting out of gray taxis and going into the King George Hotel and the Grande Bretagne next door. Tourists sauntered by, a man passed selling sponges, a Greek boy carrying red roses encased in cellophane. A nice-looking elderly American couple sat down two tables away and she heard the man order a club sandwich, the same thing she had ordered her first time in Athens four years ago. She was tempted to warn him that it was a mistake, the bacon would be raw. Three Americans loaded with cameras sat down at a table in front. The younger woman mentioned a salad. Then they left. The man next to her, a Greek, expensively dressed, had a gold cigarette lighter on the table and amber tinted glasses with gold rims. He was sipping a lemon drink and kept glancing over.

Two American sailors came up the steps of Constitution Square. Shore patrol. The Greek man lit a cigarette with his gold lighter and coughed. A fat lady tourist in slacks got in a taxi. A black, chauffeur-driven Mercedes pulled up. The doorman helped an elderly man dressed in black, shaking with palsy, into the hotel. There was a plain-looking woman with him, navy coat, hair pulled back in a bun. His daughter?

Another man selling pistachio nuts. If you did not buy a package, he left two nuts on your table as a sample.

She looked at her watch. It was nearly an hour before she could expect Nikos.

More tourists sat down. A thin woman in a black tweed pants suit, short auburn hair, carrying a large bag embroidered in petit-pointe and holding one hand like a claw. The woman opposite her was busy eating pistachio nuts. The Greek man sitting at the next table walked off leaving his glasses. The white-haired American, who had ordered the club sandwich, ran after him. On his plate she noticed most of the bacon. Uncooked.

Four boisterous men in polo shirts joined the woman eating pistachio nuts. They were discussing things to buy, had red faces, pot bellies, one clutched a postcard of the Parthenon. They laughed loudly, blocking the sidewalk so people could not get by. A carriage drawn by two horses decorated with red ribbons let four people out in front of the Grande Bretagne. A man selling the Athens News. "In English," he said.

"I don't want to read the paper," said a coarse-faced man in a green sport shirt and cowboy scarf. "I don't want to know what the stock market's doing."

She was getting tired now of the passing parade. She picked up the check the waiter had left when he brought her coffee and counted out the right amount of drachmas.

Soon Nikos would be here. He would tell her that it had not

been easy, but that Katina had agreed to a divorce. They could plan their future. Together.

In her room she waited for what seemed an eternity, pacing back and forth, walking out on her balcony to look at the Acropolis, then back to the telephone, as if by staring at it she could make it ring.

But there was only silence.

Had she missed his call when she was sitting in front of the hotel? But there were no messages in her box. And if he had just come by she would have seen him.

Perhaps things had not gone well with Katina, perhaps she had refused to give him his freedom. But how could a woman remain with a man knowing that he was in love with someone else? Wouldn't her pride . . . no, Greek women had no pride. They sat and waited for the infatuations to fade, for their men to return. They held the trump cards. They had his sons.

"Even if a Greek man hates his wife, he'll stay with her because of his sons," she remembered Lukas telling her. "It is better for the family."

The family. The indissoluble Greek ties. She looked at the phone again. He should have called by now. And even if she had his home number she could not telephone him there. She walked out on the balcony again and looked at the Parthenon. The Greek flag was waving on top of a nearby building, a jet flew overhead, below the noise of the Athens traffic, horns honking, people shouting. A long black limousine pulled up in front of the hotel and three fat Arabs got out.

A sense of foreboding swept over her. I hoped for too much, she thought, walking back into the room again and sitting on the edge of the bed. Could it be that the Greek wife is the safe harbor and I am just a ship passing in the night?

And then the telephone rang. She grabbed it eagerly.

"I am in the lobby," he said. His voice was strained, distant.

"Come on up."

"No, I will meet you here."

"I'll be right down." What had gone wrong? No, she was just imagining things, she assured herself, as she walked down the corridor to the elevators.

She got in the elevator. A middle-aged couple, obviously American, smiled at her. She nodded absently. The doors opened and she saw Nikos standing near the reception desk. He walked toward her and he did not need to speak. It was all written on his face.

"Let us sit here," he said, leading her over to a corner where there were two gilt chairs next to a marble-topped table.

"She wouldn't give you a divorce?" she said finally.

He did not look at her. "I cannot leave my sons. I cannot abandon my family."

Forever after she would remember the pattern of this Oriental rug, this lobby with tourists arriving, this afternoon when her life seemed to lose all color, all meaning. "I know," she said. The words stuck in her throat, choking her. "I understand."

"I could not live with myself if I did."

"I know that too."

"Ah, *Alexa mou*—" His voice broke. He started to reach for her, then got control of himself. "It is hopeless. There is no happy life. For anyone."

She turned away. Through the glass doors she saw the doorman putting suitcases in a gray taxi. A young couple, their arms around each other, got in and drove off. Happy lovers, she thought bitterly. One day will it end for them, too? Nothing lasts. All of life can be summed up in those two words. Say it over and over again until it doesn't hurt so much. Nothing lasts.

"I will always love you, Alexa," he said, agony in his voice. "*Chryso mou.* You must believe that."

The end of the affair.

Time would pass, diminish, erase. Or so they both hoped. Had he wanted to tell her in the lobby so that she would not make a scene?

If it had been in her room they would have ended up in bed. She stood up. Better to leave quickly. Like a sharp knife, it hurts less.

"Goodbye, Nikos," she said. And she turned and walked quickly toward the elevators, not looking back, for she knew that if she did she would be lost.

Thirty-Seven

She hurled herself onto the TWA plane and fastened her seat belt. She felt like throwing up two weeks of Greek food, she wanted now to forget everything Greek, the sound of the language made her want to scream. It was his voice speaking Greek that I loved, she thought, and now that everything is over forever . . .

She bit her lip and stared out the window at the Athens airport. Once she had loved coming here, now she couldn't get away fast enough. A long flight to New York, ten and a half hours, a lot of time to review the four years they had known each other, when it was all a new and fascinating world to her. Now she knew that those worlds could never meet.

"The worlds of a Greek man and an American woman meet only once place," she had read somewhere.

The engines of the plane started. I will get rid of all my Greek records when I get home, she told herself, or at least put them away with the photographs, until it all becomes a dim memory. No, it will never become dim, but at least the pain will.

The plane was racing down the runway, now they were airborne, below mountains, white houses, land that I loved because of him. Forget, forget it all.

The sea below, so blue, the harbor with ships. Forget the ships too, and how he looked commanding one, his voice shouting orders on the bridge, his voice asking softly, "Do you love me?"

I'm glad no one is in the seat next to me, she thought. I couldn't bear to have to carry on a conversation.

She looked out once more. His land is Greece, he is Greek, his roots are here, he is steeped in its tradition. How did I ever think he could change his life that much?

She had driven friends crazy with her "Greek period." She had learned the language because it was his. "I'm going to wait until the Greek god becomes 'that damned Greek'" one man who was in love with her told her.

Now below, clouds. I must not start crying on the plane, she told herself.

Once she had thought that love conquered everything, now she saw that it did not. There were other things that came between.

Since it was doomed from the start, was there some reason for our meeting, our love affair? I did a lot of traveling because of him, I saw many interesting places, there were beautiful moments between us.

All over now.

Nothing lasts with me, she thought, I'm not lucky in love. Some people find the right person and it works out, they spend a lifetime together.

I want peace and quiet now, to enjoy my home, my children, my garden, away from the sound of Greeks shouting at each other and rattling worry beads. And I have my job. I am stronger than I was after Keith's death, I can stand on my own feet now and support myself. Yes, I will survive.

I will survive.

And one day, when I am old, I can say, "Once I knew a Greek man. He came from the island of Corfu. It was a very interesting experience . . ."

But now—farewell, Greece.

Thirty-Eight

The events of mid-July on Cyprus had been brewing for a long time, but when the fighting started and the Turkish invasion came, it caught everyone by surprise.

The cruises stopped, the airports closed, and thousands of tourists were stranded with no way of escape.

The Greek armed forces were on full alert and the Athens radio was transmitting only military marches. Weddings were postponed as bridegrooms were suddenly mobilized. There was a curfew and the public was instructed to use the telephones only in an emergency. Food prices were frozen, wine festivals suspended, light and sound shows in Athens and Rhodes closed down.

Every day the news from Cyprus was worse. Turkish air strikes hit the resort hotels of Famagusta and Kyrenia, Turkish troops swept over the island, plundering, raping and killing. Archbishop Seraphim of Athens and all Greece asked the clergy to donate blood for the wounded.

On the twenty-fourth of July the hated colonels of the Junta resigned and Constantine Karamanlis returned from his Paris exile to take over the Greek government.

And in the Piraeus offices of the Delphinaki Lines a serious discussion was going on.

"We would like you to sail the *Pericles* to Cyprus to rescue the Greeks," the owners told Nikos Meletis. "With the Turks overrunning the island, we do not need to say what they will do to those who remain."

"You do not have to ask me. I will do it gladly."

"We must also warn you that it is a very dangerous mission, so that if you feel—"

Nikos shrugged. "Dangerous? Life is dangerous."

"You are our most experienced captain. Our best. If anyone can carry it off, you can."

"I will do my best." He paused. "But what of the American Sixth Fleet? Where are they?"

"They are neutral. They do not come to our assistance. They want to protect their bases in Turkey. No, we can expect no help from the Americans."

"I see."

"So it is up to us. We stand alone. Again, against the Turks."

"You can count on me. When do you want me to sail?"

"As soon as possible."

Slowly they approached Cyprus under cover of darkness. The seaside hotels of Famagusta were on fire, they could see the flames from far off and hear loud bursts of gunfire. Nikos looked through his binoculars. It would not be possible to go much closer. He gave orders to get the lifeboats ready to go ashore.

He could see groups of refugees huddled on the beach waiting. Greeks.

We are here, he thought. We will not let you down.

Turkish troops now controlled Kyrenia, the most beautiful part of the island where many foreigners had homes and British warships were standing offshore and sending helicopters in. But they were only taking British and other tourists stranded by the sudden war.

The Greeks were there, again attacked by the Turks.

The Turks had ordered that all ships must stay ten miles out, that was why the British were using helicopters on the other side of the island, and it was going very slowly. He hoped to sneak in close with the *Pericles* while they were diverted and get out as many Greeks as possible. It could be done, with luck.

Suddenly it came back to him what his aunt had told him long ago when she read the coffee grounds. "You will rise to the top of your profession. You will be honored for your bravery. You will have one great love, but it will be near the end of your life."

"Now," he ordered. "We will start sending in the boats."

There were eight lifeboats, but he could not overload them, that would be dangerous. Luckily the sea was calm.

And where were the Americans? he thought bitterly. Why had they not sent help? They could have prevented the Turks from taking over the island but they did nothing. Kissinger, he was behind it, he knew what was happening. Their friends, the Americans, had betrayed them and sided with their ancient enemy. Turkey.

The first lifeboat was in the water, now the second. Bright flames lit up the coastline.

On shore the people looked like lines of ants, waiting.

Then he heard Turkish planes. They could suspect them of bringing in Greek troops on the cruise ships. He hoped they would not strafe the lifeboats with the refugees. The Turks were capable of anything, that he knew.

Barbarians!

Already they had killed many Greeks on Cyprus, raped Greek women, driven Greeks from their homes.

And still the Americans did nothing.

He picked up his binoculars again. The first lifeboat had almost reached the shore.

The Turkish planes had gone to the other side of the island. Good. They must work fast and get out of here.

He waited, pacing the bridge, the ship in darkness.

Now, the first life boat was returning. As they came alongside the ship he could see it was filled with frightened-looking women and children. The sailors grabbed them and helped them quickly up the gangway. The lifeboat pushed off to rescue more refugees.

There was a little boy who looked very much like Fanis. He was crying.

Again he cursed the Turks.

The rescue operation continued. Now all the boats were back, the cabins of the *Pericles* were full and cots had been set up in the lounge.

"We'd better leave quickly, Captain," said the first officer.

Nikos gave the orders to the engine room. The anchor came up. The ship started.

"We have made it," the second officer said. "We got all of the people on the beach."

Nikos ordered the speed increased. There was a breeze and the sea was starting to get rough. They had finished just in time.

He went outside on the bridge and looked at the coastline of Cyprus disappearing.

Then he heard it.

The sound of a plane. It was coming closer to the ship.

He looked through his binoculars. It was Turkish.

The first officer had seen it also.

"Captain, watch out!"

Nikos turned and started for the wheelhouse.

Too late.

It happened so fast that he did not feel anything.

Only the deck coming up to meet him, the deck that was stained with blood.

His blood.

His eyes closed and it was over.

www.ingramcontent.com/pod-product-compliance
Lightning Source LLC
Chambersburg PA
CBHW011352010726
47494CB00008B/2271